Leaving Berlin

Leaving Berlin

Britt Holmström

thistledown press

Thistledown Press Ltd.
118 - 20th Street West
Saskatoon, Saskatchewan, S7M 0W6
www.thistledownpress.com

Library and Archives Canada Cataloguing in Publication
Holmström, Britt, 1946-
Leaving Berlin / Britt Holmström.

Short stories.
ISBN 978-1-897235-91-1

I. Title.

PS8565.O639165L42 2011   C813'.54   C2011-905335-7

Cover photograph detail of Elbeo Stockings advertisement
by Wolfgang Sievers, 1938 with permission from the Powerhouse Museum,
Sydney, Australia
Author photo by Amy Snider
Cover and book design by Jackie Forrie
Printed and bound in Canada

Canada Council
for the Arts

Conseil des Arts
du Canada

SASKATCHEWAN
ARTS BOARD

Canadian
Heritage

Patrimoine
canadien

Thistledown Press gratefully acknowledges the financial assistance of the Canada Council for the Arts, the Saskatchewan Arts Board, and the Government of Canada through the Canada Book Fund for its publishing program.

ACKNOWLEDGEMENTS

Thank you, Al Forrie, for wanting to publish my stories.

I am also very grateful to Elizabeth Philips for being such an excellent and inspiring editor.

And it was very generous of Mungo Jerry, alias Ray Dorset, to happily let me quote from his famous song. Thank you.

As ever, a standing ovation for Nick, Christopher and Anna for always encouraging me and putting up with me.

And while I'm at it, I would also like to doff my hat to all the people who — unaware of the fact — inspired these stories.

To Nick, my patron saint

Contents

*It is inevitable that each of us will be misunderstood;
this it seems, is part of twentieth-century wisdom.*

— Carol Shields, *The Stone Diaries*

Leaving Berlin

We left Berlin on a Wednesday evening. I don't know why I still remember that. It was mid-March 1970, the weather gloomy, already getting dark around four o'clock when we handed our remaining Deutschmark (down to the very last Pfennig, I remember that too) to Frau Paulus at the Pension. Such money manoeuvers were Henry's specialty, the counting out of exact change in every transaction in foreign currency to make sure we were not robbed of a single worthless coin.

Early on I had pointed out that people might find his lack of trust insulting. His reply had been the standard one. "Too fucking bad."

Frau Paulus was a seventy-six-year-old widow who had turned her large fifth-floor apartment into a Pension to make ends meet. She wore a different dress on each of the five days of our stay, all of them dating from the forties, very feminine, complemented with a pearl necklace and a brooch, ready for her daily social event, afternoon tea with a lady friend. Whenever we arrived back after another aimless trek, we heard the hum of their murmured conversation, glimpsed them sipping tea out of cups as fragile as the hands that held them. They nodded when we passed the door to the salon, the lady friend staring with disdain at Henry, Frau Paulus greeting us with a nearsighted smile of indiscriminate delight.

We were her only guests that week, and as we were leaving she took her time scribbling the receipt she insisted we must have, "*Eine* properly business tranzaction, *ja*?" She used an old-fashioned pen with a nib she kept dipping into a porcelain inkwell, expertly, never spilling a drop, her head bent over her task, every single white curl obediently in place. And all the while she talked — mostly in German — sometimes directing the flow of words at us, sometimes at her husband, *Oberst* Paulus, who stood attentive in his Luftwaffe uniform in a brass frame on the desk. He had been a late casualty of the war. Shot by a mad Russki, she informed us when we first arrived, illustrating the event by pointing her hand like a gun at Henry and shouting "Boom!"

Henry did not take offense, which was amazing considering that lately he took offense at just about everything. He just stepped aside and said, "Ha, ha, you missed." Frau Paulus found that extremely funny.

The small overheated room that served as her office was an aviary of stuffed birds. They sat perched on every shelf, lurked in the deep windowsill behind her, nested on the giant dresser and the desk. Every bird wore a grey cloak of dust.

Henry waited patiently beside me, very unusual for him, not a single *pianissimo* tapping foot or jittery finger, no snarky comments about why the old bat didn't keep a fucking stuffed dodo as well.

The exact moment Frau Paulus handed the carefully blotted receipt to Henry, the streetlights came on. The lamppost directly outside the window behind her haloed the two cranky-looking horned owls regarding us with beady glass eyes from the sill.

The abrupt light emphasized the dusk outside, giving the impression that it was much later than what our watches claimed, as if foreign time flowed at a different pace. Hoisting our backpacks, we said good-bye to the nearsighted Frau — she shook our hands with both of her talcum-scented ones — and with no German money we headed for the elevator to begin the long trek to Zoo Bahnhof.

We stood like polite strangers in the coffin-sized elevator, its wood paneling creaking, travelling an inch a minute down the five floors. On the fourth floor an old man carrying a snuffling Pekingese tottered in and squeezed rudely between us. His perfumed silk scarf matched his pink nail polish. Henry made faces at the dog over the man's shoulder. The dog wriggled towards him and licked his face. Henry smiled. For some reason animals loved him. The old man scowled and stuck his nose in the air, an aristocrat among peasants. By the time the elevator had laboured down to the first floor, we all reeked of his perfume.

Earlier that day I had considered exchanging some Canadian dollars into Deutschmark to be able to take a taxi, travel in comfort for a change. It was going to be a long and tedious slog from Berlin to Copenhagen. In the end I didn't bother. I knew it would be pointless. Henry would refuse on principle, because he knew what he knew: that every unshaved taxi driver in Europe belonged to a widespread fraternity of criminals whose sole purpose in a long and pointless life was to cheat Henry P. Fontaine out of his hard earned cash.

We had not taken a single taxi in any of the countries we had travelled through during our five-month trip, no matter how tired or lost, no matter how hopelessly late for the next train, bus or boat. Nor had we utilized subways, streetcars or buses.

Why?

Because Henry scorned all public transit as well. He agreed that it was inexpensive, but so what? It was jam-packed with pickpockets, con artists and the general riffraff of a decadent continent.

I was convinced we would miss the train to Sassnitz, but it turned out we had plenty of time. A clock struck five when we crossed Bundesplatz. By then I was trailing Henry by a good eight feet, a distance that made conversation impossible. Not that it mattered. It appeared we were once again not speaking. Like an atmospheric disturbance, this communication *interruptus* had changed from a sporadic phenomenon to a daily occurrence as soon as we set foot on European soil. Suddenly everything I did annoyed the hell out of him. As the days went by I watched him change from merely brooding — which was what had attracted me to him in the first place — to hostile and paranoid. The merely brooding I had always taken for angst, common in the artistic type and not without charm; it suited his persona. The hostility and paranoia I found harder and harder to interpret generously.

The *sforzando* dissonance of the trip was — like everything else that went expectedly wrong in life — entirely my fault. Okay, it was true that taking the winter off to travel had been my idea. And maybe it was whimsical on my part, but I had wanted to go to Europe since graduating from university two years earlier. Not a shocking suggestion. Europe was not outer space. Everybody went there.

There was another reason that I wanted to travel to Europe. I had never been able to get close to Henry despite having lived with him for almost a year (wondering every day why he had deigned to move in with me), so I hoped that when we found ourselves alone among strangers we would grow closer, having only each other to turn to. That he would let me inside his private sphere as we shared new impressions. The music he had composed and played when I first met him was soft and mellow and sensitive, reflecting the expression on his face at the time, and it had led me to believe that getting close to him was possible with a bit of patience. Perhaps it was a naive assumption, but in my defense, Henry did come along willingly: I did not force him, did not beg, nag or plead. "How about taking the winter off and going travelling?" I had asked.

To which he had lifted his fingers a quarter of an inch off the piano keys, shrugged and asked, his voice pleasant enough, "Where?"

"Europe?"

This was followed by another shrug and "If you insist," before he lowered his fingers onto the keys and continued playing. There had been no frown, no acid in his voice.

The moment we found ourselves in Europe, the questions and accusations began, as if the ground beneath his feet had grown unstable. Why did I insist on dragging so much goddamn luggage around?

Because we're going to be here for five months and we need more than a change of underwear.

Did I have to stuff my face every five minutes?

Twice a day is not every five minutes.

Did I know what that dried up fucking sandwich cost in Canadian money?

Yes, a dollar fifty.

And what was it with my moronic habit of smiling at strangers? How clueless was I?

You tell me.

He had grown more distant with each day that passed. I had felt increasingly ostracized. More often than not he treated me like a troubled stranger who had forced herself on him, some demented nutcase talking to herself. I wanted to yell, "It's me! Don't you recognize me?" But I never did, I was afraid of what his answer would be.

To soften him up, I tried harder, talked more, talked faster, laughing more shrilly with the strain. The harder I tried, the more I failed. And the more I failed, the harder I tried, succeeding only at fueling his contempt. His contempt invalidated me, and I discovered how difficult it is to function when you've become invalid. People sense it and treat you accordingly.

Later that sullen Berlin afternoon as we stopped at a red light across the street from the Zoo Bahnhof, an elephant began to trumpet. It was a sudden desperate bellow. Another elephant responded, equally vexed, and together they continued to vent their anguish which reached a *fortissimo* crescendo when the piercing shriek of a tropical bird made them fall silent.

Not on speaking terms, Henry and I exchanged no comments about this, but I noticed his shoulders tensing. He was listening to the elephants as if interpreting a message. As if he was in psychic contact with them, sharing their pain. Maybe he was.

We had visited the Zoo two days earlier. That was when I discovered Henry's peculiar weakness for elephants. Peculiar only because he seemed to retain no weakness for anybody or anything else in life, apart from his music, that is. If there were only pachyderms plodding this planet, Henry P. Fontaine would plod among them, a harmonious man.

We stood for the longest time staring at a sad-eyed grey bulk of African elephant. A chain around its right back leg was attached to a pole, preventing its cumbersome body from moving freely. Henry stood dead still before it, his fists rammed deep into his pockets. After a while he started tapping his left foot, *largamente*, as though it, too, was chained. He never took his eyes off the giant. The elephant kept moving its trunk back and forth, back and forth, like a metronome while Henry followed it with his eyes, adjusting his rhythm accordingly.

Afraid he would disappear deeper inside himself, I finally said, "Let's go, please, Henry. I'm cold."

He mumbled, sounding for a moment like an awkward child, but did not object.

I wished I were an elephant.

When we reached the ape house I suggested we go in, if only to warm up. Henry looked as if he had not heard a word, but when I pulled open the door he said "Okay" and followed me meekly inside, head bent as if in sorrow, hair hanging in his face, preventing me from seeing his expression.

The pungent building was deserted but for a handful of badly dressed people who all looked like they were there because they had nowhere else to go. An old man in blue overalls was busy hosing down the area between the barren cubicles and the rail marking off-limits. He performed his task with meticulous care, taking his time, as if his work was of vital importance. After a while he got to where we were standing, in front of the stark cell that was home to a large orangutan lying in a corner looking more dead than alive.

Then in the unkempt pile of fur an eye flipped open. It was an eerily intelligent eye, out of place in that mangy pelt. Sliding from left to right, the eye surveyed the supposedly superior *Homo sapiens* gawking back at it, but it was only when it spotted the old man that its supreme indifference gave way to alert recognition.

Henry tensed beside me. I took his hand. He pulled away.

The orangutan came to life, dragged itself up, shuffled to the front of the cage and came to a stop face to face with the old man. Its gaze was inscrutable, but something was going through its mind. This was a creature with a plan.

The old man, unperturbed, turned off the hose at the nozzle and raised his head to meet the steady gaze of the ape. As he did so, the orangutan pressed closer. With a rapid movement, a hirsute arm shot out between the bars. The leathery hand went straight for the man.

The handful of people gasped. So did I. Henry did not make a sound.

Instead of putting a safe distance between himself and the ape, the man stepped closer, moving with the leisurely pace of a person who has not had reason to hurry for a long time. When he got within reach of the outstretched hand, he stopped. The orangutan cocked its head. Its eyes softened as it gently touched the man's face, stroking his cheek several times before hauling the arm back in as if overcome by sudden shyness.

The man said something in German with a heavy Slavic accent, then he held up the nozzle and pointed to it. The orangutan began to bounce up and down, smacking its lips, pressing its face to the bars. It looked like it was dying to be kissed. The old man turned on the hose and gave it a long drink of water. When the ape had had enough, it took a step backwards and bared a row of yellow teeth in a gleeful grin.

"*Ja, ja. Du bist sehr geistreich, mein Liebling,*" cooed the old man. He smiled at his clever darling, a melancholy twitch of a smile, and continued hosing away straw, bits of rotting vegetables and fruit the inmates had thrown out onto the concrete floor beneath the cages and the rail.

The orangutan, never blinking, watched the man until he was out of sight, then shuffled to the back of the cage and flopped down. Eyes closed, it once again turned back into a fur rug.

During the entire episode, Henry never stopped drumming on the rail, *adagio* at first, then faster and faster, reaching an *agitato* finale when the orangutan stroked the man's cheek. When the ape once again looked dead to the world, Henry continued drumming, *diminuendo* now, unevenly as though his fingers had broken from the strain.

Waiting for the light to turn, I wanted to remind Henry of the episode, make a conciliatory remark, string words over the abyss between us, approach him on them like a tightrope walker without dignity. As usual I had no idea why we were not speaking. Only Henry knew what warranted these punishing silences.

The light turned green and we crossed the street, Henry striding ahead, wading through a group of Turkish *Gastarbeiter*, seven men dressed in black leather jackets. At least I assumed they were Turkish; one had a Turkish flag glued on the back of his jacket. They were having what sounded like an argument. Whatever it was, it involved a lot of shouting and arm waving. Close by, somebody kept honking a horn. I watched as Henry put his hands over his ears and started running, his backpack bouncing against his back, the fringes on his suede jacket dancing around his hips as he fled.

The inside of the train station lacked the dignity of the ape house. It was early evening, and in Berlin come evening, transvestites and whores, perverts and pimps and what have you, emerged out of nowhere, all dressed up and perfumed, slinking out of the shadows like the undead at sundown. I never understood why so many transvestites favoured the old train station with its glaring lack of ambiance, when the city offered an unlimited number of spas for the morally infirm, dimly lit places where I got the impression that every manner of perversion had been raised to an art form. I saw a woman try to French-kiss her dog. In Berlin you were spoiled for choice not only where to pamper your particular predilection, but with whom and what with.

"There is," Henry had pronounced on our first night getting to know Berlin, looking around in the first of the clubs we stuck our heads into, sounding like a research scientist confirming his hypothesis, "something unnatural about Germans having fun. I mean, look at these assholes."

I am not sure what he meant by that. (I'm half German.) The people he was referring to — men and women alike — were all staring at him, some with delight at the sight of the dark-eyed brooding stranger, others with a perverse sort of dread and longing, assuming no inhibitions in the long-haired freak before them. A man grabbed himself at the crotch and threw Henry a kiss, a woman pulled up her blouse and exposed her breasts, wiggling her hips. Henry ignored them.

Never had I felt such a rube. The club we went to on a dare the following night had shown pornographic cartoons on a large screen above the bar. In *Snow White*, the prince resuscitated the heroine with more than just a kiss while seven horny dwarves looked on, friskily masturbating in rhythm to the thumping glass coffin. They were well-hung dwarfs, I will give them that, but they came up short compared to the Prince. No wonder he could wake the dead.

Henry had watched it with a patronizing smile. I kept sneaking glances at the rest of the clientele, expecting I don't know what. A glassy-eyed masturbation orgy? Most of them, no more than a dozen, looked half asleep. A well-dressed hunchback was snoring face down at a table in a corner, clutching a half eaten peach in his left hand, a limp red satin tie dangling from his neck.

When I wanted to leave, Henry insisted we finish our beer. "This piss cost an arm and a leg," he lectured, pointing to his mug.

I sat down. We stayed until our mugs were empty.

At the station I decided to pop down to the *Damen* before we went in search of the train bound for the Sassnitz/Trelleborg ferry. As I had no German change, I waited outside an occupied cubicle, ready to grab the door when it opened. Having observed local custom the past few days I knew this was the common manoeuver for sneaking a free pee. It was in order to please Henry that I had become an expert at crossing my legs long enough to keep five *Pfennig* from ending up in enemy hands.

The toilet flushed and the door opened to reveal a six-foot-plus transvestite, his teased blond hair sprayed into a stiff beehive, his cherry-red lipstick clashing with his blue eye shadow. He wore a fake mink coat draped over his shoulders over a blue satin dress tight enough to reveal an endowment similar to Snow White's cartoon prince.

Outside a man's voice sang out. "*Veeeera! Kommst du schon?*"

"*Ich komme jetzt!*" bassooned the baritone blonde, winking at me as he held the door open to bequeath me his throne. He had pissed all over the seat, which, as a lady, he had seen no reason to raise.

You would think that as a lady, he'd piss sitting down.

All at once I longed for home. Only another week to go. We were on the last leg of our disintegrating foray, a northbound army of two fighting itself, on our way to Copenhagen to visit some Danes we had managed to befriend in Spain the previous New Year's Eve. Befriending people was a daily challenge in Henry's company, but Jens, Inge and Hans had been so gregarious, so easygoing — so unlike us — that we came to depend on them for a good mood, needed them to stand between us like a jovial buffer zone. New Year's Eve had been the best day of our trip. Having sampled the wines in all the twenty caskets in a bodega in Motril (including four kinds of sherry), we had ended up blind drunk and inseparable, misty-eyed as we belted out *Auld Lang Syne* like there was no tomorrow, quietly drinking Spaniards — all men, there were no other women — staring with contempt at our performance. By the time the church bells tolled and the new year began, Henry and I had forgotten who and where we were. When he kissed me I imagined that he meant it. Imbibing twenty kinds of wine in less than four hours does cloud one's interpretive powers.

By the time we arrived in Berlin, New Year's Eve was a distant embarrassment.

The wall sliced the city in two jagged halves, barbed wire coiling atop the length of it. Large stretches were decorated with impressive graffiti. There were machine gun-toting soldiers staring mindlessly from the guard towers at Brandenburger Tor and Checkpoint Charlie, soldiers who looked too young, the machine guns too heavy for their bony shoulders.

Henry found this concrete monument to man's inhumanity thoroughly fascinating. It confirmed his worst suspicions about mankind and that always had an uplifting effect on him. "That sucker is twelve feet high and more than a hundred miles long, did you know that? In some places it goes right down the middle of the fucking street!" The numbers made his fingers spring to life, searching new rhythms.

"And what is it you find so intriguing about that?" I wanted to understand his fascination.

"The thinking behind it. The twisted reasoning of the human mind. The sickness it is capable of."

"I see."

"No, you don't."

He was right.

The wall was a looming threat the night we crossed into East Berlin from the neon jungle of the West. The train hurried headlong into stark emptiness, leaving behind the human zoo of masturbating dwarfs and satin transvestites. On the other side of the wall it was as if everybody had fled long ago.

Not a gaudy freak as far as the eye could see, no con artists doing card tricks, no beggars and street performers, no movie houses, restaurants, bars, strip clubs and discotheques, no refugees selling useless knickknacks on dirty blankets on the sidewalk. East Berlin was a ghost town. There was nothing and nobody at all. It was as if the gaudy half of the city had sucked all colour and energy out of its ailing twin and left it for dead.

"It looks like an abandoned movie set," reflected Henry. "Must be what inspired those black and white spy movies where it always rains and men in bad suits slip across the wall to save mankind from communism."

Unsure if he was talking to himself or to me, I offered no reply.

The train drew to a stop beside a desolate stretch of platform. After a while two uniformed men came marching out of the station building.

"Vatch out, Fräulein! Ze batt guys are comink to get you!" This time Henry was talking to me. A door slammed further down the train. A few minutes later the same two men pulled open the door to our compartment and shot a single word at us: "*Pässe!*" We handed over our passports. From the vague amusement with which they inspected our Canadian documents, one would have thought we had presented them with hand drawn amateur forgeries.

Then I got worried. People in authority took an instinctive dislike to Henry. It never failed. Apart from his scowl, which now was quick to take up position, he had long dark hair and an attention-seeking moustache. He wore a fringed suede jacket he had got cheap by bargaining a pissed off Algerian to the ground at a street market in Marseilles. In fact, Henry looked more like an ill-tempered Mexican bandito than a basically honest, if dysfunctional, Canadian composer/musician.

The taller of the two uniforms decided it might be strategically advantageous to search Henry's luggage. That was all right. Henry looked like the type who carried a ton of illegal drugs, but he didn't. He carried no drugs at all (though he would have brought a stash of weed, had I not put my foot down), and he was smuggling neither weapons nor government secrets. All we hauled around in our backpacks were clothes and the odd souvenir to prove that we'd been where we'd been. And books. Blessed books. The less we had to say to one another, the more avidly we read. Books make excellent shields.

The taller uniform won the treasure hunt. He pulled two books out of the bottom of Henry's backpack with a triumphant grunt and held them up, his arm straight in the air. One of the books was Albert Speer's *Inside the Third Reich*, the other Mario Puzo's *The Godfather*. We had bought them one rainy afternoon in Torremolinos in a small bookshop on Calle San Miguel. Afterwards we had hurried to a café and ordered tea and toast before taking shelter behind our new books, avoiding each other in a civilized manner.

The uniforms stepped out into the corridor to confer. Their expressions were those of men who had stumbled upon all the military secrets of the Soviet bloc about to be smuggled out by a shady bandito and his clueless moll.

One of them disappeared, the other returned to our compartment and slid the door shut. He did not return our passports. Without a word he sat down beside Henry and stared hard at the ceiling. Mimicking him, Henry stared in the same upward direction. As he did so, he began clicking his heels, producing perfectly the *staccato* approach of a goose-stepping army.

Ignoring them both, I contemplated the unexpected turn of events, wondering how the uniforms would react if they decided to ransack my bag to find Doris Lessing and Kurt Vonnegut pressed front to front atop my dirty underwear.

The platform remained empty. East Berlin was without sounds — apart from Henry's goose-stepping — until a few minutes later when a train door slammed farther down the platform. Purposeful feet marched in our direction, never missing a beat, echoing in the train corridor. Henry kept thudding his heels, keeping pace, until the other uniform pulled open the door again. He had brought with him a third official wearing a much fancier get-up. *Der Kommandant*, as Henry would refer to him.

Der Kommandant was a tall, elegant man. He occupied the doorway for a moment, allowing himself to be beheld for an appropriate length of time. His back was straight, his uniform immaculate, his deportment arrogant; he was fully aware of what a striking figure he cut. Looking first at Henry, then at me, he wished to know, pointedly: *"Sprechen Sie Deutsch?"*

It was not a question as much as an order. Judging by his countenance it would be advantageous to answer in the affirmative. Best to confess then.

"Ja, ich spreche Deutsch," I said. Half-assed *Deutsch* anyway. My mother was born in Frankfurt. Should I tell him that? Would it win me favour?

My gut instinct told me not to bother.

My affirmative reply made *Der Kommandant* raise one thin eyebrow in my direction. He stepped through the door into what suddenly felt like a prison cell and sat down beside me. Gingerly he placed his right leg over his left before folding his hands over his knees, executing each graceful gesture with slow and studied perfection. Having achieved the precise position necessary for whatever he had in mind, he proceeded to interrogate me, pleasantly aware of my fear.

Where did we come from? Where were we going? And why? Why were we in possession of this propaganda material? He pointed to Speer's book. Where had we got it?

"Why this unhealthy interest in the affairs of the Third Reich? Why should this be of interest to Canadians? Is it not a bit . . . how to put it . . . perverse? Hm? Answer me please."

The questions, though asked unhurriedly, were fired in a sharp tone indicating that we had committed not only an illegal act, but one of unparalleled stupidity. The gravity of our crime was unpardonable. We were to expect no leniency. There were no mitigating circumstances in a case such as this, and if we did not understand that we were even dumber than we looked.

I offered no excuse for our wrongdoing. I had none, only the bland truth that when we had been looking for something to read in an English bookshop in a winter-deserted tourist trap in Spain a few weeks earlier, Henry had thought *Inside the Third Reich* looked interesting. So had *The Godfather*. It was, as I pointed out in our defense, on every bestseller list in the free world.

Der Kommandant's eyebrows fluttered ever so slightly at "the free world."

Ignoring his expressive brow, I rambled on, explaining that, as the choice of books had been somewhat limited, we had bought these two because we had needed something to read that afternoon, you see, *Mein Herr*, and the next day on the train to Barcelona, and later on the bus from Barcelona to Geneva, and on the train from . . .

Here I raised my doomed head and looked into a pair of eyes so supremely indifferent to my rambling that I clammed right up.

Henry, who had been treated as invisible during the interrogation, burst out with a helpful, "Tell that fucking asshole we've done nothing wrong. Go on, tell him!"

After giving Henry a look so icy cold it actually shut him up, *Der Kommandant* repeated every single question again, enunciating each word with such pedantic accuracy it was as though he had an obsessive love of language.

Once more I repeated what I had already struggled to communicate with grammatically bungled phrases about our plunge into a life of international crime. By then more than half an hour had passed since the train stopped. They had yet to return our passports. The compartment was cold. I was sweating.

Surely there were other people on the train? Impatient people fidgeting in their seats, checking their watches, swearing in various languages, livid at the delay? Why were no voices raised in protest, no enraged passengers spilling into the corridor demanding an explanation? Why were we surrounded by silence?

I realized I was terrified. Soon I would be writing to my parents from an East German jail cell to inform them that I would not be returning home.

It pleased *Der Kommandant* enormously to see the terror in my eyes. I detected a flicker of amusement in his.

"So, kindly remember in the future, young lady, that it is forbidden to import this kind of propaganda into East Germany. Attempt to learn the rules of a country before you decide to visit. Understood? Hm?" Bored with the game, having had his bit of fun, *Der Kommandant* suddenly spoke English. It was as flawless and precise as his German.

"Understood."

"Good girl."

As he got up he reached out and touched my cheek with a smooth hand that smelled of cigarettes. It was not so much a pat as a slap just weak enough to pass for a gesture of kindness.

One of the other uniforms flung our passports onto the seat beside Henry. Taking his leave, *Der Kommandant* informed us that they were confiscating the "propaganda material." *The Godfather* was included under that heading.

Henry's scowl was severe. He spat a sentence at me. "You realize those were the same robots goose-stepping for Hitler during the war?"

The train had left Berlin and was chugging north towards the coast, headlong into a squall sweeping down from the Baltic Sea. Furious rain lashed the window.

"Never mind," I said. I felt faint with relief. "We're free."

"Whoopee shit."

"And we've read the books."

"What the fuck's that got to do with it?"

"Nothing. So why don't you let it go?"

"Bet you those bastards couldn't wait to read *The Godfather*. Notice *Der Kommandant* spoke English after all?" Henry's agitated fingers started drumming on his knees, out of rhythm with the rain, accompanying a frenzied fugue only he could hear.

"Well, you enjoyed it."

The drumming stopped, fingers halting in midair. "Are you trying to piss me off?"

"No."

I pissed him off with no effort at all.

He started drumming again, faster this time, *accelerando*, like feet running.

I spent the night alone in the train ferry cafeteria. It was jam-packed with drunks shouting and singing in what I assumed were one or more Scandinavian languages. Everybody chain-smoked and chain-drank throughout the night, from teenagers to pensioners. Where did they get the energy? Every table except mine was overflowing with beer bottles and schnapps glasses, the floor soaked with spilled drinks. The smoke was so dense it obscured people's faces, but at least it was warm in there.

Henry huddled out on deck in the privacy of the windswept rain, a quixotic figure facing south to where the lights along the German coast grew ever distant. Only Henry would choose to sit in cold drizzle, shoulders hunched, convinced he was proving some significant point that I in particular and the world in general were too shallow to grasp.

He did not budge all night. The wind kept tugging at his wet hair, tearing at the fringes of his jacket.

We reached Copenhagen early the next afternoon. With our friends as buffers we had a wonderful five days. The sun was shining, the beer was cheap, the Danes blessed with a natural knack for enjoying life. Nobody was in a hurry. It was springtime, there was music in the air, a million tulips and Easter lilies drenched the parks and the markets. Jolly citizens zoomed around on bicycles with bouquets of spring flowers in the front baskets. We were told that it was not unusual to see the Queen of Denmark pedal her bike about town.

Even Henry found it difficult to dislike a country whose queen rode a bike. That all the pretty girls flirted with him also helped soften his heart. They had a way of pressing their gregarious boobs against him when having a conversation, flicking their Danish blond tresses over lissome shoulders, asking him brazen questions in a singsong accent. None of them wore a bra.

Henry pressed back and turned downright sunny.

One night in a jazz club, amazingly, he let himself be persuaded to have a go at the piano after somebody discovered that he was a musician. He ended up performing to an enthusiastic crowd — half of them blond and bra-less and horny — until closing time, jazz tunes not his own, melodies full of life and energy and toe-tapping rhythms, smiling to himself the way he always did when his fingers gamboled over piano keys, that blissful smile I did not have the power to invoke. Perhaps smiling also at how easy it was for him to seduce a room full of people when he felt like it.

Mistaking his private universe for mine, having drunk too many Tuborgs, I thought, "Why, that's him! There he is!" as if he'd been gone for a long time and had only just now returned. As if he was back to stay.

He wasn't, of course. I was being my usual optimistic self. All the pleasantries were but an interlude. I was just one of the fools easily seduced. By the time we sat strapped into our seats on the charter flight from Gatwick to Toronto we were once again, for reasons as befuddling as ever, back in the trenches, not speaking. Except for halfway over the Atlantic when he turned to me and said, "Hey, want to get something to drink?" and I tiredly said yes even though I wasn't thirsty.

Later that day heading west from Toronto, I peered out the plane window with jet-lagged eyes and discovered to my consternation our relationship sprawled down below. It must have fallen out of the plane somehow, because there it lay, a barren expanse, hard and cold and flat, with large patches of ice like dead skin on its cracked surface, too far gone to survive. The shadow of the plane slid across it like a knife.

Henry didn't notice, the same way he never noticed that I had stopped wearing a bra, never noticed the way I flicked my brown tresses. He was engrossed in the new copy of *The Godfather* I had bought for him at Gatwick, tapping a foot as he read, drumming his fingers, *mezzo forte*, never stopping.

I wanted to break his fingers.

It was dark when we arrived home.

"We're home."

"*You're* home," he corrected me, shoving the book into his pocket. "*I'm* not from this fucking backwater."

I had hoped to see friends and family waiting, smiling people eager to fold us to their welcoming bosoms, this despite the fact that we had not informed anybody of our arrival. Henry had requested there be no embarrassing display of touchy-feely shit. My family was too extroverted for his taste.

His own estranged family, "limited and middle class, what's there to describe," lived in Ottawa. He refused to tell me what they did for a living. (I have since learnt that they are very rich.)

Arriving back in Regina after half a year was confusing. I had expected everything to look different, if only to mark the passage of time. But nothing had changed. My grade ten chemistry teacher, Mrs. Arbuthnot, a woman famous for never shutting up, was greeting relatives by the luggage carousel, mouth flapping faster than ever. Mr. Hodgkins, the childless widower who lived across the street from my parents, was pacing up and down, craning his short neck in search of somebody.

My hometown. An insular world where it's impossible to pass through the airport without spotting a familiar face.

And still in the grip of winter. A savage wind tried to tear the skin off our faces as soon as we stepped outside.

"Welcome home," muttered Henry. This time he did not hesitate to jump into a taxi, where he crouched in a corner of the back seat, glaring at the naked trees leaning south in the wind. Just as we pulled up in front of the apartment building, it started to snow. Small hard flakes ripping by in gusts.

"Looks like you brought back bad weather," grumbled the cabdriver and turned on the windshield wipers. They screeched against the glass. "Won't be no spring this year."

"Like that's my fucking fault." Henry got out and slammed the door.

Blushing, I tipped the driver too much as apology for my partner's lack of grace.

The next morning I woke up to the sound of the piano. Notes fell as atonally cold and brittle as ice crystals. It was still snowing. The city had turned white. I forgot it was late March and began preparing for the winter ahead, dragging parkas and boots, mitts and hats from the back of the hall closet.

It snowed for two days.

Henry spent the entire time at the piano, building a dirge out of crystalline notes that fell dead long after the snow stopped.

Spring arrived eventually, it always does, even around here. The earth warmed up, the wheat sprouted green, and Henry and I went our separate ways.

On the last day of April he headed back to Ontario. He loaded his grand piano onto the back of a truck with the help of two musician friends, tied it down and covered it with a tarp, saying as a way of farewell that we were incompatible. He had tried, he assured me. We just did not belong to the same species. He looked pained, but wasted little time getting into the passenger seat of the truck. There he sat, staring ahead, shoulders hunched, arms crossed, not knowing what to do with them if his hands were not near piano keys.

Turning my back on him, I went upstairs.

I had expected the living room to look desolate without the piano. Instead it was roomy and bright. I had feared that heavy silence would fill it and weigh me down, but the air was as buoyant as an impromptu waltz. Inspired, I danced by myself on the dusty floor where the piano had stood. Danced and danced in the room that was mine.

It happens sometimes, if I see a copy of *The Godfather* — or an orangutan, an elephant, or a dwarf — that I think of Henry. Henry P. Fontaine, the composer. When I do, I wonder if he still enjoys being free, if still he smiles only when his fingers gallop over an open stretch of piano keys. His long fingers lacked the ability to be still, forever beating out the distress signals I never knew how to decode.

He has had some success with his music career, producing six CDs over the last two decades. Some critics use clichés like "tortured, but brilliant" when they attempt to explain his compositions. Others indulgently describe the way his music "reflects the disturbed cacophony and the ever present dangers of modern life."

I have yet to listen to the first five. There are some things in life one is better off avoiding. But a few days ago I relented and bought his latest CD. It was the title of it that intrigued me. It's called *Leaving Berlin*, the name of the first number featured on it.

It starts out *largo* — reluctant, suspicious notes that without warning collapse into a dragged out tedium. As they capitulate, a pronounced frustration bubbles to the surface. Flashes of atonal anger glide effortlessly into disgruntled chords that sigh. The chords keep on sighing with deliberate exaggeration, while throughout, somewhere within this misery, furious fingers beat a dogged rhythm, *forte, risoluto*, intent on escape. They never cease, those despondent, hurrying fingers. The notes they produce are sardonic to the point of snarling.

The music paints an emotional landscape so forlorn, that when I hear it I want to give in to an immediate need to distance myself from it, to flee, *risoluto*, before I, too, get stuck in that bleak place.

Towards the end, the subdued basses grow tired and fall silent, but then, just as the fatigued, brave cellos are about to give up, a small brass section erupts in a startling, joyless *crescendo* that makes my heart skip a beat every time I hear it. In that *fortissimo* howl I hear once again how the elephants trumpeted as we waited, not speaking, for the light to turn green.

The Blue Album

She had surprised herself in March that year by walking out on the man who was her husband. That was how she had come to think of him since the day they got married: the man who is my husband. As though he had been allotted to her.

Her sudden departure made the marriage a brief one; still there had been ample time for her to learn to recite — backwards, forwards and sideways — the list of her flaws. It was a list, the man who was her husband was fond of reiterating, that was twice as long as his arm, which, to illustrate, he would raise in a semblance of a Nazi salute.

She would look at him and think how a Hitler-inspired moustache would not have gone amiss over that prissy little mouth of his.

The subject of her flaws had begun eating at her husband as soon as he found himself with a wedding ring squeezing his finger. Within weeks he had begun to deplore his failure to notice her blatant deficiencies prior to tying the knot. He had been, in his parlance, wrongfully conjugated. He should have paid more attention, but he had a very hectic schedule, didn't he? He could deal with only so many frustrations at any one time, he was only human. He was a travelling salesman for a company that sold orthopedic equipment, artificial joints and such. His busy mind had a lot of essential facts and figures, dates and names, to keep straight from day to day.

Brenda, unambitious miscreant that she was, spent her days poking seeds into dirt in an overpriced greenhouse. Probably the only kind of work she could be trusted with, considering how inept she was.

Inept how? Timid Brenda used to wonder, numbed by his behaviour.

Well, the wrongfully conjugated man would reply, if she didn't know that, then her condition was even more terminal than he'd suspected.

Whether he had planned it or simply seized the moment that morning, he used the comment as an exit line, accompanied by an expression of disdain that served only to emphasize that he did not sport much in the way of a chin. With the key to his new silver Pontiac shining like a dagger in his fist, he slammed the door.

The house shuddered and fell quiet.

There was newly fallen snow powdering the ground, covering a treacherous layer of ice. Normally Brenda would have called out — it's what a good wife does — for him to drive carefully. That day she watched in silence as he flung open the car door and hurled his pigskin briefcase and a pile of glossy brochures into the back seat where he kept samples of the latest model of an artificial hip joint. As he bent over, she noticed his spreading butt straining the seat of his pants.

In the next stupefying moment she found herself trespassing in someone else's head, peering out of a pair of wide open eyes far more discriminating than her own, at a complete stranger. With a clarity that was clinical in its brightness, antiseptic in its smell, and as sharp as a scalpel, she stood nose to nose with the fact that she did not know the round-faced jerk cramming himself behind the wheel of his beloved car.

Nor did she want to know him.

It was in this state of lightheaded awareness that she made the impromptu decision to get the hell out of the house, of the marriage, of the role she was playing. Not at some point in the future, but there and then, before she was forced back into her own wishy-washy head again. Yes, she would flee, and she would take with her only what was hers. Apart from her clothes, few of the items in the house were hers: a non-stick frying pan, an oriental vase, an ornately framed small still life featuring grapes and a dead pheasant, a handsome unscratched mahogany desk and a rocking chair that had once belonged to her maternal grandmother.

The rest belonged to the man who was about to no longer be her husband. He had inherited the bungalow from his grandfather. ("Lock, stock and barrel, you name it, *I* own it.") Nothing but his, from the liquor cabinet — containing half a bottle of Jim Beam — disguised as a globe on a stand, to the mustard yellow shag carpet in the living room, where a stag's head hung over the TV. His father had felled it with a single bullet. Every night its melancholy eyes glowered at Brenda while she tried to escape into her favourite shows.

I didn't shoot you, she often reminded the severed head, but it kept glowering.

The name of the man she was leaving was Desmond. She had never been crazy about the name.

Before slamming the door to Desmond's bungalow for the last time, Brenda had to face the humiliating reality of her situation: she could not afford a place of her own. She would have to share. Go live with a stranger.

Another stranger.

She checked the ads in the previous day's paper with trepidation, knowing it might take greater courage than she possessed to call an unknown, faceless human being to inquire about possible cohabitation. The world was full of sex maniacs and serial killers and perverts in general; it was another of the verities of life that Desmond had alerted her to.

She read the twenty-four ads twice, confirming that there was only one safe-sounding possibility: one that appealed for a "responsible roommate to share spacious second floor apartment in a duplex." The ad said to call Donna. Brenda liked the reassuringly feminine name. After five minutes of breathing exercises to induce calm — and getting pleasantly dizzy — she dialed the number, remembering to keep breathing, to make her voice sound business-like, brushing her ineptness under the shag carpet. Hoping this Donna would be at home early in the . . .

" . . . Hello? . . . Is this Donna? Oh, hi there! M . . . my name's Brenda . . . I'm calling about the ad for a roommate?"

Donna hogged the conversation from there on, driving it expertly, chatting as if they had known each other since kindergarten. She confided that Brenda was the only caller she'd had who didn't sound like a masturbating pervert.

They both interpreted this as a favourable sign.

Taking into account the dearth of potential tenants, Donna said Brenda was welcome to move right in, place unseen, should the spirit move her. "I mean, like, what the eff, eh?" It was a bit risky, she supposed, but Brenda sounded like a decent human being. And it was a real nice apartment, promised Donna, who sounded nonjudgmental and easygoing and had the morning off.

Brenda decided to take the chance and move in. Non judgmental, easygoing company would make a change. Might give her an opportunity to grow a spine.

After she hung up, she ran a finger through the Services section in the classifieds. A man with a pick-up truck was advertising small moving jobs at a reasonable price. She called him at once. His name was Ernie Bryner and he confessed to having a slow day, it being kinda the crappy season for moving, what with the weather and all. He would be able to pick up her stuff around ten or thereabouts.

Next she called the greenhouse where she worked and told them she was not feeling herself at all. Considering the circumstances, this was not a lie.

Her thirtieth birthday was the following Saturday. Come the weekend, she would enter an age by which one is supposed to have accomplished something.

Turning her back on that myth, she hurried off to pack.

Ernie Bryner was half an hour late. He saw no reason to apologize for the delay, but generously offered her the seat beside him when she told him she had no car. Brenda accepted the offer but declined when he held out a crumpled pack of Export A.

"Youse don't smoke?"

"Trying to quit," she lied, wanting to appear worldly enough to have bad habits.

"Good for you. Fucking killing me." To illustrate the approaching asphyxia, Ernie did his best to cough up a lung.

Less than two and a half hours after Desmond's Pontiac had torn out of the driveway, Brenda had left for good. Already the year and a half of marriage — and what a bland stretch of days it was — looked unfamiliar. Moving from one life into another, aided by a gasping chain-smoker in a green Chevy pickup, proved such an easy manoeuver it never occurred to her to that this rash decision was the greatest milestone in her life to date.

The address where the pick-up truck pulled to a stop was a red brick duplex on a leafy street full of identical duplexes east of the downtown core. Not that it mattered where it was, the man who still was, technically speaking, her husband would never come looking for her, not here, not anywhere. Just as she knew that, should she return to plead forgiveness, he would have changed the lock on the door of his domain. He would be sitting on his couch in his living room staring at his TV under his stag's head, pretending his wife Brenda did not exist. Watching some sitcom, laughing at jokes that weren't funny.

Donna O'Hara was six years divorced and favoured sleeveless tops that exposed frayed bra straps. Not prone to navel-gazing, she had never ever entertained those punishing thoughts that were more inescapable than the black holes in space, the holes Brenda kept tripping into while manoeuvering herself into the future.

Donna was blessed with a constitution so cheerful it bordered on annoying, unhindered in her *joie de vivre* by obstacles such as moral principles and firm opinions. God knows she was more than easy to get along with, but her middle name was not Dependable. (It was Angeline.) This became evident during the first get-to-know-each-other-days. Brenda realized that should she ever need somebody to be there, if only to lend a sympathetic ear, Donna would not be the one lending it. Donna would be off dyeing her hair, shoplifting underwear at Zellers or — if it was after dark — picking up lost men slouched in bars where ambiance was not a priority.

On the other hand, the rent was cheap, this not yet being the neighbourhood of choice for the upwardly mobile.

Most of the time Brenda had the place to herself, which was fine, she really did not mind, she liked to pretend she lived alone. Fridays after work she stopped at Safeway two blocks east to shop and to treat herself to a bouquet of flowers. Carnations with a sprig of baby's breath, that kind of modest arrangement. The flowers, when placed in the centre of the kitchen table, provided the undersized kitchen with a glimmer of hope. Sometimes she lit a candle while she ate supper. Watched the flame cast an ambiguous glimmer on the surface of her soup.

Making the best of it, Brenda learned to relax again, day by day, muscle by muscle. It wasn't easy, but she managed and she was proud of that. Had she felt like frying a pork chop for dinner, she could have done so without a frowning person dangling it on a fork at arm's length, snarling "What the fuck is this lump of fat supposed to represent?"

"It's an uncanny replica of your face, my beloved," Brenda had never dared reply.

The man prone to dangling pork chops was the same man who had once bought her flowers hard to come by out of season, flowers not available in a plastic bucket placed at Safeway's express checkout counter. The man who, when asking her to marry him, had professed to be drowning in the sapphire ponds of her eyes. She had assumed him a poet for saying that, unaware that clichés and poetry did not walk hand in hand like dreamy-eyed lovers. The way he had thrown his money atop the bill after dinner had humbled her. The tip had been so scant as to be absent, but she had failed to notice that, gratefully beholding the strong take-charge personality of the man called Desmond.

His last name was Gorchek.

Inexperienced, and in constant need of assurance, it had never occurred to her to say no when he proposed a few weeks later, as though it would have been bad manners to disappoint him. As if he was expressing a well-intentioned kindness that deserved a reward. Once he shared his last name with her, she had hoped his indelible assurance would rub off.

It had not. His romantic deportment had been an act — a bad one, looking back — and for reasons she would never fathom. What she had not been able to figure out was *why* he had kept up the determined act just long enough to get her to marry him, *why* he had wanted to marry her when it soon became blatantly obvious that he did not like her. It was nothing personal, he just did not have a high opinion of women. Maybe he wanted to prove to himself that he could marry if he wanted to marry.

Equally puzzling was why it had taken her so long to see through him.

That aside, and may it rest in peace, she was once again, for what it was worth, Brenda Jones, independent nonentity.

Though time had no reason to linger, it did not pass rapidly, still the weeks and months did plod by in an orderly fashion. The black holes in space did not conveniently disappear, but they did begin to shrink. Brenda stumbled into them less readily.

It was on a Friday night the following September, just as she was washing her soup bowl and spoon, that there came three sudden raps at the door. The door — the only entry to the apartment — opened straight into the kitchen from the back stairs. It was such a flimsy door, its hollowness gave power to the most timid of knocks. These three raps were hard and to the point, violent explosions in her private evening space. Brenda considered not answering, thinking for a fleeting moment that it was Desmond come to claim her, knowing full well he would never waste the energy.

No, it would be Donna who, having once again forgotten her key, was desperate to hurry her beer-bloated bladder to the toilet.

Better open the door then.

Haloed under the porch light stood a squat, solid figure dressed in an overcoat that had been fashionable long before he was born (and he was not that young), a woolen coat speckled grey like his hair and adorned with a quaint black velvet collar much too small for its bulk. With its round soft edge, it added a perversely childlike quality to the stranger's appearance. The unshaved face above the collar gleamed with an oily sheen, as if its owner had travelled without rest, but with a great deal of anxiety, for a long time over a great distance. Maybe he had; his cheap shoes were dusty enough. The way the thick fingers of his right hand gripped a small suitcase gave the unacceptable impression that he had come to stay.

Whoever the stranger was, a wrecking ball would be needed to budge his solid hulk from the narrow gap of the door that Brenda was desperate to slam, bolt and board up. Any second now the terror charging up her spine would hurtle out of her mouth in the form of a giveaway scream. That would not be good. Predators are turned on by fear.

She pressed her lips together. As she did, the apparition looked at her and smiled. The smile distorted his features. It may have been a smile meant to reassure, but it made him look as if overcome by acute toothache. Staring at his cracked face, she knew for sure that the door would not withstand him, should he decide to charge. He looked like he would be able to bulldoze his way straight through it without so much as ruffling that boyish velvet collar.

Then he spoke. The sound of his voice was not unlike coarse sandpaper being rubbed against uneven concrete. "Hi. I'm Gordie. Donna's brother? This *is* where she lives, right? Donna O'Hara?"

When she first heard about this fabled brother, Brenda — an old-fashioned romantic — had imagined a young Marlon Brando, or better still, a Steve McQueen look-alike, a brooding rebel, handsome and misunderstood.

Donna had put a swift end to that delusion by describing her brother, scars, broken nose, missing teeth, and all, as "built like a brick shithouse."

It was an apt observation, Brenda now realized. The man *did* exhibit the dimensions of an average outhouse.

Come on, Brenda, answer his question. *Never heard of her.* " . . . Yes . . . she lives here, b . . . but she's not home yet. Can I . . . ?"

"Mind if I come in and wait? Thing is, see, I really need to talk to her, eh? I'm only in town for the weekend." The plea was followed by another painful smile. By then he was already inside.

Yes, I mind! "I suppose," mumbled Brenda, despising herself for the cowardice that was ten times the size of her fear.

"Thanks. Sure appreciate it. Know when she'll be back?"

"I've no idea." *It's not like Donna keeps a schedule, is it?* Brenda wondered if this man actually knew his sister.

Still, she made an effort, figuring she had no choice. She inhaled and pulled herself together, stood up straight, determined to shoo away the word "inept," shoo away not only the word, but the contempt it had for her.

I should offer coffee. It's what you do when you have company. Yes, that's what I'll do . . . She exhaled. "So . . . w . . . w . . . would you like some c . . . coffee? Or tea?"

"Say, coffee would be great! Thanks. Kinda cold out there, eh?"

"Yes."

"What's your name?"

"Brenda."

"Hi Brenda."

"H . . . hi."

Gordie put his suitcase on the table beside the toaster, blocking the view of the red carnations she had treated herself to that evening. That done, he remained standing by the door, unsure what to do next.

Trying to ignore him, Brenda plugged in the kettle and prepared to make instant coffee, unwilling to waste the good stuff, her secret stash that she drank only when alone. The stiffness in her arms made her gestures robotic and clumsy. There was no ignoring Gordie O'Hara. It was a small kitchen and he took up most of it. Scared witless, she made no attempt at conversation, too busy spilling first the coffee granules, then the sugar. Just as she handed him a mug, the phone rang. She lunged for it, splashing coffee on both the floor and Gordie.

"Hello!" *Help!*

"Brenda?"

"Donna!" Her words were so frightened they dared leave her mouth only in the safety of a group. "Donnayourbrotherisherewhereareyou?"

"Whoa there! Slow down, for chrissake! Whatcha mean, my brother? Which one?"

And Brenda remembered that Donna had four. One was dead. The other two, according to their sister, were "assholes aspiring to pseudo yuppiedom in some fucking plywood mansion in the suburbs."

Then there was Gordie.

"Gordie."

"You shittin' me! Gordie? What's he doing there?"

"How should I know? Where are you anyway? When will you be back?"

"Well, that's kinda why I'm calling. I won't. I'm up in Kingston."

"You're WHERE?" The escaping hysteria whistled like an air raid alarm in the confines of the kitchen. Brenda wished she had a shelter to flee to.

Oblivious to the alarm, Donna continued. "In Kingston. At my aunt's. Got so fucking bored this morning, I skipped work after lunch and hitchhiked up. Just got here. Took me more than seven hours. Thought I'd call you and stuff."

Brenda ceased to breathe. *I'm going to kill you.* "When are you coming back?"

"I dunno. Whenever. Monday. Maybe Tuesday. Haven't decided."

A flame of fury licked Brenda's gut and continued up her spine to her brain. It had a scorching tongue. It felt good, that tongue, cleansing and pure. Expletives formed unbidden in her head. She welcomed them. *That fucking slut.*

Then she decided Donna could *not* be in Kingston. Donna was simply not paying attention. Once she caught on, she'd be back in Hamilton.

"Aren't you listening, for God's sake? Your *brother's* here to see you!"

"I heard you the first time. Wonder what he wants? Put him on, eh?"

Brenda handed Gordie the phone telling him the obvious. "It's your sister."

He grabbed it eagerly. It looked small and defenseless in his hand. "Hey, Donna! Yeah! Don't I know it, eh! How you doing, kiddo!" His face cracked into a smile. By the looks of it, his toothache was abating.

Brenda wished she could hear both sides of the conversation.

"No shit!" Gordie was saying. "Is that right? Oh, jeez. Now, that ain't good. See, I was really hoping to see you."

That makes two of us.

"Well, ah . . . thing is, see . . . I'm . . . well, kinda . . . you know . . . off to the slammer again on Monday." An embarrassed side glance.

Don't let me keep you. Hang up and I'll call you a cab. Or a squad car.

"Oh, well, you know . . . The usual . . . What? Yeah, don't I know it, eh! Huh? Well, I'll tell you about it sometime, it ain't no big deal. No, just eighteen months this time. Actually, a social worker might be getting in touch with you. That's what I wanted to talk to you about, see. It's kind of imp . . . what's that? Oh sure. But say, Donna . . . I . . . "

I'm alone in my home with a violent felon. Was it common to let criminals roam free the weekend before starting their sentence? And if so, why?

"Are you sure?" asked Gordie. "No kidding? Well, jeez, Donna, that's real nice of you, I guess. I sure do appreciate it."

Appreciate what?

"You too, kiddo. But say, could you maybe . . . What? Yeah . . . yeah, you too. And say hi to Aunt Connie, eh? What's that? No, I don't, I was . . . Really? You sure? Jeez, that's great! Yeah for sure, I'll do that." He handed Brenda the phone, looking apologetic. "Donna wants another word."

Donna's voice in her ear was cheerful. "Hey, Bren? Listen, I told my brother he could stay there for the weekend. He can use my bedroom, 'kay?"

"You WHAT!" The flame flared up and blinded her.

"Well, hey, come on, he's got no place to stay, does he? It's only for two nights, for fuck's sake. And he's a good guy, don't worry. Trust me, really, it'll be fine. I told him you're not busy this weekend."

"You did WHAT!" *When I lay eyes on you again I'm going to grab you by that dry bleached frizz of yours and bang your empty head against the wall until your skull cracks open and all the air escapes. Gordie can teach me the best technique for this, it's right up his alley.* It was the most violent thought Brenda had ever entertained, and she relished every bit of it.

"Well, you're not busy are you? Figured it'd be a bit of company for you. Oh, come on, Bren, for chrissake, you don't *mind*, do you?" Donna's voice was too indifferent to pretend otherwise.

"Of course I freaking mind!" *Oops! Oh, shit! Oh shit, oh shit! Now he'll kill me!*

"Oh, come on. He's my brother, for fuck's sake."

What a glowing recommendation that was.

There they were, facing their imposed weekend rendezvous, Brenda Jones with a shiver and a stiff smile, acting like she didn't mind a bit, Gordie O'Hara pretending he'd gone momentarily deaf and missed her protestations.

Outside the force of the cold wind had increased, whistling disrespectfully through the frame of the kitchen window.

The radio had talked about a first frost.

Gordie was still lodged in his coat, mug in hand, coffee untouched. For some reason Brenda had expected dandruff flakes to litter the velvet collar like an early snowfall, but she couldn't see any. Maybe they had stuck to the grease in his hair.

After shuffling his feet, rubbing his free hand on his coat for a bit, Gordie put the mug down and asked, not looking directly at her, if it would be at all possible for him to have a shower. "Been sitting on a bus for the past three days."

If you make it last until Sunday. Her obliging "Of course!" sounded as insincere as it was. She rushed off to fetch him two of Donna's candy-pink towels.

As soon as he was in the shower, she hurried to her room and got her big black shawl out of the bottom drawer of her dresser. Not knowing exactly why, she spun it around herself. Securely cocooned, she drifted into the living room and sank onto the couch. Grappling with the fact that she was alone with a felon, a "crazed man with a troubled soul," it occurred to her that her bedroom door did not lock.

She warmed her hands on the lukewarm coffee mug and stared out the window. The darkness was so heavy she might have been crouching on the bottom of the ocean, waiting in resignation for a hungry shark to glide out of the shadows and sink his teeth into her.

Across the hall the faint splashes from the shower came to a stop.

"I brought my photo albums. I was gonna show them to Donna, eh?"

Gordie stood in the doorway dressed in jeans and a clean shirt. His hair was wet, his shirt collar damp. He was clutching a photo album in each hand. A red one and a blue one.

"Pardon?"

"Wanna see some pictures?"

No. "Sure."

What kind of photos do men like him collect? Jailhouse pictures? 'That's my bunk on top. And that's Psycho, my cellmate. He got life for raping and mutilating his sister's roommate. He's my hero.'

Gordie came over and got comfortable beside her on the couch. The blue album he put on the coffee table, the red one he placed on his lap. His sitting down uninvited was not a predatory move, rather that of a child getting cozy beside Mom with a favourite book before bedtime.

Confused by the absurdity of it all, she noticed that he had helped himself to her special soap. He smelled like a big ripe peach.

Eager to get started, Gordie flipped open the album and for a moment it was as if he disappeared from the room. Brenda sat rigid beside the shell he left behind, politely glancing at a meaningless series of images. Parties and backyard barbecues, the odd camping trip. Flabby guts displayed like badges of honour. Stacked beer cases towering beside picnic tables. So many grinning faces, one could easily be fooled into thinking the world was a slaphappy utopia drenched in sunshine and tattoos, laughter and free beer. Photos from the part of Gordie's life not spent in jail. Packs of cigarettes and lighters tucked up T-shirt sleeves, yet more beer bottles.

Peach-scented, brick shithouse Gordie was in the merciless throes of nostalgia, clasping his album the way a Christian might a Bible when the seven angels blow their trumpets.

It took a while before he resurfaced. When he did, he pointed to a photo of a blonde dragging on a cigarette, hair rolled tight in large curlers, eyebrows unevenly drawn, cellulite thighs spreading over a lawn chair with impunity. "That's my ex-girlfriend Joline," Gordie said. The face challenging the camera was hard. Stare at her for too long and she might reach out of the photo and knock your teeth down your throat.

"So what happened to her?"

"Well, she got married, eh? To this other con, Jeff, that I knew. Thing was, see, she already had a couple of kids with him, so . . . "

"Oh. Made sense then, I suppose." *Well, what else to say?*

"I guess."

Several pages later, he pointed again. "And this is my other ex-girlfriend. Tamara." A proud finger landed atop a skinny brunette dressed in leather pants and a polka dot bikini top. His finger covered most of her body, the ragged nail following the curve of her left shoulder. She was sitting astride a Harley, a mickey of vodka in her right hand.

"And where is she now?" It was obvious that he wanted her to ask.

"Dead. Crashed her bike. Wasn't wearing a helmet, eh? Plus she had a bit of a drug problem." He left his finger on the image of the girl like he was trying to keep her warm as the September wind got angrier outside.

"Oh . . . I'm so sorry."

"Yeah, well. It was pretty bad. But what can you do, eh? I'd only known her for, like, three weeks, so . . . "

"Not long."

"You said it."

He put the red album on the table and grabbed the blue one. It was only half full, as if here his life had petered out. The photos repeated the previous scenes, same faces, same beer, same cigarettes, same barbecues, but no more girlfriends.

And at the very end, alone on a page, carefully centred in a nonexistent frame, a photo of five children. Presumably Donna, Gordie and the three other brothers. Four boys lined up in a row, wearing identical little red and green checkered vests, bowties and starched white shirts, awkward in their enforced finery. Sitting in front of them, a tiny Donna in a ruffled dress, white socks and shiny red shoes, stared big-eyed into the camera. A red satin ribbon held her wispy brown curls in place. In the background, the branches of a sparsely decorated Christmas tree threw a shadow on a bare wall.

Gordie lit up. "Lookit this, eh! This was when we was kids. My uncle Vern took it. That's my brother Dean to the left there, and that's Ricky right next to him. And see: that's me in the middle, that chubby little guy. And that's Jim to the right. He died ten years ago. Car crash . . . "

"I know. Donna told me."

"Yeah? But say, don't Donna look cute? She'd just turned three that Christmas."

"Just adorable." Brenda studied the gap-toothed expectant grins, the freckled little noses, the five pairs of round eyes staring at the camera. Gordie's bow tie was crooked. Jim's hair stood on end. Donna's underwear was showing. Their innocence saddened her.

"That's all I've got." Gordie closed the album. It was unclear if he was referring to his collection of photos or the sum total of happy memories.

Brenda feigned interest. "No more pictures from when you were kids?"

"No. Mom didn't have a camera."

The impromptu walk down memory lane had taken up a fair chunk of the evening and for that Brenda was grateful. But when Gordie reluctantly put the albums back on the coffee table, he wanted to talk. What it was in Brenda's demeanor that inspired the trust to make her his confidante, she never would understand. But there he was, right next to her on Donna's fake leather couch, looking straight into her eyes, earnestly, as if in them he had discovered the lights of a temporary haven.

Doesn't he realize he's mistaken? How do I explain that I want him to go away?

She kept quiet and listened as he shared with her the emptiness that overwhelms a man when he no longer has a reason to give a damn. What it's like to crouch like an animal in solitary confinement days on end. Gordie snagged inadequate descriptions wherever he found them and offered them to her, looking ashamed, knowing they were not suitable gifts for a lady. "Thing is, see, there ain't nowhere to go. Just fucking nowhere, pardon my French. You need to talk, there ain't nobody gonna listen. So at some point, what happens is, you lose it. It's the way it is."

Trying to explain his handicap made him short of breath. He struggled to describe his experiences, searching for words that kept eluding him, making him frustrated. He shook his head, rubbed his hands on his knees. Once again there was an acute toothache in what passed for a smile. "See, it's always having to look over your shoulder, like, to check who is after you this time. It's what gets to you, is what I mean. Having to be paranoid. Places like that, there's always somebody out to get you."

Violence turned cliché.

Brenda glanced at his face then, at features lamenting that he had been capable of no other life but the one gone wrong. Felt her own frustration. There was nothing she could do for him.

As the clock ticked steadily towards midnight she learnt tidbits about men in incarceration that she would have paid hard-earned money to remain ignorant of. Suppressing shock and disbelief, setting aside ready judgment, she concentrated on being a gracious hostess. Took cheap comfort in the realization that however little she had to offer, it would be far more than he was used to.

When he eventually fell silent, a sigh escaped him. Brenda suppressed her flicker of compassion, instead taking the opportunity to call it a night. She worked up the courage to bid him goodnight, thinking it best to do so without mentioning the word "bed." Readjusting her black shawl to a tighter fit, her face somber, her voice void of emotion, she left the room, trying to look like she had grown fangs and was floating off to sleep in a coffin.

Closing the door to her room, she jammed a chair under the handle in a noiseless, covert operation. She had a perfect right to feel safe in her own home, yet the barricade nagged her like a shameful secret.

Apart from the man named Desmond Gorchek, to whom she still had half-forgotten legal ties, she had never been alone with a man at night.

She lay so rigid in bed she barely touched the mattress, alert to the slightest noise. Every time she heard Gordie turn over in Donna's bed, she was ready to leap up and toss herself out the window. Imagined herself turning into a bat, flitting off into the darkness, strong elegant wings silhouetted against the moon.

Soon the only sound from Donna's bedroom was a steady snoring punctuated by soft grunts.

He could be faking it to lull me into a false sense of security.

The minutes dragged.

Brenda woke up to find the sun splashing anemic light through her window. From the street came reassuring Saturday morning noises. Kids shrieking. The neighbour's dog yapping.

Mrs. Rosato's loud voice talking on the phone downstairs. The wet whoosh of traffic up on Main Street indicated it had rained during the night.

The apartment, on the other hand, was dead quiet.

Aware that she could not stay barricaded all weekend, she forced herself out of bed, put on her floor length bathrobe and tied it securely with a double knot. Soundlessly she removed the chair from under the door handle, slapped a semblance of a smile on her face and went to see what her guest was up to.

Gordie was sitting in the living room, fully dressed, drinking instant coffee, smoking and staring at the TV. The TV was not on. His eyes did not come alive until he noticed her standing in the doorway.

"Oh . . . Morning, Brenda! Say, listen, I made myself some coffee." He held up the mug: exhibit A. "Is that all right?"

What if it isn't? "Of course. You must make yourself at home . . . Would you like some toast?" *Well, he has to eat, doesn't he?*

"Say, that'd be real nice!"

You'd think he'd been offered Beluga caviar and champagne the way he's grinning.

His vote of confidence provided the burst of mental energy she needed to make toast, using Donna's sliced Wonder bread, put out plates and knives, jam and peanut butter. She even put on a tablecloth, making it special.

All too soon they were facing each other at the breakfast table like it was their regular morning routine, Brenda on the left hand side, Gordie on the right. Gordie downed three cups of coffee and five slices of toast in no time at all. When he was done most of the jam and peanut butter were gone.

A squirrel appeared on the windowsill. Noticing movement on the other side of the glass it stopped in its tracks and peered in at them with alert black eyes, nose twitching.

"Lookit that little guy!" Gordie beamed and pointed. "He thinks he's at the zoo."

And you're grinning like it's your firstborn come to visit. "Squirrels are a real pest around here."

"A pest? Cute little guy like that?"

Don't contradict him, for God's sake! "No, no, not that one! That's a different kind."

The squirrel turned around and jumped onto the nearest tree branch, its tail a waving plume.

The incident changed the dynamics of the breakfast, adding something that made Brenda awkward again, insincere. She wished she too could scoot up a tree and disappear. Felt she ought to apologize to Gordie for not wanting him there.

"So, Bren . . . whatcha up to today?" The question was diffident, his face expectant. "You busy? I mean . . . whatcha usually do Saturdays and all? . . . Not like I want to be in the way or nothing, I just want you to know that. So, you know, if you're busy and stuff . . . "

"That's okay. Really." *I never do anything much. Once I was married and planned for the future. Now I can't seem to get organized.* "I usually take a walk downtown to the market. You know, get some veggies and fruit and things." *Women's stuff, nothing you'd enjoy.*

"Yeah?" He stared at her, intrigued.

You'd think I just described a trip to the moon. "Yeah. It's a nice, big market. They have fresh fish and seafood too." *Then I spend the rest of the day doing nothing. Wondering if the phone will ring. If it doesn't, come evening I heat a can of soup, have a salad, and drink too much wine. Then I fall asleep in front of the TV.*

Gordie lit up. "I like fish. Mind if I tag along?"

You bet I do. "No . . . no, of course not . . . You don't mind walking all the way there and back?"

"Won't be doing much walking where I'm going, will I?"

Damn! "Oh . . . Sorry."

"That's okay." His smile at her discomfort was kindly.

Gordie insisted on doing the dishes while Brenda showered. It was the longest shower she had ever had. When she was done, Gordie had both washed the dishes and dried them. "I put the clean stuff on the table, didn't want to mess around in your cupboards."

Afterwards they headed downtown, talking about this and that, how Hamilton had changed over the years, which part of it they had grown up in. The conversation was not without awkwardness, but somehow it flowed easier out of doors. Brenda strolled slowly with the intention of making the trip downtown last as long as possible. The usual half hour walk took nearly an hour.

Once they entered the market, Gordie transformed. Stepping lightly and sprightly all of a sudden, he kept stopping to admire the scenery, acting like he was in some glorious wonderland. What the hell did he find so fascinating? The red hills of plump tomatoes? The yellow and orange citrus fields? The green rolling meadows of broccoli and cucumbers? Those foothills of red and orange and yellow peppers leading to a bumpy eggplant mountain? What was it his shining eyes beheld?

"Say, Bren, what are those purple things over there?"

"Eggplant."

"Eggplant? I never heard of those."

His solid bulk softened as he made his way from stand to stand, Brenda following a step behind. He took his time, his fingers stroking every surface, from the smooth satin eggplant to the unshaved coconuts. He wanted to taste everything, he declared, buy everything. And he tried his best, insisting first on familiar fruits, apples and pears, oranges and plums. "Just one or two, eh?" Then a bit of broccoli, peppers, lettuce, tomatoes, cucumber. Bananas and raspberries. A jar of homemade jam. Rhubarb and strawberry the label said. "Sounds good, eh, Bren?"

I thought you had no money. "I don't need all that food."

"Oh come on, you can always use jam, can't you? Seeing as I ate all yours for breakfast?"

" . . . I guess."

A loaf of homemade bread and then two pieces of baklava because the name intrigued him. Beaming now, he told her not to worry, he would pay, he would carry and, "Hey, what are these here weird little lumps?"

"Chestnuts."

"Chestnuts? No kidding? You can eat those?"

"Yes. This kind you can. You roast them in an open fire, or in the oven, until the shell cracks."

"Is that right? Say, let's get some and do that, eh! You guys have a fireplace. Can we roast them in there?"

Well, it's something to do. At least he's easy to please. "I suppose."

"And Bren, what are those green and red things over there? The ones the black woman in yellow is selling?"

"Those are mangoes."

"What?"

She explained what mangoes were. He insisted they get one.

"Mangoes," he mumbled, savouring the name. "Mangoes. It has a nice sound to it."

"They're delicious. And see those yellow ones beside them? Those are papayas."

"Popeyes?"

She was about to smile, but caught herself. "Papayas. They're a fruit too."

"Well, what do you know? Wanna get one? You only live once, eh?"

They walked over to the stand. The Jamaican woman's eyes slid inscrutably from Gordie to Brenda and came to an unspoken conclusion. She saw no reason to hide her amusement.

They ambled on through the crowd, Gordie's lips moving silently, a little smile twitching his lips. Papaya. Mango. The sheen had become visible on his face again, that slightly greasy coating of the weary traveller.

The woman at the fish stand was intent on selling them fresh oysters. Demonstrating, she held one up, pried it open and let its live slippery content slide down her throat. "Good for making babies!" she hooted, smacking her lips.

Gordie blushed.

The woman laughed.

Brenda found her gesture obscene. *He's not my husband! I'm just con-sitting. He's going to jail on Monday. For aggravated assault! If not worse, for God's sake! Murder even!* Ashamed of her thoughts, she declined the raunchy woman's offer, instead choosing two rainbow trout, cold, grey and dead.

After that, unable to carry any more, they headed east on King Street with their loot, an odd couple on their way home to prepare Saturday evening dinner. Brenda hoped they wouldn't run into anybody she knew. So far she had been lucky. Then again, she didn't know very many people.

It had turned into a sunny afternoon. The leaves on the maples in Gage Park sported russet and gold, dancing in the breeze. "Pretty as a picture, eh?" said Gordie. The sky was cloudless and blue, though already the sun was showing signs of fatigue. The shadows were lengthening.

Soon this day will be over.

She was desperate for a glass of wine to dull the edge of her anxiety. A glass? Make that a bottle, a jug, a cask. When they passed by a liquor store she stopped and said, "Let's get some white wine to go with the fish."

Gordie told her awkwardly that he was not supposed to drink alcohol, but figured maybe a small glass of wine would not affect him like a case of twenty-four.

"Are you sure?"

"I'm sure." His smile was friendly. "Say, Bren, don't sweat it, eh?"

Oh, I'll sweat it. "It was a stupid idea. Let's skip the wine," she said. "There's pop in the fridge."

He looked embarrassed — there was a blush in his cheeks — but he did not object.

Gordie parked himself in front of the TV while Brenda prepared dinner. He did offer to help, but she declined, wanting to be alone. Besides, this was *her* job. First she made — no, she didn't make, she created — a lavish salad that included most of the vegetables he had insisted on buying. Topped by thin slices of peppers in autumnal yellow, orange and red, it was a work of art. That achieved, she whipped up a cheese sauce for the broccoli, using two kinds of cheese, provolone with a bit of parmesan, taking her time, stirring until her arm hurt.

However I look at it, this is my life. It will be what I make of it. I have a guest for dinner tonight. He might strangle me later, but there must be no lumps in the sauce.

She grilled the fish with butter, lemon and slivered almonds. It was to be followed by a fruit salad. Papaya and apples and pears, oranges and plums, arranged in a manner designed to impress, topped with a handful of ruby raspberries. She left out the mango. That one she would slice for breakfast, its flavour best enjoyed on its own.

When called to the table, Gordie sat down and for a suitable length of time let his eyes behold the splendor. Then he threw manners to the wind and applied himself to the food like an industrial vacuum cleaner. The expression on his face was one of weepy pleasure. Which was as it should be. It was the most generous meal she had ever prepared, a lavish exhibition of something she did not feel.

A bottle of chilled chardonnay would not have gone amiss.

Afterwards she brewed some of her good coffee to go with the baklava. Later they watched a movie on TV. It was an old Cary Grant comedy, *Arsenic and Old Lace*. Twice she caught herself laughing along with Gordie.

When the movie was over they roasted chestnuts. Gordie pronounced their taste too weird, but had serious fun roasting them, insisting Brenda eat them all. By then he looked so goofy with contentment she decided she better halt the harmony and bid him good night.

"See you in the morning." Once again, acting as though the stroke of midnight would transform her, she swept herself in her black shawl and floated down the hall.

Having silently slid the chair into place under the door handle, she lay in bed feeling wretched.

In Donna's room Gordie was soon snoring.

Brenda lay awake for a long time, thinking that when dawn arrived, it would be Sunday. Gordie would be leaving to go to jail where the familiar sound of metal gates would slam shut behind him. While she would get her freedom back, be able to relax and think unhindered whatever thoughts came to mind. She had been a gracious hostess, and it had worn her out.

A lackluster light was seeping into her room when a sudden noise jolted her awake. It was the creak of Donna's bedroom door quietly opening and closing. Followed by the sound of Gordie's heavy footsteps. They were coming her way.

No.

He was heading in the opposite direction, towards the kitchen. A few seconds later the door slammed and footsteps tramped down the stairs. Gord had up and left.

He didn't even say thank you.

She was still lying in bed pondering the unexpected development twenty minutes later when slow footsteps came up the stairs. The kitchen door opened and closed. There was the scraping of a kitchen chair against the floor as somebody, presumably Gordie, sat down. After a while — eleven minutes and sixteen seconds according to her alarm clock — there was another scraping of chair before footsteps headed down the hall.

This time they were coming straight towards her room.

No.

They continued into the living room, stopped briefly, then returned to the kitchen, in no great hurry. There was a moment of quiet, then a very loud crash made the house tremble ever so slightly. It was followed by dead silence. Brenda lay in rigid terror until she heard the back door shut quietly and the sound of feet plodding back downstairs, heavier this time.

Now she dared get out of bed. She ran to the window, aware of the lightness in her movements. Leaning over her desk she could see him. He was heading towards King Street, away from the wind, head down, ox-like shoulders hunched. The posture of defeat, the gait of an old man. As if he had aged so much overnight he'd had to escape to hide it. Not once did he look back or slow down. The childish velvet collar was turned up, a useless shield against the wind. The suitcase hung like a dead weight in his hand. Swirling autumn leaves, like taunting street urchins, followed close at his heels.

The sun, too, had run out of steam. It looked as if the day would not grow any brighter.

A minute later he turned the corner by the gas station and was gone.

There was a deep dent in the wall by the kitchen door where Gord had slammed his fist before leaving. Some tiny red spots indicated that he had broken the skin of his knuckles from the sheer force. Bits of plaster lay scattered on the floor below. Brenda stared at the mess while she made a pot of her good coffee. She poured a cup, grabbed an apple and went into the living room to puzzle over her guest's sudden, ungrateful departure, and what he had hoped to accomplish with smashing a fist into the wall. The room smelled of stale cigarette smoke; she had not dared ask a chain smoking felon to butt out. Later on she would give the place a good airing. While the fresh air swept through it she might go for a brisk walk, put some colour in her cheeks, before vacuuming and doing the dishes. Eat lunch. Leftover salad and fruit.

She almost did not discover the ivory envelope propped discreetly against one of the empty coffee mugs on the cluttered table, half hidden by the plate where only some crumbs from last night's baklava remained. Her name was neatly printed on its front. She picked it up and held it unopened, weighed it in her hand like a clairvoyant. Mulled over the fact that Gordie had sneaked out, thinking she was still asleep, to go down to the all-night drugstore and buy her a card.

She tore open the envelope. The front of the card featured a rotund guinea pig, bashful but jolly, holding out a basket heaped with flowers. Roses and daisies, lilies and bluebells. Dapper in a checkered vest and bright red bow tie, the guinea pig stood smiling at her.

She almost smiled back.

Inside Gordie had put into words what the weekend had meant to him. How swell it had been. Going to the market to buy all that great food. How weird it must have been for a terrific lady like her to be stuck with a guy like him. He wanted her to know how 'greatfull' he was. It was the only misspelling and she was not proud for noticing it. "I hope you don't mind I took some fruit to have on the bus?"

The card was signed "Gordon O'Hara."

She stared at the guinea pig for a long time, imagining Gordie on a bus somewhere in rural Ontario, cradling a leftover mango on his lap, stroking it like he might a favourite pet, his grazed knuckles red and swollen.

From the card in her hand, the irritating rodent stared at her, adoringly, provokingly, continuing to offer his basket of garden-fresh blooms. Brenda kept hoping its outstretched arms would grow tired, but it was a tough little critter.

THE SOUL OF A POET

"LET'S MOVE," SAID MY HUSBAND ONE NIGHT at supper, twirling pasta with his fork, slopping sauce on the table cloth.

"Okay," I said.

It was neither a flippant suggestion nor a mindlessly rash answer. Decisions of that magnitude may sound sudden when uttered, but they never are. Thoughts — be they pro or con — percolate cautiously in the subconscious for a long time before your gut instinct takes that final step it was planning all along. That was why his suggestion made perfect sense. Our three grown children had built their own middle class fortresses, producing families and mortgages of their own.

"I mean, we've done our bit," reflected my husband, as though family life had been a job contract that had run out. "Time to buy a smaller place, don't you think? We're shrinking, not taking up as much space as we used to."

I twirled some pasta of my own and said, "Let's do it."

Clearing out a place that has been home for thirty-four years is a daunting, frustrating, thankless, near impossible labour. Things accumulate: odds and ends and broken bits, stuff that "might come in handy." All the stuff that piles up along the road from infancy to the grave. The stuff that tells us who we once were, or thought we were, lest we forget.

Last week I spent an entire day going through the contents of all the boxes long forgotten down in the cobwebbed crawlspace, boxes that had obviously mated and reproduced in the dark over the years, boxes full of treasures once too important to part with. The first one I tore open contained stacks of outdated sewing patterns — some never used, folders of old bills for the repair of cars sold for scrap decades ago, a bag of old party hats and partially burned birthday cake candles, the kids' schoolwork, a gallery of bad drawings dating back to Kindergarten.

Some of those I decided to hang on to.

Hours later, at the very back of that dank space under the kitchen, that dungeon holding the boxes filled with the most forgotten bits of the past, I came across a damp mess of papers and folders spilling out of a collapsed box that had burst at the seams. Imprisoned in this mildewed neglect under a bunch of essays from my university days — marks ranging from C+ to B+ (and one A) — a small notebook demanded attention, clutching at the uneven hem of my memory. I picked it up, wondering why a four by six inch notebook had been so important that I had felt it imperative to preserve it.

I never kept a diary. My life was never that interesting.

Studying it, I recalled that this particular notebook had once had a shiny purple cover, smooth to the touch. I don't know why I remembered that. I opened it. Loopy scribbles crowded every page from top to bottom. The scribbles were mine, yet I had no recollection of what they were about.

A quick scan revealed that whatever I had written, it was not about me. The one name that cropped up on almost every line was Eleanor, Eleanor, Eleanor. Eleanor said this, Eleanor did that, and isn't that just sooo typically Eleanor? The letters kept changing shape and size and direction as if I had been unsure of my identity or whatever role I was expected to play apart from narrator. Oddly, in my scribbles, Eleanor does not resemble the Eleanor I knew as much as the Eleanor she imagined herself to be, the personification of eccentricity and clever illusion.

Seeing her name in the faded limelight on every page, I remembered what happened. Eleanor went mad. At some point in time Eleanor made the stubborn decision to go stark raving bonkers. I also remembered that Eleanor was not the kind of person who would go nuts unless she decided to.

The past was a far distant place. It had been years since I last gave Eleanor Griffith a thought. Now here she was, unsullied by the fingers of time. This notebook was where I had chronicled the details of the persistent dreams I had once been subjected to. In the here and now, when I flipped through those densely filled pages again, the writing so purposeful, so intense and diligent in its energy, each one became as clear as if I had dreamt it last night.

They had appeared with frequency, those dreams, staged in a specific time and place, following a script as if a director had shouted impatient commands offstage for me to for god's sake get it right. I had often had the notion that somebody else was conjuring up that parallel world inside my head, a notion so strong that at times I had woken up feeling used.

I had recorded my observations about Eleanor, and the never changing details from dream to dream, obviously under the assumption that such singularity had to be of monumental significance. And here they still were, neatly dated for posterity, a stretch of fifteen months between the first and the last entry. I opened the book at a random page and there she was: "Sometimes Eleanor is too preoccupied posturing, too busy speaking in private tongues, to acknowledge my existence. She does this on purpose, banishing me from my own dream while she holds centre stage. And I think, 'Why, you fucking bitch!' I never say it out loud, for if I did, she'd be terribly hurt. 'I've no idea what you're talking about,' she'd say and look wounded. Eleanor's wounded look is a work of art. Her eyes are round to begin with, and her glasses are so thick, they magnify her hurt and make an impact. That's the way she is, her own creation, every detail meticulously seen to."

I carried the notebook upstairs. I had no choice; it would not let me put it down now it had been found. It clung to my hands like a needy orphan.

Well, I would give it attention. I was curious.

Still, how peculiar. When I think back, the only Eleanor I remember is the one she invented. So why had I succumbed to serial dreams about her? Why had I allowed her such possession over my mind, letting her use it to help fulfil the twisted notions that were — for lack of a better word — her guiding philosophy? Letting her stage her frequent dramas in my brain?

Ours was a fairly brief, if meteoric, friendship. For less than two years Eleanor and I were one soul in two bodies. That was how Eleanor put it at the time. Then again, she was a master of affected images. "Our souls," she explained, entwining her manic hands for effect, "are Siamese twins attached at the brain." It was because of the way she gazed into my eyes when she presented me with such statements, nearsightedly and vague, as if to quell any hurtful opposing opinion, that I never had the guts to dispute her theory, though I had always assumed that twins were alike in some way or other. But what did I know? She was much smarter than me.

It was a friendship exhaustingly intense despite the fact that we had absolutely nothing in common. I had endured high school and been duly rewarded with grades that helped me scrape into university. Eleanor, the prodigy, had been admitted to university a year early. She could strut her learned stuff at the drop of a hat, quote at length famous philosophers and writers I still have not heard of.

I was introverted. Eleanor was not.

I had no sense of self. Eleanor was full of herself.

I looked so steeped in melancholy — I have that kind of face — that people were convinced my soul was as black as my duffel coat. Manic Eleanor appeared to bring laughter and light to the world. She smiled a lot, was quick to laugh.

I, the silent type, listened; she never stopped talking.

Her restless hands were thick and solid, like those of some medieval peasant. My hands, slender and white, were docile, too timid for expressive gestures.

Eleanor always said she wished she had my hands. Why? I'd ask. They're so delicately old-fashioned, she'd say. Meant for embroidery in a lady's chamber. And she'd smile, the way a kindly teacher might smile at a dimwitted student who tries hard.

Turning the pages in the notebook, I once again became convinced that it was she who had directed what she wanted me to dream on any given night. God knows how, but somehow she was still in control, as she had been back then, for a while at least, when we used to skip through the city in the fading summer light, I, the faithful Miriam, hasting eagerly in Eleanor's flitting footsteps, hoping to find the secret fountain of such joy and exuberance. Grateful that we had met, convinced that now life would bestow greater gifts upon me.

Here are some of more impressions of the dream-Eleanor that I found essential to preserve:

— "How Eleanor loves wearing weird clothes! When I ask her about it, she explains that antique garments give her access to the past. It must be true what she says, for the older her borrowed frippery, the more highfalutin her language, the more stilted her behaviour, the more calculatingly distant the look in her eyes as they gaze past me, seeking attention in a more worthwhile dimension. She does not expect a person of lesser intellect to understand such a concept, but benignly takes the time to explain it all the same. When I respond that she looks like a neurotic ghost from the days of yore (borrowing her expression), she's delighted, for *this* is the precise absurdity she means to project. It charms her (and surprises her, I can tell by the twitch of her eyebrows), to find me capable of that level of insight."

— "I dreamt last night that Eleanor was not so much wearing, as being held up by, a constricting Victorian dress made of stiff satin, its noisy folds a faded purple. I imagined her legs dangling under the skirt, kicking the air, not reaching the floor, but then I noticed a pair of sadistic black boots, newly polished, poking out from under the prudish hem. She had draped a lavender scarf over the dress and had pulled together the look with a black fedora and sunglasses. This is vintage Eleanor. Eleanor is so studiously vintage."

— "The apartment where she exists in my head is endless, inexplicable and old, a dimly lit separate universe where time and space have yet to form a continuum, a labyrinth of hallways and rooms. It's red and dark and empty, except for the cavernous chamber somewhere in the middle where Eleanor lives in attention-seeking solitude. It has a dull echo of voices belonging to people who were only ever present in Eleanor's baroque delusions. There's dust everywhere, a thick layer muting the glow from the various lamps tucked in shadowy corners. Strange how one room can have so many corners. It is reminiscent of a stage setting from a Strindberg play full of repression and frustration. *A Dream Play* would be fitting. We performed it once in the drama club where I first met Eleanor. She, of course, is still performing, she never stopped. She claims to worship Strindberg, mainly because women are not supposed to. She's perverse that way.

'The sons of dust in dust must wander,' she quotes when I point out the dust, letting that annoying faraway look steal into her eyes, allowing a hint of superior smile, adding, 'and the daughters too. Mustn't forget about the daughters, must we, Miriam? NO! Don't touch anything or you'll break the spell. If you do, everything will implode.'

So I sit very still, minding my own business in my very own head, beholding Eleanor's choreographed gestures, which is exactly what she wants me to do. I'm obedient, sensing that I must be. If I, too, have a role to play, this is it."

— "Eleanor adores throwing lavish parties in my dreams. At last night's party, people were welcome only if they were dressed in fetching costume and chattered ingratiatingly about Life and Art to emphasize how superficial and phony they are. Eleanor insisted on this, because she secretly hates them. She walked silent in their midst, looking straight at people, staring right through them, finding nothing in them, nothing behind them, saying she was disappointed, but not surprised. She has named such gatherings Epic Theatre. (Must be another reason why she doesn't invite Strindberg, for how would he cope?)

Often she'll begin to sing in the middle of an amusing anecdote some guest is telling, performing the deliberate offense looking so beguilingly innocent that her interruption is never disputed. When the captive audience turns its attention to Eleanor, she stops singing and walks off to refresh drinks and empty ashtrays, her smile that of a perfect hostess, her hands performing their tasks with the resentful movements of an untipped waitress. In my dream last night she had invited the Rolling Stones, but she had locked them in the bathroom to prevent me from meeting them."

— "Sometimes Eleanor has small, formal tea parties with people long dead, using only the finest china and silverware. She adores having Strindberg for tea in her dusty chamber, that windowless centre of her universe that is like an internal organ the light cannot reach. Why a long dead Scandinavian misogynist? She claims they suffer from the same halluci-nations. They both have a fierce need to be driven mad by 'the hell that is Love.' For make no mistake, Eleanor, too, is a misogynist. Eleanor needs to look down on women, especially those less clever than her. And all those prettier than her. That is, most of the women of her acquaintance."

— "With me Eleanor talks mostly of Love, of how she worships Love. It is, she indulges, and not for the first time, a state of mind. Only through this State of Mind will she, Eleanor, become Pure. The reason she talks of Love with me is because in her perceptive eyes I am a simple soul who relates, without too much strain, to basic emotions. Which, of course, is ironic, in that this is the very condition Eleanor herself so hopelessly strives for."

— "My dreams about Eleanor are growing shorter. It's as if a battery is running out. She talks less, has less time for me. A bit arrogant on her part, considering she's acting out her fantasies in my head. That aside, I'm looking forward to not being burdened with her and her predictable antics. I'm tired of her. There: I've said it."

— "I haven't dreamt of Eleanor for more than a month now. I wonder if she's left the dusty chamber in my head at long last, perhaps to go and hunker down in somebody else's head. (Who'd have her?)"

— "I think she's gone for good. These days I wake up feeling relieved of a burden."

Vignettes of Eleanor, as invented by Eleanor. Was that the person she saw when — if ever — she scrutinized her face in the mirror? Did she hurry her eyes past her immediate reflection, so wholesome and plain, to some deeper place, extracting a more alluring essence than the mirror's meager offering?

Outside my — her — dreams, she lived in a minuscule student apartment on Hutchison. Textbooks stood in a precise row on the single shelf above her desk. Her bed was always made: matching pillows arranged atop a bedspread where every wrinkle had been erased like a dirty secret. There were never any unwashed dishes in her sink, never a speck of dust anywhere. The place was so spotless and so austere she could not abide spending time there. Nor could she stand not keeping it pristine.

Also, outside of my dreams, she dressed dowdily: white cotton underwear under sensible skirts — she never wore pants — and sturdy walking shoes. She never wore miniskirts or make-up like the rest of us as she considered both vulgar. "Whorish" was the term she used. Her attitude did not make sense. Makeup, part of an actor's mask, ought to have been her preferred tool. And considering that she fucked both friend and foe with undiscriminating zest, sometimes having to persuade a potential lover — ply him with booze — to come home with her, she was in no position to talk about whorish.

At the time I blamed it on Eleanor's upbringing. It had been strict in tradition and heavy on etiquette. She knew how to dress right for every occasion, the correct way of setting a table and holding a cup, which knife and fork to use first at that correctly set table. She knew which books one ought to have read, pretend to have read if one had not, knew how to conduct a debate about their meaning. (She never read books that were within the intellectual grasp of the general public.) She was fluent in both English and French and well versed in Latin. She could listen to a piece of classical music and name not only the composer, but opus and movement and major and minor and what have you, in order to critique the quality of the particular recording, to then compare it unfavorably to the famous recording of so and so.

I blamed her in-your-face plainness on her upbringing, but it was no doubt an expression of her general perversity.

Yet it was the other Eleanor who was real to me now (possibly back then too), the frenzied dream version Eleanor who wore clothes from a different century and took tea with dead lunatics. I rifled through my memories for the real Eleanor, but kept drawing a blank. She was not there.

I put the notebook aside and returned to the stolid present. But Eleanor, having escaped the notebook, had no intention of going away. A few days later she was back. I was tackling the closet in the guest bedroom at the time. On the floor, under a carton of out-of-date computer programs hid a shoebox. In it was a pile of envelopes held together with a rubber band that disintegrated as soon as I pulled at it.

The name of the sender on each envelope was Eleanor Griffith. No address. I no longer recognized the handwriting, but seeing the name gave me a thrill, as if here was confirmation that she *had* indeed existed. The letters were dated from July 1966 to January 1968.

Surely it was more than a fluke that I should run across her letters so soon after the notebook? Who orchestrates such coincidences?

Is there a dream version of me preserved in Eleanor's head, wherever she is? And if so, what do I look like? How do I act? Does she have folded into old envelopes the person I once was? A stack of envelopes stating "Sender: Miriam Duval" tied with a piece of sturdy twine. (The real Eleanor would never use a pretty velvet ribbon.) If she ever reads them, she will know more about what I was like then than I ever will.

Some letters we stamped and put in a mailbox proper, others we delivered in person, too impatient to wait. Sitting with friends in one of the usual hangouts, we would slide promising envelopes into each other's waiting hands under the table. Above the table we would exchange private smiles, twins with rich secrets.

Having secrets elevates you above the masses, Eleanor used to say.

I had a sudden flashback: one letter she threw at me from the open window of a bus. I was forced to chase it as it sailed westward along the south sidewalk on Sherbrooke.

I release the first letter from its pale yellow envelope. The envelope has a proper stamp and is dated July 5, 1966.

Eleanor is on holiday with her parents and two younger brothers. They have rented a cottage from a fisherman in Nova Scotia. The Griffiths are firm believers in annual family holidays, Mr. Griffith being a busy man the rest of the year. Distancing herself from something so deplorably bourgeois, Eleanor's condescension turns those three words, "annual family holiday," into something ludicrous, something best not spoken of in circles of bohemian refinement.

The letter informs me that McPherson, the fisherman, talks funny and scratches his neck when holding forth about meaningful matters like the price of fish. He wears overalls. Eleanor's description is one of lofty amusement.

She lets me know that often she stands alone on the eastern rim of "the immense spread that is our country," her feet immersed in the ocean. In this position, she frees her gaze to travel the great distance to the horizon. "How unattainable it is." Standing there, she contemplates Life at great length. These solitary moments fill her with a deep and sweet melancholy. Happiness, she is now convinced, is "as impossible to reach as the horizon."

I imagine her standing barefoot in that old full length fur coat she claimed was her grandmother's, though we all knew she got it at that kitsch secondhand store on Saint Laurent near Ontario. We all bought our rags there, how could we not know? It was made of squirrel skins, had a green satin lining and was ripped in four places. She called it her Satin Nutkin.

The letter continues with two pages of blathering that postures to the point of incomprehension. So typically Eleanor, I think, until I get to page four where she reveals that the previous paragraphs were excerpts from a book she is reading.

The kind of book she was never seen without. Eleanor loved to read in order to enrich her soul. She tended to her soul as though it were a prodigy for whom she had great hopes.

I have no idea what the excerpts are about, but at the bottom of the page follows an explanatory note. "And these are only two ways to describe death."

She mentions people I do not remember.

Frederic? Who was . . . ?

. . . Oh, Frederic!

That idiot. He was tall as a lamppost and thin as a toothpick. He had no front teeth and the laughter of a hyena. He was married to a long-suffering woman whose name was . . . let's see . . . Deidre or Desiree? Yes, that was it, I think, Desiree, and she despised him, something he greatly admired her for. "Dessie has spunk," he would say, howling his gap-toothed howl. Rewarding his insight, Eleanor would buy him another beer. He preferred imported brands.

Eleanor was convinced for a fleeting moment, the feeling self-inflicted like all her feelings, that she loved this feckless moron with a Love that was Steadfast and Pure. According to her logic, the more unworthy the object of her affection, the more Pure and Noble her Love.

Well, Pure Love was her prime ambition, wasn't it? Always in capital letters, make no mistake. This was where she and her friend Strindberg parted ways. "I hate to say it, but Strindberg was wrong," she would point out. "Love is not a sin. Love is a virtue." Eleanor was virtue's bride. It turned into a stormy marriage when it turned out Love had a mind of its own.

Her letter continues with another cryptic offering: "You sought a woman and found a soul — you are disappointed." She is quoting this with regards to some man named Jeffrey.

A vague outline of this person begins to unfurl at the back of my head.

Jeffrey . . . Was he that stereotypical intellectual? Read Sartre, at least in public places? Smoked a pipe? Leather elbow

*patches, beard, the whole nine yards, proud of the shallow pond
he mistook for his depth?*

*Yes, I do believe that might have been him. Jeffreyish enough
anyway.*

Eleanor's mind was always busy searching for Truth, also
always with a capital T, while cunningly evading it, lest it find
her first.

*I often wondered if Eleanor ever used her considerable
intelligence for any practical purpose. Often she treated it
as a handicap she was ashamed of, especially around men,
pretending to be ignorant of facts and events that she was
far better versed in than the pompous twits spouting lengthy
opinions on everything. She would claim not to have heard of
a writer, all of whose books she had read and whose theories
she had analyzed without difficulty. She would mispronounce
words — transmongolfry instead of transmogrify — as if to put
herself in her place, being humble when there is no reason to.*

Her next letter is dated two weeks later, mailed in a pink
envelope with a perfectly symmetrical daisy drawn on the
back.

She is still on holiday and wants me to know that today
Life is indescribably beautiful. Every day she greets dawn by
dancing across flowery meadows in graceful, secret ecstasy,
fishermen scratching their mundane necks at the sight of
Eleanor Griffith, soul in hand, twirling towards the endless
ocean. An ocean that imparts its wisdom only to Eleanor,
because "only *I* am willing to listen, Miriam. Only *I* take the
time." She inhales the wisdom with the salty air and comes to
an insight. "I embrace Life! Life embraces me!" She is enfolded
in a great Peace.

"Burn the previous letter, Miriam. Burn it! It was too black. More important, it was more revealing than I would have liked it to be."

It revealed nothing. Then again, Eleanor would have found it too revealing to be found to have revealed nothing.

She will be back in Montreal in a few days, she writes, inviting me to dinner at the usual place, The Place, on de la Roche just off rue Rachel by Parc Lafontaine, the kind of tavern where everybody turns up sooner or later for lack of anything better to do.

I wonder if it's still there?

She is expecting a detailed account of what I have been up to in her absence. "Behind my back" is how she puts it. With a frosty hint she hopes I have not been within sniffing distance of the aforementioned Jeffrey. Here her handwriting becomes uneven as if hit by a violent gust of wind.

If I had been sniffing around some elbow-patched poseur, I would probably have a clearer recollection of him. My love life, if worthy of that description, suffered a sorry lack of passionate intrigue. That I remember. Despite my "whorish" makeup and short skirts, I was a paragon of virtue. A virtue I seemed unable to shed, mostly for lack of trying.

Next is a hand-delivered letter dated mid-September. It is tucked in a plain white envelope. A homemade stamp features a rose drawn in purple ink.

With the same purple pen that drew the rose, she quotes Brecht, Mallarmé and Pushkin in an exuberant jumble.

But of more immense importance is this: she is longing to see Philip whom she has just recently met. PHILIP! *He* is the cause of her exuberance. PHILIP! She cannot stop pouring out his name. Philip! Philip! Philip! It gushes from her pen.

"He has such lonely eyes. Eyes that see but that cannot accept. Oh, Miriam, how he suffers!"

Philip never suffered in his life. He was too lazy. "Fucking Philip" was how people started conversations about him. "Fucking Philip has done it again."

Done what?

You name it. Had sex with his best friend's girlfriend. Shoplifted. Given his wife another black eye. Pissed in a public place (one of his favourite pastimes).

All of the above.

Yes, that was when it started, after she met Philip. I always thought her decline was partly my fault, for after all I was the one who introduced her to him. This is how it happened. We were sitting in The Place early one evening, a month or so after she got back from the annual family holiday, a dejected Thursday evening when nothing was happening. It was raining heavily, a regular monsoon, and there was nobody around. I can't remember why the hell we were even there.

Then the door opened and out of the downpour emerged a drenched Philip. Being wet made him look vulnerable. His moustache drooped, his hair hung into his eyes, raindrops ran like tears down his emaciated cheeks. He looked around, searching for somebody, saw me and came over. "Hey Miriam, long time no see, how are you? Say, have you seen Ben?" (Or was it Harry?)

Eleanor's reaction was insidious and unexpected. She kicked me hard under the table, demanding attention, meaning to hurt me if she didn't get it, while above the table her eyes went eerily blank. Her mouth opened and hung unhinged in a drooling sort of manner. So I introduced her. It was no big deal.

I had known Eleanor for half a year by then. We had met when we enrolled in the drama club the previous fall. I had known Philip for six years. We had met at The Place through mutual friends, but a while back he had disappeared for several months. One rumour had it he was in a mental institution. Another rumour said his wife had stabbed him to death.

"Fucking Philip," people concluded. "With him anything is possible."

Before she met me, Eleanor had not known The Place existed. It was not the kind of demimonde hangout she had been brought up to frequent.

She took to it like a fish to water.

That Thursday evening I found myself in the company of a different Eleanor. She grasped Philip's hand and held onto it, gazing up at him as if he were the Pope come to bless her, and not an alcoholic misfit who at age twenty-eight had drowned his litter of ambitions to avoid the tiresome responsibility of having to look after them. For a moment I was sure she was going to kiss his hand.

Philip was in a hurry and didn't really see her, the same way the Pontiff does not notice, indeed cannot be expected to notice, the individual faces in an adoring crowd.

"Say Miriam, can you spring for a beer?" was all he said. Before I said no, Eleanor offered to buy him one. She ended up buying him seven.

The letter continues with the announcement that she does not love anybody but Philip, will never love anybody but Philip. Philip. Philip. Then she asks, "Am I honest, Miriam? You see, I don't think I am."

No, Eleanor, you were never honest, though God knows you thought you were. You meant to be. You thought you sincerely meant to be.

On the next page she becomes sentimental, earnest.

"Remember last summer, Miriam? Remember our walks in the park, barefoot, carrying our shoes in our hands, rolling in the grass, laughing and singing? Remember that perfect morning when we stayed up all night, sitting up on Mount Royal by Belvédère? Remember how dawn came so very early, sneaking over the rooftops, bringing light, making the river glow? How the birds sang in that gentle light when we were the only ones awake in the entire world? How the new day was ours alone? How the city belonged to only us, the only ones worthy of it? The artlessness of our happiness? It was fleeting, but it was there, wasn't it Miriam? There was guileless joy at times like that, wasn't there?"

That wasn't a dream?

Words like falling leaves. "Summer is over, Miriam. My heart aches with the loss. But I will always cherish the memories of it. Remember the time we had been to a party in Griffintown and ended up throwing stones into the Lachine canal in the middle of the night? The quiet plopping sound in the dark water, shattering the reflection of the moon? Standing on that little bridge? Walking fearlessly the dark streets back downtown? We owned this summer, Miriam. Especially the nights we haunted like happy ghosts. And I'm so glad we did. Aren't you? Now there's a chill in the air and all the magic is gone."

Thinking back, remembering, yes, I am glad, too. Back then the world was so full of possibilities each new day, if only at the very moment when the morning grew bright in the east. Sometimes it was so magical Eleanor forgot to act.

We looked in the mirror at faces that were so young we were sure we were immortal.

At the end of the letter, "It's so difficult to love."

I always found it far more difficult to be loved.

The next letter was hand delivered, tucked in a wrinkled brown envelope on which is drawn a stamp featuring an erect, slightly crooked penis.

Must be Philip's, all worn out and bent.

The letter is two pages long and consists of several poems: fragmented, unfinished thoughts. Eleanor was well aware that I was no fan of the kind of poetry she found deep enough to be meaningful.

And then: "Miriam, listen, I have found something. What is it, you ask? Only this: an incredible calm. Suddenly everything inside me is a sea of calm. There is a God. Not a separate God, but one that is present in all of mankind. There is no duality. I no longer need anybody to love me. There's so much infinite Love inside me I do not need it reciprocated."

Too much by half, but that's what she was like. If and when it was convenient, Eleanor found and claimed God for herself, flowing over with His Love, saving her own for later. Other times, if God was unavailable, she flowed over all the same.

"It's winter now." Eleanor is sitting by her window watching snowflakes float by in the haloes of the street lights, aching with the white, cold beauty of their slow descent on Hutchison. She does this while waiting for the figure of Philip to appear in the halo directly below, his long black scarf wound twice around his neck, but as ever without gloves or a warm coat. She is ready to rush down and let him in, to offer him food and wine, a bed and a body for the night.

The next hand delivered letter is dated April 30. The envelope is green and has a heart drawn in the little square pretending to be a stamp.

Wasn't that the day I was standing by the bus stop on Sherbrooke, the one opposite the Music Building, and a bus, the wrong one, stopped and there was Eleanor tossing me a letter out the window as if she had been expecting me to stand there, gormless and patient, my sole purpose in life awaiting the imminent arrival of her latest outpouring?

It was written during an exam for a film class. She is feeling stupid, she says, she never had enough time to study, what with tending to Philip's tortured soul full time. She shares with me "the most postmodern" question from the exam. "Discuss, from a historical and esthetic point of view, film's relation to drama and the novel."

How on earth, she asks, can she be expected to concentrate on such irrelevant trivia? She will be seeing Philip later. They will drink wine and talk about matters of significance. Together they will reach new depths, new heights. Expand the universe.

Philip! Philip! Philip!

Did she write the letters of his name slowly, revering her feelings for him? Or fast and hard, following the heralding thumps of her heart?

"Tonight, Miriam, do you know what I'm going to do? I'm going to listen! Yes, I am. I'm going to sit silent and listen and absorb. All night I shall listen to what other people have to say, not just Philip, but everybody. And I shall learn. Oh, I'm so very, very happy!"

She does not elucidate the reason for her happiness, her unselfish plan to lend an ear to the thoughts of others for a change, but there is no need, is there? The reason is Philip.

She continues: "Frederic has explained to me why Philip can never be satisfied with only one woman, why he can never be satisfied period. He assured me that Philip does not humiliate me on purpose.

"Now that I understand, Miriam, I shall be patient."

And then: "Something is happening, Miriam, something so momentous I stand humbled before it." She does not share what it is, but page after page of undisciplined emotions dance and shout, too full of admiration for their own grandiosity to notice the beat they are twirling to. A chorus line of exclamation marks dance in their wake.

There are no more letters until September that year. By then she is in a terrible state, as fragmented and incomprehensible as the poems she loves to quote. I no longer recall what went on in the interim.

No, wait . . . That must have been when I started to see less of her, that fall when her deterioration was well under way, her eager plunge into masochistic madness, catalyzed by Philip, who was already beyond redemption. Of course, had he not been beyond redemption she would not have Loved him.

"Never is Love more Pure than when it has to redeem," Eleanor assures me, and not for the first time. "Miriam, no doubt you'll think this letter egocentrical, like all my letters to you, but I have to write this pain, this disease, out of my system. I need to direct it to somebody who will not turn away from me in disgust and disappointment."

Tediously, it is all about Philip — who else? — so full of anger, so weary of the prolonged exercise of survival imposed upon him daily.

Everybody said he was a poet. It was true that he did write some poems once, published in some long defunct literary journal. Eleanor knew he was a great poet. He had not written anything for years, be it a poem or shopping list, but this was apparently beside the point.

As Eleanor used to say, he does keep a notebook just in case.

"He suffers, Miriam, he suffers." Eleanor is frightened. She has almost run out of tears. "It would be so easy to die tonight. I need to see Philip, to talk to him, to tell him he's wrong about me. Tell him that I'm *not* the punishment for his sins. I'm the one who wants to take his pain away. I am the balm on his wounds. He must understand that.

"The days are growing darker, Miriam. So is my soul."

It was around that time I started to grow tired of her self-inflicted pain. I never knew pain could be so narcissistic.

A hand delivered November communiqué sits in an envelope that is the same dull grey as an early winter sky. This time she has not bothered to draw a stamp.

She accuses me of lying, though it is not clear about what. Somebody named Tom is upset and it is apparently my fault. There is something I should not have done.

I have no idea what she is on about. It sounds as though she is superimposing the drama of her own turbulent love life onto mine. I do not recall having an actual love life, only wanting one desperately.

Was this Eleanor's generous way of making me think I had one?

"Notice," she writes on the second page, returning to a more interesting topic, "that I have not mentioned the name of a certain person." She ends by saying she hates to see the gloom of December punctured by gaudy Christmas lights. "There is a reason for such gloom. It should not be tampered with."

A January letter in a white envelope addressed to "My Friend Miriam" contains several grim statements.

Philip has left her. He is with Janet now.

Janet?

Oh, that Janet. A prematurely flabby, vulgar broad (Eleanor's evaluation), loud, but always cheerful. The crowning glory of whorishness, pronounced Eleanor, who went out of her way to make friends with her, fawned over her until she made her feel ill at ease. Eleanor measured herself and her rivals by the purity, the valour, of the love for the man who was the object of their self-effacement.

"Oh, Miriam, how can I live another second without Philip in this cold, dark world? My agony is killing me." She has been sneaking off to church again, to L'église du Gesù for some reason. It must have had the right props. Only in church does she find peace now. I have to promise her not to tell anybody about this naughty habit of hers.

Did Eleanor go to church regularly or were her meetings with God always so clandestine? I suspect that, too, was an act. She set the stage, and the stage was a church. She then entered and performed, expecting God to play along. Her Love for God was not Pure, it was utterly mercenary.

There are three letters left. The next, a yellow envelope, was delivered by hand in February 1967. The stamp she has drawn features a coffin and a cross. It's a childlike drawing.

"Time again for a self-centred letter. Do try to forgive me, Miriam, please, please! Somebody has to, and I know you will. You always do, that's why I need you."

She is still in torment because of Philip, whom she has not seen for a while. She fears he has sought refuge with his enduring wife. Or that he is still with Janet. Or Yvette or Helen or Carrie or Yolande. "Is there no limit to the degradation one can subject oneself to?"

It would seem not. Eleanor's degradation was abject on the grandest of scales and stubbornly so. Never have I seen a human being so willingly subject herself to debasement. And why? In order to prove that her version of Love was more Pure than anybody else's.

That was when I knew she was lost. Lost to herself, lost to her friends, lost to her family who knew nothing of what was happening. I could do nothing for her. She had no intention of letting compassion stand in her way.

She took to sleeping on the floor below the rumpled bed where Philip, if he had the energy, had blasé sex with Janet, who, like Eleanor, was merely another passing victim eager to save a poet's soul through human sacrifice between unwashed sheets.

In the morning Eleanor would go down to the dépanneur on the corner and buy milk, eggs, and flour to make pancakes, nutritious food to make the gaunt Philip strong enough for a repeat performance the following night, if not with Janet, then with Yvette or Helen or Carrie or Yolande. Or somebody new. Sometimes the poor man would have to visit his wife for a bit of rest.

Each word in her letter is doubled over with pain. The pain is real. If it was not real before, it is now.

And she reveals the reason for her new torment: she is pregnant. The child is Philip's.

He had already spawned three children, all boys. There were no doubt others with women forgotten. Men like Philip never do anything useful on this planet, but for some reason they reproduce with the ease of vermin.

"I dare not tell him. Oh, Miriam, how I want Philip's child! Our love child. But not without a father. What should I do?"

Unfortunately my sympathy had run out by then. That I remember. It's not something I'm proud of. Nor ashamed. She didn't really want it.

Second to last letter. The once white envelope is smudged. It has no stamp, real or drawn.

It is March, cold and rainy. Eleanor hates the cold, hates the rain.

Yesterday she told Philip that she was carrying his child, hoping for some miracle no doubt, for her illicit friend God to step out of the shadows and put things to right.

Philip's response was not unexpected. He became theatrical, derisive, his entire body staging a sardonic collapse. His eyes rolled heavenward in mock horror. He lamented. "Oh, the tedium of life! The tedium of love! The fucking tedium period!" Having thus performed, he borrowed twenty dollars and stormed out.

Whether it is from the shock of his lack of remorse, or something else, five days later Eleanor wakes up in pain. This time the pain is physical. She is having a miscarriage. Afterwards she takes a couple of sleeping pills and sleeps for two days alone in her room. She keeps the windows closed, curtains drawn, "to shut out the sound of children playing in the yard below."

There was no playground anywhere near. No kids either.

She still loves Philip with the Pure Love that is her nemesis.

With her talent for Love it was sometimes hard to tell the pure from the tainted, the virtuous from the sinful.

Her last letter is dated April 22, 1967. The envelope is the shade of dead leaves and feels just as fragile. The first sentence is a news headline.

"Situation with Philip resolved." There is mention of a man named Ben who "is a dear, dear friend, who's been there for me through the entire ordeal with Philip."

I remember Ben. Normal, friendly Ben. He was a violinist with considerable talent. Yet he was a friend of Philip's. One of the numerous friends, who for inexplicable reasons always burdened themselves by paying for Philip's wine and cigarettes, letting him sleep on their couches and puke in their toilets (or on said couches), screw their girlfriends and eat their food. Who would say, "Well, fucking Philip. You know what he's like."

Why were they so malleable with him? Was it pity or contempt?

Eleanor longs for summer. Suddenly she wants to live again. She has finally had enough of Love. She now craves Culture, she longs to Travel, go to London and the National Gallery, Paris and the Louvre, Madrid and the Prado.

I wonder if she ever went to any of these places?

In August that year I moved to the West Coast. I flew back to Montréal for a visit the following Christmas, expecting nothing to have changed in so short a time.

I did plan to call Eleanor during my visit, but I ran into her at a party my second day back. The change in her was drastic and complete. She had grown so thin her face consisted of nothing but eyes, new eyes bruised and hard. She was no longer wearing glasses, peering blindly at a world she no longer wished to see. Only sharp, cutting edges remained of her body. When she opened her mouth, her teeth appeared smaller, sharper, rodent-like, ready to bite. Her every gesture was threatening.

It was as if she had annihilated the Eleanor I had known, turned her to dust. The daughter of dust wandering in dust.

Is then all that remains of my friend Eleanor the words left behind in these nine letters?

People at the party whispered about how she was slowly killing herself. It was, of course, over Philip. Once in a while he would take her back to further humiliate her, ease his boredom by seeing how low he could make her go. And each time she would bow her head, touch her forehead to the ground like a contortionist, accepting whatever obscenity he chose to dish out, as if he did it out of kindness to help her build character.

Fucking Philip.

No doubt Eleanor suffered, but she considered suffering an Art. Who knows what she got out of it? Who knows which she loved more, Philip or the pleasing image of her own martyred soul?

I was happy that Christmas. My happiness was of a bland and contained nature, but visible all the same. Feelings of that calibre were new to me and I no doubt handled them with inelegance. Three months earlier I had met Anthony, my future husband: he was the cause of my clumsy bliss. Anthony accompanied me back home to meet my parents, and managed to charm them, even my snobby English mother of the bloodline.

Eleanor tried (and failed) to seduce Anthony at the party, cornering him in the bathroom. It was, he said, a cold and uninspired attempt, driven by a need so blind that it was as if she did not even see him. (Without her glasses she probably did not.) The incident left him feeling perplexed and insulted.

I tried not to let her see the pity in my eyes. She would have despised me for it.

When we parted that night, Eleanor gushed her "indescribable joy" over my newfound love, badly mimicking the person she imagined I would have preferred her to be.

It was the last time I saw her.

According to rumours, Eleanor at some point moved to New York in pursuit of something or other. Whatever it was, it was not Philip. He had committed suicide a few years later. I found this out through Ben, whom I ran into on a visit home shortly afterwards.

He shot himself at a party. (What is drama without an audience?) But, as Philip's wife had reminded Ben at the time, Philip had the soul of a poet, so it was hardly surprising that he came to a sticky end. She blamed his downfall on all the pathetic women who constantly demanded his attention, preventing him from putting the brilliance of his wisdom into immortal stanzas.

"And that bitch Eleanor!" Philip's wife had become apoplectic at the memory. "Remember? That scrawny, nearsighted bitch! Having the nerve to show up at the funeral! At *my* husband's funeral! Did you see the way she acted like *she* was the widow, dressed all in black, an actual veil and the whole bit, gliding up the aisle with her head bent, hands clasped in prayer? I mean, can you believe the *nerve*?"

I can.

Was God by Eleanor's side in church that day? Was His hand on her elbow, steadying her as she walked down the aisle towards the dead object of her Pure Love?

Thinking back, it occurred to me that this happened around that same time that my dreams began. As if Eleanor, having removed her widow's veil, hovered restlessly in her minuscule apartment, found my letters, perhaps by chance, untied the sturdy twine and, for something to do, read through whatever it was I had had to say. And then — amused or bored stiff, but at a loss — she had an idea and said to herself: "Now, *here's* a place to hide and heal my wounds. Good old Miriam, my meek twin, she'll help me out. I'll go and dream a more worthwhile version of myself inside her sturdy head." Knowing I would not have the heart to throw her out.

Feeling used, her last letter still in my hand, I rebelled. I gathered the letters and the notebook in a paper bag, marched out back and hurled them in the garbage container in the back alley. That would teach the bitch.

I had trouble falling asleep that night, turning this way and that in our nearly bare bedroom, attempting to get away from the image of Eleanor's face the last time I saw her. Those sharp rodent teeth glimmering in the remnant of her face where predator and prey had become one.

At three in the morning I got up, put on my slippers and bathrobe and sneaked out to the back alley to retrieve what was left of Eleanor. Shivering in the damp night air, I hoped nobody was looking out the window to see good old Miriam rooting through the garbage, ass in the air like a full moon.

I found the bag with the letters and notebook a foot deeper from where I had thrown it, pulled it out and scurried back inside. In the kitchen I sat down and put the letters in the proper sequence before tying them together with a length of leftover red and green Christmas ribbon from my sewing box that I had yet to pack. I put these remnants of Eleanor in a plastic bag to protect them and tucked them away in the bottom of the sewing box, secure for the future, put the box in the bottom of a large cardboard box I had left out on the counter for the next day's packing. The gesture was not so much altruistic as voyeuristic, but Eleanor would have approved of that.

Doing Laundry on a Sunday

THE TWO YOUNG WOMEN ARE ALONE in the Laundromat. They have just begun pulling staticky garments out of adjacent dryers, oblivious to the synchronicity of their movements, when The Perfect Beauty sashays through the door.

She is not wearing a sign around her neck announcing her as such; it is how they will think of her afterwards. They will do so separately and with vague resentment, never acknowledging to each other that they so much as glanced at The Perfect Beauty as she entered their lives that hot, humid Sunday afternoon.

Her sashay, cocky to start with, is made cockier still by a pair of taupe cowboy boots. She is not wearing any other western accoutrement — a cowboy hat, for example — as might have been expected considering her footwear. Instead she sports a round felt hat with a floppy brim. The brim shivers when her heels slam the floor. They slam hard as if she likes the noise they make. Her clothes match neither the boots nor the hat: she's wearing a pair of cutoff jeans and a tight pink, nipple-revealing halter stained with what looks like a chocolate smudge on the front. An uninspired, tacky ensemble, but who is going to fault her for that when her beauty is flawless?

The hat's soft brim drapes an indulgent shadow over a profile so exquisite it spellbinds Katrina, the taller of the two women, rivets her attention to the point that when the brim trembles, so does Katrina, imperceptibly, for *that* is the exact profile she has always dreamt of one day discovering in the mirror through some overdue miracle.

Having seen such ethereal features only in old movies, Katrina has always assumed they do not exist in the three-dimensional reality she is confined to. To discover otherwise in a Laundromat of all places is disconcerting to say the least.

Her friend Doreen pays no attention to the hat. Not a Stetson, it's not her kind of headgear. Doreen's gaze hovers at floor level, glued to the stitched pattern twirling over the boots. She is thinking, her heart leaden, that boots like that belong in stirrups.

This magnum opus of a beauty ought to have been preceded by heralds trumpeting a fanfare, followed by an entourage of fawning admirers tripping themselves in their zeal to kiss her saucy boots. Instead she has only a single yokel in tow, an acne-scarred, scrawny specimen. Maybe a younger brother or some adolescent stray enlisted to carry her cargo, a ripped garbage bag crammed with dirty laundry.

The Perfect Beauty stops by a washing machine to count the change she digs out of a pocket in her cutoffs. Her nails are chipped, but the two women furtively sizing her up pay no attention to such an irrelevant detail. In between covert glances they are too busy pulling hard at their laundry, shaking it roughly, punishing it for something it did not do.

Katrina and Doreen always do laundry together on Sunday afternoons. It's an arrangement that started some eight months back when Doreen, a pretty young woman, hobbled into the Laundromat on crutches, dragging a canvas bag. The only other person in the place, the thin, pale faced Katrina engrossed in a Marlene Dietrich biography, felt obliged to get up to help the newcomer load a washing machine. The woman on crutches — round-faced and cheerful, a head full of dark curls — introduced herself as Doreen Riley and explained her misfortune: she had recently been in a car accident.

Surprisingly, considering her cool demeanor, the tall attractive woman was quick to provide sympathy. She had once broken her left ankle slipping on the icy sidewalk, she said, right outside her apartment building, so she knew how it felt to be stuck in a cast. She introduced herself, "I'm Katrina Ferguson," offering the additional information that she lived in the high-rise on Brock Avenue, not very far away, did Doreen know the one? Doreen said she did, but surely such a swank building had laundry facilities?

"Oh, there's a laundry room, but it's in the basement and has no windows. A creepy dark place. I had my sheets stolen once, if you can believe it. And by the way, if there's anything I can do to help out, please let me know." Katrina did not elaborate that she prefers this Laundromat because it's always deserted on Sundays.Doreen, being a chatty sort, and touched by the kindness of the stranger, said that she had just two days ago moved into an attic apartment in a house a few blocks south, and yeah, no kidding, it was goddamn tricky getting up the stairs. "And thanks for offering to help. I just might take you up on that."

Though they have done laundry together every Sunday since, they have to date not exchanged phone numbers.

Doreen's attic is located on Halifax, in a big brick triplex owned by a friendly Vietnamese family who, judging by the aromas wafting up from their kitchen, spend their entire days preparing and eating various mouthwatering foods. When Doreen is too lazy to cook — about five days out of seven — she happily snorts these aromas while chewing bland peanut butter sandwiches. She is convinced the weight she is gaining is from the aromas, not the sandwiches.

The best feature of her new home is the skylight in the living room. It gives her the impression of sitting under the stars at night. During the day it floods the room with enough light to enable fourteen potted plants to thrive directly below. They compete for space with a secondhand sofa and a brand new coffee table. Nine of the plants are cacti, some quite imposing. The rug underneath is the colour of desert sand. The walls enclosing the rectangular room are lined with framed posters advertising Westerns, close-ups of various men in Stetsons that obscure the vistas that go on forever behind them. Alan Ladd. Clint Eastwood. John Wayne. Weather-beaten, horse-riding men who are quick with a gun, should the situation call for it. Brave, silent men who know what they know but keep it to themselves.

Doreen is going to hook up spotlights above each poster to illuminate those manly, trustworthy faces at night when she sits under the stars among the cacti watching westerns on her VCR. She is saving up for a DVD player and a wide screen TV to do the scenery justice.

Off the living room is a kitchen the size of a chuck wagon. Tucked behind it is a small bedroom containing a twin bed covered with a Navajo blanket. Above the headboard she has mounted a guitar she doesn't know how to play. Bought at a garage sale recently, two strings missing, the back cracked, it still looks right and that's what counts. The ceiling slants like a tent. It does not flap when it's windy outside, which is a bonus.

Doreen is already so devoted to her attic she has decided never to move again — just as well, as she is convinced, based on experience, that this is as close as she will ever get to her dream.

Doreen is prone to daydreaming.

She has not told her new friend any of this, nor does she plan to, convinced that Katrina would be far from impressed with someone who has recreated the Wild West in the attic of a triplex owned by a food-loving Vietnamese family down the far end of Halifax Street.

The Nguyen family refers to Miss Riley as "the cowboy girl on top." They are convinced that she is a bit simple and treat her kindly.

Katrina's one-bedroom apartment is located on the tenth floor of the high-rise on Brock. It is a monochrome world up there, dimly lit. The walls are white. One wall in her bedroom is decorated with hats, all with brims, most of them floppy. They are a bit dusty, because although she plans to wear one any day now, to date she never has, apart from the most expensive one that she recklessly bought on her one and only holiday abroad.

The hats are either black or grey. Soft grey, dove grey, lead grey, rainy day grey, plain grey, mouldy grey, smoky grey, leaden grey, tedium grey. It's hard to imagine that many shades of grey all at once, but there they are. When they get dusty enough they will all turn the same colour. Necklaces hang from little black hooks in between the hats. A white pearl necklace here, a silver medallion there, that kind of thing. When the sun spotlights the wall in the early morning, the hats and necklaces create a pattern of lines and circles, strange shadows that look like a coded message. Sometimes she pretends to decipher it.

In her living room a row of tall white bookcases holds an impressive collection of videos and books about film. Publicity photos from old European movies line the other walls in a symmetrical row. The room is a study in black and white tempered only by the dove grey sofa pillows and smoky grey carpet that looks as if feet have never touched it. As if Katrina, when she is at home, floats through the air, in and out of time, like a spectre. The thick curtains, as white as the walls, are always drawn, in case the bright lights of the twentieth century fade the nonexistent colours.

Katrina's decor — like Doreen's — is a tribute to wishful thinking, but Katrina's domain is far more forbidding, much harder to reach. Real life does not stand a chance in Katrina's private chambers. She never invites company for that very reason. She, too, prefers to daydream.

She is not about to confide this to Doreen. How could Doreen, so down-to-earth, so well grounded, possibly understand the fragile nature of a non-existent dimension?

Doing laundry together on Sunday afternoons continued in an unplanned fashion after their first chance meeting. Somehow they sensed it would be so. Two o'clock, laundry time, and there they were. Only later did it occur to them that they had created a tradition. The idea pleased them both. Traditions have a past and a future. And Sundays are sometimes void of meaning.

Yet despite these weekly meetings on which they both depend a great deal more than they let on, they have to date never got together during the week, never gone to a movie or a concert, never met for a drink after work. Katrina has never set foot in the Wild West. Doreen has never been invited back to the monochrome forties.

Only on Sundays, while their dirty laundry gets clean again, do they go for coffee at the diner a block down from the Laundromat. There, in the Sunday lull when traffic is light, they sit by the window at a scratched Formica table and talk like old friends about work and fashion, films and music, this and that, and how was your week? They agree on everything during these conversations, giving the impression that they have a lot in common, making it appear as if they live ordinary lives. Behave as if they have nothing to hide. Comfortable in their Sunday personas they get along splendidly.

Sometimes, if the day stretches too long from where they are sitting, they say, what the hell, let's have something to eat, and they order grilled cheese sandwiches and fries, always the same, food they never eat at any other time, dipping each oily fry in plenty of ketchup, taking their time.

It is of some importance that these personas not lose face. And that is the reason on this particular Sunday that Katrina pretends not to notice the hat and the luscious shiver of its brim, the reason Doreen tries to stop herself from beholding for too long the saucy boots, as The Perfect Beauty enters their stage and renders meaningless their carefully crafted scripts.

The Perfect Beauty, having counted her change, issues an order to the yokel, not bothering with so much as a glance at either him or the two young women: "Dump it all in one, 'kay?"

Katrina has always dreamed of being the kind of beauty that graced the silver screen in the thirties and the forties, a heroine of black-and-white movies, presenting to the world a Dietrich or Garbo-like profile under a hat's sculptured brim. Wavy hair with a polished metal sheen, black glossy lips, endless legs in high-heeled shoes, unwavering seams down the back of silk stockings. Striding in those high heels (long legs always stride) down city streets where gaslights refract into scattered gems on rain-soaked pavements, her slender silhouette crossing a bridge as church bells toll midnight.

Katrina is unsure if church bells ever toll at midnight, but that is really beside the point. This being *her* fantasy, cathedral bells will toll whenever she needs them to, to warn of danger, or simply to reassure, softly but with resonance, for the audible effect is as essential as the visual. She is convinced that sounds were gentler in those days, less imposing. Full of foreboding when foreboding was in order, the ominous echo of the staccato of her heels along deserted pavements is equally foreboding.

If there is background music, it's distant and discreet, at times a hesitant violin or muted alto sax, nothing else.

At other times she pictures herself in a bar or café, sitting alone at a marble-topped table, absentmindedly twirling a glass of red wine or cloudy Pernod. It's an elegant hand doing the twirling, long and thin and pale, her nails as black as her lips in this world without colour. She never drinks the wine or the Pernod. The drink is a prop.

Her face does not reveal that she is waiting for a man in a trench coat. He will arrive late. Without a word of greeting he will slide silently onto the chair opposite hers, his hair and shoulders wet from the drizzle. It's always autumn at times like this, the melancholy season; it rains every evening. Greeting each other with a hint of a smile they will after a moment's silence begin an enigmatic conversation, their voices low, while mist begins to roll in from the sea, or the river, depending on the location. Soon a thick fog will dim the lights out in the street where enemies lurk.

It's important that they keep their voices down, Katrina and this nameless man who is her lover, or would-be-lover, but either way, a spy, a secret agent, a hero on the run. Somebody is after him. He is in grave danger, but brave and unafraid to die. The fact that he is being chased is important. For whatever the details of the setting, their affair is doomed, as all the best ones are.

This tableau is Katrina's favourite, this *noir* wartime brand of realism where hope feels out of place and lovers remain stoical. *Le Quai des brumes* meets *Casablanca* meets *The Blue Angel* meets . . . the choices are endless. It may be old-fashioned and vague, but it's the kind of vagueness in which lie innumerable possibilities, depending on Katrina's mood. Apart from the romantic aspect, doomed though it is, it makes thoughts of the future superfluous.

Katrina's mother, Eva, fled Hungary with her family when the Soviet army invaded Budapest in 1956. Eva Fenyvesy was ten at the time. Eventually the family left Europe for the safety of the big, unknown faraway country called Canada where tall blond Eva came of age in the sixties, the decade when narrow-minded thinking gave way to free love and miniskirts. And yet despite these temptations Eva managed to retain the old-fashioned way of dressing that favoured the red lips, string of pearls, clip-on earrings and the cloche hats that her mimicking daughter would later grow up to fancy herself weaving webs of feminine allure in. Eva's elegant prewar style had been determined by what *her* mother had worn as a chic woman sweeping in and out of the fashionable cafés of Budapest, a bright-eyed fox stole slung like fresh kill over her shoulder.

Katrina has never set foot in a Budapest café, has never set foot in Budapest period, but has eagerly adopted the legacy of a faded elegance she can ill afford and has nowhere to flaunt.

Once when Katrina was little, she and Eva watched a documentary on TV about the Hungarian revolution. Eva had insisted Katrina become acquainted with the tragedy of her family history, the continuing bloodshed of Eastern Europe, so easy to forget in comfortable North America where everybody lives in a nice house and has a good job and a car.

When the camera focused on three young men helping a bishop out of a manhole from the sewers where he had been tucked for safety, Katrina's mother let out a piercing yelp. "My God! That's cousin Joska helping the bishop out of the sewers!" A few days later, Joska had been shot by the Russians, she told Katrina, shot down like a dog, just like his brother, Árpad, a week earlier. "Such brave young rebels they were, those two!" Eva, distraught, remembered a photo of the three of them, taken on Árpad's fifteenth birthday, and ran to get the album to reconfirm her past.

After the program Eva wept for the rest of the evening, turning pages plastered with photos of what was no more, pointing to faces Katrina would never meet. For Katrina the event was a watershed, a confirmation that she truly *was* meant for a dangerous life, truly *was* meant to wear high heels and a hat, a fox stole, frequenting cafés with an inscrutable clientele. It was in her blood, just as she had always suspected. Here was the proof.

She hugged her mother and kissed her wet cheeks.

Watching the old movies Eva was addicted to helped put the icing on the cake. Thus the fog. It came from *Le Quai des brumes*, their favourite. It was the movie that made them heave the most sighs. The living room echoed like a haunted house when they went at it, according to Katrina's father, Albert. As soon as he heard the movie soundtrack he fled to the safety of the garage to tidy his workbench and clean his tools.

Though born and bred in Canada, Albert is of hardy Yorkshire stock and thoroughly proud of it. Quiet and humourless, there has never been anything vaguely romantic about Albert (though he adores his wife) except for one vital fact: he bears a remarkable resemblance to Jean Gabin, star of *Le Quai des brumes*. This is not a source of pride. The way he sees it, looking like a dead Frenchman is nothing to write home about.

Katrina is as humourless as her father, but takes after her mother in appearance. Attractive, tall and blond, she identifies only with the fascinating part of her family history — the Hungarian one. Those hardy Yorkshire folk never did anything but work, eat, sleep, and toast the queen on her birthday.

Having chosen the appropriate identity gives Katrina licence to walk down deceivingly deserted streets, alert to the danger that always lies in wait. Licence to spend time in nonexistent cafés, tapping restless black nails on quartz tables while waiting for a man in a trench coat, a haunted, hunted man whose eyes reveal the knowledge of the tragic fate that awaits him.

Katrina has not told Doreen any of this. Doreen is far too realistic to appreciate a dream life inspired by a largely forgotten movie made in 1938 in grainy black and white.

Doreen is entrenched in dreams of her own, dreams as intense as Katrina's, but of a different genre. She is given to roaming the Wild West under a sky far more immense than the one back home, surrounded by a landscape that never quits, arid and empty and merciless, an unyielding land inhabited only by coyotes and rattlesnakes and wild-riding buckaroos in black boots and Stetsons. Their horses are palominos, their saddles handmade. Doreen has such a keen eye for detail, if she closes her eyes she can smell that soft leather, the sweat of both the horses and their photogenic riders.

Sitting firm in such a saddle, she races across grasslands, painted deserts, up buttes, into valleys, lighter than tumbleweed. She is one with the horse, a steed so fast its hooves barely touch the ground. In such a landscape Doreen is as feisty and fearless as they come.

This is a West that is Wild yet aesthetic, made with only the finest ingredients.

The most handsome cowboy, the one with the whitest teeth in the most sunburned face, invariably falls in love with her, the kind of manly love that does not demand a lot of verbal input. A man made of quiet, jaw-clenched potency, stereotypical yet ruggedly individual. He tends to be called Chuck or Buck or Wild Bill, but never Adrian or Sebastian. Sometimes her hero has brown eyes, sometimes blue, but whatever their colour, he plays the guitar and yodels cowboy tunes that send shivers up Doreen's spine, always starting with her favourite, *The Old Chisholm Trail*. When he comes to the line *Goin' back home to see my honey* his gaze lands on Doreen with profound longing. In his eyes, be they brown or blue, shines the firm promise of a ranch nestled in hills teeming with antelope and mule deer.

At night they lie stark naked (apart from their Stetsons, somehow) in a sleeping bag made for two under a million stars, while the campfire crackles and dies and the leftover beans form a crust in the pot. Coyotes howl in the hills, horses snort in their sleep. The moon, once so distant, perches like a giant Day-Glo orange atop the silhouette of a jagged butte.

Soon the only sound heard on the planet is the wind sighing in the tall prairie grass.

This is Doreen's idea of heaven.

Doreen's mother, Lydia, was born and bred in New Brunswick, a stone's throw from the Bay of Fundy, "where we never once locked our doors." A bustling person with a fierce need to nurture, she knits sweaters and crochets more doilies than the planet has any use for. When not busy with balls of yarn, she bakes bread, cakes and cookies, humming as she does so, for she was born exuding contentment. Whatever has caused Doreen's western bent, it has not sprung from her maternal seaside genes.

Possibly it originated in her paternal chromosomes. Doreen's father, Bernie, is a big burly Irishman whose parents hailed from County Cork. He is an ex-steelworker, having recently retired. These days he spends most of his time watching TV in his doily-infested recliner, eating more baked goods than is good for any man.

During her formative years, Doreen often watched Westerns with her father in the hope of getting to know him. Bernie, although purebred Irish, was never big on words in mixed company. On the other hand, he was — still is — a devoted admirer of John Wayne and has always extracted deep meaning from movies where men are men and women are women, the way the good Lord intended them to be.

This is the reason Doreen grew up learning how (but never why) women who knew their worth adhered to a code of beguiling helplessness, trapped in cumbersome dresses that any normal female would perish in under that burning western sun. Some of those non-sweating women, albeit virtuous, were uppity, but only until someone like John Wayne straightened them out. The impossibly uppity ones rode horses (despite their dresses) and were harder to tame. Even Mr. Wayne had to struggle, though he always succeeded in the end, breaking them the way he would a wild horse, with the reluctant respect a hero feels for a lesser creature.

Such ladies were labelled feisty. Sometimes they even sweated.

For as long as Doreen can remember, she has wanted to be feisty. She is willing to sweat. She has the right build and does not own a dress.

But, as Bernie initially took pains to point out, movies where men are men were not for little girls. Doreen, a stubborn child, watched the movies all the same — for educational purposes — and her father never made more than a halfhearted attempt to stop her. He was proud of his taste in cinematographic art and deep down it pleased him that his daughter had inherited his discerning eye.

Doreen has not dared reveal to Katrina her dreams of sitting tall in a handcrafted saddle, a Chuck, Buck or Wild Bill wooing her by the campfire. Katrina is far too serious, far too sensible, to appreciate Technicolor illusions set in rattlesnake country.

A year ago Katrina spent a couple of weeks in Paris with three colleagues from work. The trio had approached her when a friend of theirs was forced to cancel and they needed a fourth person in order to keep the two double rooms they had booked. Katrina made a spur of the moment decision to join them. She had always longed to see Paris. To see herself in Paris. In Paris she would fit in.

She did her utmost to look the part while she was there. Tall, blond and elegant, she donned high-heeled shoes that were murder to walk in, bought an expensive hat and perched it on her head at fetching angle. And still those damn Frenchmen appeared oblivious to the significance of her presence among them. She became increasingly desperate and decided something had to be done. Precious days were slipping by.

Finally, one afternoon — they were heading for the métro to return to the hotel in the 18th *Arrondissement* to rest before an evening of possibilities — she worked up the courage to cut loose. She told the others she needed time to shop for presents for her family and that she would meet them back at the hotel.

Kisha, Lorraine and Melanie encouraged her independence. They were tired of Katrina, had been since day two when, not knowing any better, they had consented to be dragged halfway across Paris to some bone yard Katrina claimed was world famous. Had wasted more than half a day in order to pay tribute to some dead old bag named Colette who didn't even have a last name. One of France's greatest writers, according to Miss Know-it-all Ferguson who made them take several pictures of her standing by this Colette-person's grave wearing the stupid hat she had bought earlier that morning.

Visiting Colette was what Katrina had promised Eva, who never got to travel. Katrina's father abhorred the idea of foreign places.

There stood Katrina, trying to look French — at least semi Hungarian — beside a black gravestone reading *Ici repose Colette* 1913-1981. The red stone beneath stated *Fille de Henry de Jouvenel des Ursins et de Sidonie Gabrielle Colette*, so she knew it was the right place. There was another Colette in the adjoining grave.

Jean Gabin was not buried at Père-Lachaise. She had no idea where to find him. Then again, Jean Gabin was not his real name — that much she knew — but she had forgotten his original one. His remains could be anywhere.

The other girls were not interested in hanging out with dead people. Apart from Jim Morrison, of course. It gave them a cheap thrill to see his grave with its graffiti, empty bottles and reverently toking hippies. A quick thrill, but no more. Famous or not, hot or not, the guy was dead. What Kisha, Lorraine and Melanie loved best was to sit at sidewalk cafés and laugh and flirt with real live men, then hope for the best. Like Lorraine pointed out, "It's what you're *supposed* to do in Paris, for fuck's sake!" Most evenings after dinner and a few bar stops, the girls would hit yet another auspicious nightspot with very loud music and an undulating mass of sweaty, fashionable people.

That time of night was when Katrina bid them goodnight and took a taxi back to the hotel to lock herself in the room she shared with Kisha. Her preferred pastime at this late hour was to stand by the window and survey the street below. First she switched on the bedside lamp. Its faint glow turned her into a mysterious shadow beside the blue curtain. She wore her hat as she stood there, waiting, in a state of readiness. Could she have chosen background music for the tableau she would have picked a softly wailing trumpet. Miles Davis, *Générique*. Had the fog rolled down rue Burcq, and had a strange man in a trench coat passed under the streetlight below, looking haunted, Katrina would have known what do to. As it was, she waited in vain, disappointed, yet not utterly surprised.

Well, she thought, peering down, pretending time had slid backward fifty odd years, *Le Quai des brumes* was set in Le Havre. No doubt it is foggier on the coast.

Still.

Her solitary afternoon became critical. She was now impatient to see if reality would deign to conform to her fantasies just this once when the setting was spot on. Parading her persona along the Seine that afternoon, she turned onto Pont-Royale where she stopped and rearranged her hat to offer a more suggestive contour. Exuding allure, she remained at the exact centre of the bridge, giving passing pedestrians a chance to admire her elegant profile. And she did not go unnoticed, it wasn't that. Men eyed her. Men in suits. Less well-dressed men. None in a trench coat though, none of them right.

On boulevard de Sébastopol, too anxious to walk any further, she sat down on a bench to await Destiny. She did not expect Destiny to be punctual, but was fairly hopeful it would not let her down, not *here*, not *now*, not when taking into account her family history and the circumstances that had converged to deposit her on this very bench.

A man in a trench coat did amble by eventually, an old man in dire need of a bath, carting his belongings in two plastic bags. He was too busy having a querulous conversation with himself to notice Katrina. His coat was ripped. A very handsome man strolled by, making kissing noises with pursed moist lips into his cell phone while winking at Katrina. Three gesticulating Arabs passed by, dressed in *kaffiyeh* and long gowns. Students of various nationalities, Rastafarians, Nordic blondes, Slavs with bad teeth, Africans with impossibly white teeth, old codgers with no teeth. Young boys on rollerblades. Every male stereotype of *Homo sapiens* a tired evolution had coughed up. Many of them glanced at her, ready to connect, but she averted her eyes. None of them featured in the script. The right man would recognize her instantly. Having dreamt the same dreams he would know his lines.

Come on, she urged Destiny, don't let me down! I only have four more days! Send somebody my way!

Please?

When the tall woman blazed around the corner, steady on four-inch heels, the colours of Boulevard de Sébastopol paled. To Katrina, the woman looked like the kind who normally sleeps during the day. That big red hair, that make-up prominent at twenty paces, those gregarious boobs half revealed so you knew they weren't soccer balls shoved down her dress to grab the attention; every part of her spoke of lurid night time activities. She was brazenly out of place on a busy daytime sidewalk, yet looked as if she owned it.

When she noticed Katrina in solitary splendour on the bench, she stopped dead. A salacious grin ignited her face. Katrina turned around to see at whom the woman's sudden lust was directed, but found no one. By the time she turned her head again, the woman was sitting next to her, pressing an affectionate thigh against hers. Her gaze held Katrina's as her mascara coated lashes whipped meaningfully up and down.

Katrina stared unabashed. Her mouth hanging open gave her a certain slack-jawed charm. The larger-than-life woman parted carmine lips and released a flow of words. Judging by her purring dulcet tone and slightly raised eyebrows, she was proposing something. Alas, it was entirely unclear what she was on about, for Katrina spoke no French, apart from seven useful sentences memorized from her phrase book. None of them dealt with this kind of situation.

A second later the tête-à-tête was nipped in the bud. Before the woman could melt Katrina's frozen shock, a third party intruded from somewhere behind her. Katrina became aware of the interruption only when the apparition's passionate demeanor switched off. It was as though the woman's grin had never been. Her thigh withdrew. Her face grew chilly and disapproving. Pointing to Katrina's watch, impatient now, her gesture demanded to know what time it was, *vite, vite*!

As Katrina held up her arm, displaying her wristwatch, she noticed the sagging skin beneath the woman's chin, how brittle that skin. She looked like a cartoon ghost about to fade. Katrina tried not to stare as the woman nodded a formal *merci* and stalked off on her stilts, back to whatever dimension she'd escaped from.

Katrina glanced over her shoulder. A police car had pulled up to the curb. Two amused *gendarmes* were holding a mumbling exchange, staring in her direction through the rolled down passenger window. Recognizing an *ingénue* when they saw one, the young *gendarme* in the passenger seat leaned out and treated her to a lewd wink before his colleague depressed the throttle and eased the car back into the sea of cars that was rush hour Paris.

It was all too absurd. She was in Paris, for heaven's sake. It was autumn. Golden leaves fell onto the sidewalks on cue. And *this* was all the city had to offer? She had been striding down miles of boulevard on sore feet, *soignée* in her new hat, autumnal grey and soft with just the right kind of bounce in the brim, purchased in a boutique on boulevard Saint Germain. It matched her angora sweater which came from a small boutique on rue de Rivoli. Both had cost a wad of cash so immense it did not bear thinking about, but she was convinced such fashionable items were well worth it. She looked gloriously sophisticated.

And then this.

Ordinarily she did not mind a solo existence, quite the opposite, but being alone in the world's romantic hot spot, crammed with bars and cafés suitable for covert meetings, how could she feel anything but cheated? How could she not feel an abject failure?

Her adventure had been short and bizarre. Worst of all, it had been humiliating. As she had watched the woman's lips, so big they could have swallowed her whole and kept on smiling, the revelation that had dazed her was that *this* would be the most astonishing event of her life.

She returned to Canada four days later, hurrying back to the place in her head where adventures played themselves out in soothing black and white.

Her daydreams continue despite the setback; she has grown too dependent on them. But for a while they were not as intense. They became blurred, slightly out of focus, the sound less audible. It took effort to get back on an even keel, but she managed.

She knows she will never wear the hat again.

Telling her new friend Doreen about the trip is out of the question.

Doreen has her own story to tell — should she choose to — for she too went looking for adventure. She travelled not east, but west, and at terrific expense. She clopped along on horseback under a sky as endless as she had known it would be, clopped along just like the feisty women that gave John Wayne no end of trouble, yes, she did, humming *Feet in the stirrups and seat in the saddle, I hung and rattled with them longhorn cattle.*

She clopped and she hummed, but only for two days.

A day and a half to be precise.

She paid more money than she will ever be able to justify to fulfil her need to take part in a cattle drive in Alberta. It was not the Wild West per se, but it *was* the west no matter how you looked at it. The west is not nearly as wild as it used to be, but why let that lessen the allure? The cattle were not longhorns, but the way Doreen preferred to look at it, cattle are cattle, a herd is a herd.

To look the part of her true self, she invested $248 in a lovely taupe Stetson, another staggering amount on a pair of to-die-for boots in a coordinate shade. And she *did* look the part. Her image in the mirror struck her as so authentic it was more than worth the expense. Had she saved up more money she would have bought a pair of chaps too, but it had taken long enough to save for the trip and the hat. As it was, the boots wore out what was left of her credit card. Roughing it in the Wild West did not come cheap.

She flew west, rented a car at the Calgary airport and headed southeast for the ranch beyond the horizon, an open map beside her, hoping Destiny had saddled its horse and was ready to take her for a lope towards a suitable sunset.

The farther she drove, the bigger the land, the mightier the sky.

It looked wild enough.

Yes! yodeled her heart. This is it, this is *it*!

At the ranch the next morning, the sun lit an accommodating infinity of rolling grasslands and craggy buttes. This truly *was* a land that did not end. Doreen was thrilled to think she would soon ride across it on a real horse.

By then she and the other city slickers were hovering expectantly by the corral, trying to meld with the setting, leaning against the fence at what they hoped was the properly relaxed angle, scanning the ground for suitable straws to chew. They were all wearing spanking new hats and boots.

When it was Doreen's turn to get teamed up with a compatible horse, the rancher picked a bay named Nelson. Nelson was a sure-footed quarter horse. Seeing as she had no prior experience, she and Nelson would make a fine match, said the rancher, hoisting a saddle over Nelson's broad back. She'd have nothing to worry her purdy little head about.

"Sure-footed" was the term cowboys used to describe unambitious steeds past their prime who favoured static grazing over forward perambulation. It was another term for "mighty slow," but the cowpokes saw no reason to burden Doreen with that fact.

Even so, on the second day, trailing the rest of the group, she managed to topple off her sure-footed companion. As soon as she hit the ground, Nelson stopped to graze, oblivious to his lost rider, content with life in general.

Afterwards Doreen reflected that her fall should not have come as a great surprise. From the beginning she'd had a niggling suspicion that nothing was going to turn out the way it was supposed to. Reality, indifferent to the authenticity of her costume, felt no obligation to conform to clichéd fantasy just because Doreen Riley had her hopes up.

First of all, the two cowpokes assisting the rancher were too short. And if that wasn't bad enough, one was scrawny and had bad breath, the other was bald under his Stetson and had two ex-wives. The bald one, Willie, looked down on women as people, he explained during a philosophical moment, though he loved them as women. This was his idea of a compliment.

The scrawny quiet one, Frank, preferred equine company to that of the complex human variety.

Neither of them played the guitar.

Among the other city slickers were three women from Toronto, all taller and prettier than Doreen, though friendly enough. One knew how to ride and made sure they were all aware of the fact, until Willie pointed out that "ridin' English don't count for shit in these parts."

The remaining two were men. One was a baby faced weasel of a lawyer from Kitchener who had come to get drunk outdoors. The other, a rotund fellow from Windsor, was too full of delusions of his own to notice Doreen and the Torontonian trio. Like Doreen, he clopped along on a sure-footed mount, clutching the saddle horn, bouncing madly, virgin chaps flapping.

The first evening it turned very cold. A mean wind came sweeping from the north howling a wintry tune. There was no lazing around the campfire that night, no camaraderie and singing of songs. They all took to their sleeping bags early, keeping most of their clothes on for warmth even after the cowboys got the wood stoves blazing in the tents. In the men's tent somebody snored as if his life depended on it. He sounded like a Harley Davidson needing a tune-up.

Despite the Harley, Doreen must have fallen asleep at some point, because the next morning she woke up shivering in her sleeping bag. The ground had grown harder overnight. The stove was no longer blazing. Outside it was so cold there was no lingering around the campfire at breakfast either. An inch of snow covered the landscape. The rancher offered no apology for the sudden change of season.

It was down with the ham and scrambled eggs, anemic coffee in a tin mug, on with an extra layer of clothing, and up in the saddle where the wind seemed stronger. Doreen's gloves were not warm enough so the rancher lent her a pair of knitted mitts to put on top.

Grabbing the reins with big red mitts just did not look right.

"Is the weather supposed to stay like this? It was not in the forecast." The lawyer, chugging something out of a pocket flask, looked like he might sue.

"The weather changes awful quick in these parts," informed the rancher, challenging any sissy to complain about nature's way. Nobody said another word. The rancher hinted that they should have had the foresight to bring long johns. He himself had exchanged his Stetson for a fur lined hat with earflaps. Wielding a spatula by the chuck wagon, he looked disconcertingly like Elmer Fudd.

Two hours after setting out, Nelson's sure front feet slid on an icy patch and Doreen found herself doing an involuntary somersault. She had not been paying attention, too busy thinking about how this ride was supposed to turn out, had Destiny bothered to keep the appointment. Before she knew it she lay sprawled atop a frozen prickly pear cactus. As she lifted her head from the harsh, hostile ground mumbling, "Oh God, let me die," she watched Frank streak up a butte on his Appaloosa to head off some stray cattle. It looked exactly like the effortless manoeuver she had planned to impress Chuck, Buck or Wild Bill with.

Then came the pain. It turned out she had broken her left ankle. The end of her career as a cowgirl was abrupt and inglorious. While she tried to get up and failed, the rancher got out his mobile phone and tucked it under the right earflap of his hat. He looked none too pleased. Forty minutes later Betsy, the rancher's wife, came charging across the grassland in a pick-up truck to remove the troublesome Doreen Riley so the cattle drive could proceed the way a cattle drive should.

Doreen could tell they were happy to get rid of her. She was a liability. The rancher had no insurance.

Betsy drove Doreen straight to Calgary with Betsy's Cousin Verna following in Doreen's rental car. The cab of the truck was warm and cozy. Betsy was cheerful and sympathetic, offering hot coffee laced with rye from a thermos, talking non-stop the entire way, telling Doreen over and over not to cry, these things happen, heaven's above, she was darn lucky to have an excuse to escape the weather, wasn't she?

Considering the circumstances, Doreen felt it would be impolite to tell Betsy to shut the fuck up.

After waving good-bye to Betsy and Verna, and having had her foot seen to in a Calgary hospital, she spent the night in a hotel room overdosing on nachos and mini bar offerings while watching dirty movies. If she watched them for a treat or for punishment she never could establish, especially as they were showing *Rio Grande* on another channel. She fell asleep during a grunting group activity reminiscent of a picture she had once seen of a rattlers' den. The painkillers combined with booze and all the limbs writhing entangled on the screen made her dizzy.

She had hoped to see a rattler while out riding, from a safe distance atop a palomino.

The next afternoon a kindly flight attendant rolled her onto an eastbound plane in a wheelchair, the taupe boots and hat shoved in the bottom of her suitcase. The Wild West had cast her out. The humiliation hurt more than the ankle.

Back home she stomped her feisty good foot on her Stetson until it was flat and shapeless, only to immediately regret it and try to reshape it. It did not comply. Like Doreen, it would never be the same. The boots ended up in the back of her closet.

Sometimes she releases them from their prison of shame and looks at them, sighs as she runs a defeated finger along the stitching. They are good-looking boots, made to last. There are still bits of mud and bits of straw stuck to the soles. They smell of the west and she sometimes hates them for it, but cannot bring herself to clean them and erase the sorry adventure.

Let's face it, she began to rationalize, she *did* sit firmly in the saddle. And a very nice saddle it was. She *did* ride across a western vista on a horse, following the lumbering backsides of a herd of genuine cattle. Nobody can take that away.

Still.

It was humiliating, getting within sniffing distance of her dream, then failing to grab hold of it. People kept asking, "Sooo . . . how was it? And what happened to your foot? Fell off the horse, ha, ha, ha?" She lied and made up a story about a car accident somewhere outside Calgary. A woman named Betsy in a pickup truck, drunk as a skunk. A head-on collision. She was lucky to survive.

While her foot healed, she spent her evenings playing cowboy songs and drinking rye. Rye was what the cowboys had said they favored come sundown.

Enough rye will eventually alter a city slicker's brittle hold on reality, and when it did, Doreen succumbed to the sloppiest form of sentimentality, which invariably ended with an inspired rendition of *The Old Chisholm Trail*. With her eyes closed she would hoist herself onto a horse, a palomino with the leaping grace of Nureyev. Her body became one with the loping horse as she lost herself in *Come a ti yi yippee, come a ti yi yea.*

Until one night, just as she got to *With my knees in the saddle* . . . the landlord came hammering on the door yelling, "Enough already!" He'd had it with her yowling. What strange goddamn medication did they give her for that broken ankle? Was she on illegal drugs? Self-medicating? He didn't want no drugs in his house. Enough was enough.

That was how Doreen found herself evicted in the middle of her favourite tune, foot in a cast and all. Once again she had toppled off her horse.

The following week, through a stroke of luck, she discovered the gem that is the attic apartment where she now lives.

On the first Sunday in her new place, without any clean clothes, she threw her full laundry bag down the stairs and slid after it on her bum, step by bumpy step, hung the laundry bag over a crutch and hobbled up to the Laundromat three blocks north. There she met a woman named Katrina, the only other person in the place, sitting as if alone at a party (apart from the book on her lap), dressed in a discreet grey dress accentuated with a white pearl necklace. Though she did not seem to appreciate the company at first, she got up and helped Doreen empty her bag into a washing machine.

In response to Katrina's queries, Doreen served up the usual lie. How could she reveal the truth? Katrina would have laughed her head off. She is far too sophisticated to indulge in fantasies. She wears pearls to the Laundromat for crying out loud.

Katrina recently met a man at the art gallery where she sometimes goes on Saturday afternoons whenever there is a new exhibit. It's something to do. The man struck up conversation in front of a piece of modern art depicting nothing but the artist's bleak lack of talent.

The man, honestly confused, wanted to know if she had the required knowledge to interpret that blue rectangle with its single dot of pink and splashes of yellow that looked as if the artist's brush had dripped paint. The painting was called *Home on the range*. Which bit was the range, he wanted to know. Was it the blue or the pink dot? Should a range not be green?

Katrina confessed to not having a clue.

Her response cheered him, she could tell by his smile.

Before she knew it, they were having coffee together in the cafeteria. A daring move, but as Katrina told herself, daring was supposedly what she aspired to. Besides, what could possibly happen in an art gallery cafeteria full of culturally minded people on a Saturday afternoon? The tables did not have quartz tops, it was not foggy outside. Several elderly women wore hats. No enemies lurked.

She now wishes she had not responded so rashly to this man's invitation, because he keeps calling to ask her out. He went through all the seventeen K. Fergusons in the phone book until he got the right one and was not the slightest bit embarrassed to confess to it. And Katrina likes him a lot, it's not that. He is a very nice man.

But he is absolutely the wrong type. He is talkative and easygoing. Laughter comes as natural as breathing to him. He grew up on a cattle ranch out west. She can tell he is not one to keep secrets. Nor is he in any danger. His type never is.

She has succumbed and gone out with him a couple of times, but she is not sure what to do about a man like that. He plays the guitar and likes country music. Katrina cannot abide that kind of twangy racket. The confidence in his stride is unhindered. His eyes are open and blue. She will never be able to mould this man into her monochrome dreams where life is perilous and women wear stockings with seams. He doesn't own a trench coat. She asked him and he looked puzzled, saying he had no idea what one looked like. He had, he said, never been in the trenches.

She wishes she knew someone who likes this outdoorsy windblown type, because she wishes him well, she really does. He is kind and generous. He wants to take her to restaurants and feed her big steaks. "Put some colour in those pale cheeks," he says, looking at her with manly longing.

When he looks at her like that, her immediate instinct is to close her eyes. He is too overwhelming, this open-faced man, too real, made of such frighteningly solid flesh.

His name is Bill.

What should she do? Leave her dreams behind for the sake of this flesh and blood man?

She has thought of mentioning him to Doreen, but the thing is, Doreen has a boyfriend already. Or a lover, more like it. Katrina is not sure how to label him, because when Doreen sometimes mentions a man named Chuck, she does so in a very possessive, off-hand manner that has Katrina convinced it's an illicit liaison, that this Chuck is married. Thus the secrecy. She feels sorry for Doreen, stuck in a hopeless relationship. Men like that never leave their wives.

Out of respect for her friend's delicate situation she does not flaunt Bill's existence.

Doreen went out with a new man last week. She met him in a wine bar where she went with a bunch of people from work. It was something to do. She doesn't usually frequent establishments like that if she can help it, she feels too out of place. She finds the piano music irritating, the urban decor disturbingly aloof, the clientele pretentious. Plus she is not crazy about wine.

Though God knows he is good-looking, this man, everybody has taken pains to point it out as though she is legally blind. But here's the problem: he is a foreigner. Doreen has nothing against foreigners per se, she just gets insecure around people who can hold forth in languages she does not understand. It makes her feel excluded, as if secrets are being kept from her.

He is from Switzerland, this man, from a city called Zürich. Doreen had never heard of the place until he mentioned it. She can't pronounce it properly, she calls it Zoorick. A man sorely lacking equine ambitions, this enigmatic Swiss, he claims to never have been within ten feet of a horse. Nor does he plan to be. No, he told her when she asked, he would not dream of sitting on one. Why would he?

Doreen is unsure where this man's interests lie; he is annoyingly secretive. His job involves a lot of travelling, but he evades any mention on what it entails.

Computers? Global corporate takeovers? Politics? Is he a spy? Gangster? Hired assassin?

His lips remain sealed. It's only work, he says. A man should never bore a woman with the tedious details of his toil. He is quaintly old-fashioned in his mannerisms. "I do not wish to bore you with my problems." His voice was soft when he said it, his accent charming, his smile enigmatic.

He does not smile very often, and when he does, his smile is always resigned, his eyes rather sad. But he appears genuinely taken with her. He buys her flowers. Red roses that look out of place in the Wild West.

It's certainly a dilemma. Doreen is fond of this man, but no more. How could she be, he is far too distant, downright ethereal at times. It's as though he is not made of flesh and blood. Nor is he likely to ever burst into song.

And his name is neither Chuck nor Buck nor Bill. It is Alexis something or other.

Should she give up her dreams and rearrange her life to try and grow closer to this man?

Introducing him to a more cosmopolitan woman, sure to appreciate this type, would solve the problem, but she can't for the life of her think of any. She considered asking Katrina, of course, he would be just up her alley, but Katrina already has a boyfriend. Or lover. Once Doreen watched as she got some change out of her wallet and saw a photo of a man wearing a no longer fashionable trench coat. He looked almost old enough to be her father. Katrina never mentions him, which means he is married for sure.

Women with married lovers keep their affairs to themselves to avoid humiliation. Married men never leave the comfort of marriage behind. Why would they?

As she would not want to embarrass Katrina, she does not flaunt the fact of the enigmatic Alexis from Switzerland.

Slouching on one of the plastic chairs by the window, the Perfect Beauty is looking bored, slowly chewing gum, eyes closed. Her sidekick is scrutinizing his dirty nails, chewing a bit off here and there. With their backs to them, defiantly, Katrina and Doreen begin to sort their lukewarm clothes in a sloppy manner. This is not at all like them. Both are expert folders and usually take their time smoothing and folding each garment as if persistent neatness might increase their chance at happiness.

But not today. Doreen shoves her clean laundry into her canvas bag helter-skelter, knowing that by doing so everything will need ironing when she gets home. She does, she tells herself, not give a shit.

Katrina takes a bit more care initially, but her folding quickly deteriorates. Halfway through she gives up and stuffs the rest of her clothes into her large tote bag. Then she bangs the door to the dryer shut. It's an angry gesture.

Doreen defiantly leaves her door open.

Together they exit the Laundromat, heads bent in shame, or so it looks.

"See you next Sunday?" Katrina asks as they dawdle on the sidewalk. She appears restless, in a sudden hurry, as if having just remembered something she must do before it's too late.

"I guess." Doreen seems equally preoccupied. Looking tired and restless, she keeps fiddling with her keys.

Katrina does not ask why this is. She feels weary and limp herself. The sky is overcast, growing darker by the minute. It's going to rain finally. It has been hot and humid for the past month. The forecast this morning warned of thunderstorms in the late afternoon. Now the entire city lies quiet, bracing for the storm that will break the heat, wash it clean and make it new. Oppressive weather will frazzle even the most cheerful constitution.

It is, they are both convinced, the humidity.

They part without a smile, without looking at each other, as though they will never meet again but can't understand why.

Inside the Laundromat, the acned youth observes the two women indifferently. Just as they walk off in opposite directions, the first fat raindrops slam hard against the window.

"D'ya see the way them broads kept starin at ya earlier?" He turns to his flawless companion, stares at the nipples looking perky under the flimsy top. "Like they wanted to, like, jump ya or somethin?"

The Perfect Beauty — she has not paid the women any attention — forms her luscious lips into a pouty circle. From the centre of the circle emerges an expanding pink bubble. The timid pink of the gum clashes with the vivid red of her lips. Eventually the bubble bursts.

"Fucken dykes," she reflects, shoving the gum back in her mouth.

The Company She Kept

IMAGINE THEIR PLACE OF WORK, if you will, the way it was before the established order of life fell apart: a large office area on the fifth floor of a teaching hospital. Desks arranged to provide everybody with equal space, democracy measured in inches. Functional furniture, cheerful colours, all brightly lit. An unimaginative, generic habitat invented by experts in environmental psychology.

Now imagine in this setting the group of women: Gertrude, Pat, Margaret, Irene and Jill. Gertrude at forty-four was the oldest, Jill at twenty-nine the youngest, Pat, Margaret and Irene scattered across the thirty something range, resulting in an average age of 36.6 years. They felt they had known each other forever. It's like that, they would have said — had anybody asked — when you're confined to identical desks in close proximity from nine to five, five days a week, when you see the same familiar faces every time you raise your head from whatever you're doing. As time goes by you either end up despising each other or you forge a bond.

All those touches added to give each generic space a human flavour become personal ads that say: "I thrive in pleasant surroundings." (Potted plants: African violets and spider plants, the odd rubber plant. Crocuses and tulips in the spring, a poinsettia at Christmas.) "I'm a devoted mother: my children come first." (Photographs of children, good luck charms, drawings, craft projects from school or daycare). "I'm divorced. I need no man in my life." (Stark absence of photos of husband, lover, brief fling.) "I'm the plucky sort who has kept her sense of humour." (Cartoons cut from newspapers and magazines, office scenes featuring the medical profession, taped to any available surface.)

Over time they had answered each other's ads. They had forged bonds.

In short: they were all divorced, mothers of an average 1.4 children. Three of them, Jill, Margaret and Irene, were overweight, albeit not greatly. Pat and Gertrude were skinny. Their average weight was 142.8 lbs, average height 5 feet, 7¼ inches. None of them were beautiful. None of them were ugly.

Being so soothingly alike, they spent a lot of time together outside of working hours with the consensus that it would have been foolish not to take advantage of a favourable situation. Also, getting together meant a more varied social life. Or a social life, period.

What did they do during these get-togethers?

They talked mostly.

About what?

You name it. This and that. Their children. Rehashed whatever had happened at work lately. Embellished the odd urban myth. Kept appetizing gossip alive. They did not aspire to great thoughts or daring actions, had no intention of discovering the meaning of life. They did not have the ambition, and besides they were too tired in the evening.

Individually they nursed tender egos held in place with the frayed duct tape of optimism, but together those egos melded into one large entity, a cushiony shoulder that was a comfort to lean on.

All in all, they were easygoing people. Tenacious survivors, the sturdy backbone of society, women who undervalued themselves as though it was their feminine duty to do so. Without the abundance of their ilk, women's magazines would fold like a bad poker hand, cliché-riddled self-improvement books and guides to instant happiness would be shipped back to destitute publishers. There would be no foolproof new diets, no calorie-free food substitutes, no exercise programs targeting problem areas. The economy depends on keeping festering insecurities alive.

The five women were well aware of these facts but never gave them a second thought, for the same reason they wasted no time reflecting on the fact that the earth is round.

Then one day Kaye entered their lives.

She did so without fanfare, standing before them one Monday morning dressed in an unassuming blue knit dress accentuated by a maroon leather belt, her neck, ears, arms and fingers free of jewelry. She was slender and willowy, her complexion translucent. Her eyes shone. Whether they shone from expectation or some kind of inner joy was impossible to say.

"I'm the new temp," she announced by way of greeting. Her smile was on the shy side, but friendly; she posed no apparent threat. How could she, she was a temp. She was there to fill in for Sharon Voss who started maternity leave that day.

By fault of design Sharon's desk was halfway in, halfway out of their enclave, the shorter part of a large L-shaped area. The longer part of the L, the territory around the corner, was inhabited by six women too young and callow to appreciate the finer points of their older colleagues' gathered wisdom. Sharon had, despite the angle of her desk, belonged to the greenhorns. She was only twenty-two.

Kaye, on the other hand, was no greenhorn. She could have been twenty-five or thirty-five, it was difficult to tell. She had a breezy air of mature sophistication about her. Therefore, as she appeared promising enough, the five invited her to accompany them to the cafeteria on the ten o'clock break. She was under no obligation to accept the invitation, she could as easily have gone with the greenhorns.

Or, as Pat later suggested, she could have taken tea with the Queen of frigging Sheba.

But she did not, she accepted their extended hands of friendship, if not so much tagging as sauntering along as if on a catwalk before an appreciative audience, hips jutting left and right with the ease of conceit. She made no effort to take part in their chatter as she sipped her herbal tea, looking quietly amused.

Why did she bother to join them, when in between broad smiles she turned out to be decidedly standoffish, dropping ill-disguised hints that their company was not quite up to her lofty standards?

"I mean, it was like the bitch was humouring us," said Irene.

"Like we were drooling imbeciles," said Pat.

After four days they found themselves more or less apologizing for being so formidably dull, never once asking themselves why they took to sweeping under the rug all talk of humdrum subjects like their lives and their children. Already they were behaving as though having procured offspring was nothing but proof of some mental deficiency or a social *faux pas*.

For years they had taken their corporate identity for granted, had assumed that due to its deep-rooted ordinariness it was beyond reproach. Now suddenly every faction of this identity was cast into doubt. They became insecure, started to fret, to suffer mental turmoil. They no longer knew what to wear when getting dressed in the morning. Their clothes had turned treacherous and frumpy in the darkness of their closets. Hairstyles were scrutinized in bathroom mirrors and discovered unsuitable for their particular features, shades of blush and lipstick re-evaluated and tut-tutted. In the beginning they didn't even realize they were doing it.

"Sorry," they would say, individually or in unison, and for trivial reasons.

With a flutter of a white porcelain hand Kaye would implore them not to worry about it, whatever it was.

Margaret, the most even-tempered, succumbed to dishonesty one day and felt forced to point out that they were not all that worried, thank you very much. Why would they be? "And say, where are you going next, Kaye? Your time's up soon, isn't it?"

The pinprick was wasted on the balloon of Kaye's confidence. She merely released a little sigh. Her sighs, although of a delicate nature, were such that each exhalation made her look thinner.

"I simply can't decide," she confessed, looking relieved to finally be able to share a cumbersome burden. She was forever being deluged with offers of permanent positions and the offers put quite a pressure on her. At the moment she was tempted to accept one of them, though if she did, it would put an abrupt end to being a free spirit. And she so treasured her freedom, that was the thing, she was sure they understood, but on the other hand, the position was so well paid it would be damn near criminal to refuse it. Not only that, it involved a lot of travel. Kaye had a passion for travel.

So did Gertrude. "Really? What countries have you visited?"

"Well, you name one, I've probably been there."

"India?"

"Five years ago."

"China?"

"Last year."

"Tierra del Fuego?"

"Oh, I just love Terra! I went to Club Med there two summers ago."

Gertrude shut up and got busy stirring sugar into her coffee, forgetting it was not her habit to do so.

Afterwards Jill was heard mumbling, "Terra, my ass."

A week later a memo announced that Sharon Voss, having given birth to twin boys, had quit her job in favour of full-time motherhood.

The memo did not reveal that Kaye, already ensconced at Sharon's desk, had been offered the permanent job as Dr. Billington's secretary, nor that she had accepted without a nanosecond's hesitation. Kaye announced that tidbit herself.

Five pairs of dubious eyes hit her like hail during coffee break. "So what about the job that paid twice as much?"

"Oh, don't think I didn't give it a great deal of thought," she said, letting another of her helium sighs float heavenward. Kaye explained her decision to stay on. Not that it was any of their business, but she had accepted this job because in the long run it would be less hectic. Her health wasn't all that great, if they must know. "No, no, nothing serious, but chronic, quite debilitating at times." She preferred not to talk about it. "And, promise you won't tell anybody, but I just might settle down soon. Family obligations, that kind of thing."

She was sure they understood.

They were sure they did.

Days went by, still Kaye's desk remained barren of individual expression. Not bothering with Personal ads, her desk sprouted not the smallest African violet, no special penholder, no figurines, no framed photos of the family she had obligations towards.

They would have suspected her of not planning to stay, had it not been for Kaye's ear-to-ear smile, which flared up whenever Dr. Billington strolled through the door. It was a smile brimming with teeth and promises. A flush highlighted her cheekbones most becomingly. Her eyes grew lustrous. Hints of untold secrets twirled like smoke around her irises. God knows her eyes looked feverish at the best of times. According to Jill, eyes like that belong to people who are in the regular habit of popping something not available over the counter at Shoppers Drug Mart.

"That's a serious accusation," warned Gertrude.

"Prove me wrong," snarled Jill.

Pat's theory was that Kaye polished her eyeballs with Windex every morning.

Whatever the reason for her shining orbs, being around Kaye seven hours a day required effort. She was so highly strung she wore out both herself and her surroundings.

The five women stopped inviting her for coffee, but she came along anyway. When they succumbed to a tryst with a donut on Friday afternoons, Kaye sipped herbal tea, pinkie finger out, saying how that kind of indulgence was not for her. She had to stay in shape. Most of her girlfriends were fashion models. Hanging around them you had to aim for perfection or you might as well be dead.

"Perfection, my ass!" said Jill, later on.

"Why do we put up with her?" Irene wanted to know.

"She intrigues us," was Margaret's hypothesis. "We need intrigue in our lives."

"Are we that pathetic?"

"Apparently."

At Halloween Gertrude decided to host one of her famous dinner parties. Gourmet cooking had been her hobby for as long as they could remember and she was the unchallenged queen of sauces involving cognac, cream and crucial timing. They were all gussied up for the occasion, including the kind of full evening makeup warranted only for a promising date.

But like Irene said, "There's nothing wrong with feeling festive, even if it's just us."

Kaye had been invited as well, despite vociferous protests from the other four. Gertrude had to remind them that she was not one to leave people out.

Not that it mattered. Kaye's response had been, "Sorry gals, I've got other plans." She was off to a party at some famous actor's pad in Toronto. An actor she had known for years, a dear, dear friend. "He has this amazing loft in a renovated warehouse. The view is absolutely to die for!"

"Anybody we've heard of?"

"Hal Watkins." Kaye's eyes smirked their triumph.

"Who?"

She was appalled to discover that they had never heard of him. By the way she closed her eyes and shook her head, they knew with sinking hearts what gormless provincials they were.

It was the knowledge of this deplorable fact that caused them to get thoroughly pissed at Gertrude's Halloween dinner, the reason they commenced bitching like there were no tomorrows, even though the future consisted of nothing but. The art of bitching was not foreign to them, but that night they swept the board, collected the money and did not go to jail. Drunk as skunks, they became convinced there was not a single tomorrow left to be had.

So why not get wasted?

Besides, who the hell would reward them if they stayed sober?

Kaye had wreaked havoc with their self-esteem. They judged it an unforgivable crime. Enough was goddamn enough, was the unanimous decision. Around midnight Jill finished the last drop of the last bottle of wine, thumped her stockinged feet on the coffee table, raised her glass and hollered, "Fuck that bimbo!"

Margaret hissed, "Jill!" with a glaring lack of conviction.

Pat, twirling her glass, mumbled, "I'll drink to that."

Jill stared morosely into the empty bottle. It held no message.

Irene — she had stopped smoking six months earlier — mooched a cigarette from Gertrude who said she better go make some strong coffee.

A week later Kaye announced that she was throwing one of her notorious bashes and had to take an extended lunch hour to pop downtown to buy a large punch bowl.

Would they mind covering for her?

They had been unaware that she was famous for throwing bashes.

"Oh yes! You better believe it!" Her tone implied that they ought to have known this. As if there had been extensive coverage in the media.

The reason for throwing this one was simple enough: she had found a recipe for a rum punch she just *had* to try. "Just listen to this! Apart from rum it's laced with Cointreau and Grand Marnier and a dash of tequila. Does that sound good or what?"

They supposed it did.

"So you guys just *have* to cover for me!" Kaye was breathless with excitement. Her cheeks were on fire, her eyes the size of golf balls. Her body hummed and vibrated.

This was when Gertrude recalled that she had a beautiful Waterford crystal punch bowl with a dozen little cups, a most darling set she had bought in England years ago at great expense, having transported it back home in her hand luggage. Kaye was welcome to use it.

Kaye said, "Oh no, I couldn't possibly!"

Gertrude insisted. That was the way she was, doing her maternal best to usher everybody in the direction of potential happiness. In the end, mostly to please her, Kaye accepted her generous offer but took a two-hour lunch all the same.

"Must be some shindig she's planning," mumbled Margaret.

They were all looking forward to the bash, but it turned out they were not invited.

The following Monday Kaye forgot to return the punch bowl.

The party?

"Oh, it was a total riot!" It had gone on until four in the morning when as a suitable finale Hal had performed a striptease on the dining room table. "He looked too darn cute, wearing only black boots and the empty crystal bowl for a hat.

And, listen to this: a red ribbon tied around his you-know-what, flicking it provocatively hither and yon! Can you believe it?"

They didn't even try.

"I'll show you the pictures when I've had them developed," promised Kaye. "You'll *adore* them!" She had been forced to sleep through Sunday in order to survive. "Well, you know how it is. So . . . anyways, I never got around to cleaning the bowl. But I'll bring it tomorrow, I promise."

"That'll be fine," said Gertrude. Her unwarranted understanding narrowed her friends' eyes. Their faces turned grim.

Shortly afterwards Jill, Pat and Irene gathered for an impromptu conference in the ladies' room where the general agreement was that Gertrude would never see her imported at great cost frigging English punch bowl ever again and that it served her right. The consensus was that Gertrude damn well knew it but was too big a wuss to say so.

Resentment obliterated their smugness on Tuesday morning when Kaye brought back the box with the punch bowl and twelve little cups, looking suitable grateful when she once again thanked Gertrude.

Wednesday was elective surgery day. With no doctors in the office, work was light. Rain poured from morning until evening, confining them to an island of fluorescent light in a world of semidarkness. Gertrude and Irene were the least busy and took a half hour coffee break to break the tedium.

"So . . . was your punch bowl in one piece?" asked Irene.

"You bet. And the cups too."

"And clean?"

"Clean as a whistle."

"I'm surprised."

"Not as surprised as I was. Want to know something funny?" Gertrude asked, staring out the window at the curtain of rain. Her left hand was playing a solitary game with a plastic spoon.

"What?"

"Kaye never used it."

"What do you mean, she never used it?"

"Just that: she never used it. I took all the stuff out of the box to see if she'd cleaned it properly. You'll be happy to know I didn't trust her. All the cups were still in their original wrappers inside the bowl, still securely taped even though the tape was old and dry. She never even opened the damn box. When I lent it to her I neglected to mention that I'd never actually had occasion to use it myself. For stupid reasons, I might add. I was always afraid I might break something."

"Are you serious?"

"Would I make it up?"

"Well, no. It's just too weird."

"And it raises a puzzling question: Why did she make such a big thing about her friend wearing it for a hat, and not having time to wash it? What the hell was the point?"

They pondered this mystery for a while, staring at the rain. Life ticked on.

A few weeks later Kaye let it be known that she was hosting a fancy dinner party and needed to stretch another lunch hour in order to purchase a large salad bowl. The woman seemed to suffer a dire shortage of bowls. This time Margaret offered to lend her one. After the usual resistance, Kaye accepted in a manner suggesting she did so only to indulge Margaret.

Again, they were not invited, though Kaye did share the terrific news that she had decided to cook French. A Breton feast, to be specific. She was already agonizing over what kind of wine to cook the mussels in, not wanting to waste anything too expensive on cooking, but fretting that cheap plonk might ruin rather than enhance the flavour. Details like that were just *so* important.

"You know what I mean?"

They assured her they did.

Later that day Gertrude and Margaret held an unscheduled conference in the Xerox room. The door was firmly shut.

The following Tuesday Margaret got her salad bowl back. Later that night the news swept like a brush fire from house to house: Kaye had not used the salad bowl either. Following Gertrude's advice Margaret had stuck a piece of transparent tape in the bottom of the bowl. Had the bowl been used, the tape would have been removed prior to use. Even if Kaye had failed to notice it, it would have been damaged in the wash. But there it was. A half inch piece of virgin tape.

Saturday night they got together at Pat's for wine and cheese. Rather a lot of wine; it had become the norm. Kaye was off to Toronto that weekend, to the premiere of a new avant-garde feminist play called *Shakespeare Never Cleaned a Toilet*. A dear friend of hers was in it, playing the all important role of the toilet. She and the gang had first row seats.

"Toilet seats?"

Sarcasm was wasted on Kaye.

"Is your friend Al in it?"

"His name is *Hal*. But no, I'm talking about Trevor Harfield. You wouldn't know him."

There was to be a huge cast party afterwards at Trev's penthouse.

"Penthouse, my ass," said Jill.

Pat checked the *Globe & Mail* and damn it if there was not a premiere in the offing. The cast even featured an actor named Trevor Harfield. Gertrude, who indulged in cultural endeavors on the side, said she had seen the play two years earlier in New York. It was, she assured them, such a load of pretentious crappola you would for sure need a toilet once you got the hell out of there.

Monday morning they inquired about the play. Kaye said it had been absolutely fantastic. Jill wanted to know what it was about. Kaye threw her a scrap of plot that made Gertrude's eyebrows hit her hairline. Kaye, she proclaimed later, was "so full of shit it wasn't funny."

It was unlike Gertrude to use that kind of language.

Did Kaye fabricate a fake existence?

Did she have no friends?

They were forced to discount that theory. She received constant personal calls at work. At all hours of the day, there she was, babbling and laughing, cooing and bickering. In between, she was busy sending replies to a daily onslaught of e-mails. Unlike her five resentful colleagues, she was the ultimate social animal.

So why lie?

Did she borrow stuff and make up stories just to rub in their faces the fact that they were a bunch of losers? Why were their bowls not good enough? Did they have such deplorable taste? Was that it? And why did she find it necessary to go to such extremes to taunt them? Was her contempt for them that deep?

Was she a sadist?

Or was she suffering secret trauma? Had somebody died? Had she broken up with her beloved? Had he left her for another woman, absconding with all their bowls?

The time had come for serious snooping. It did not take long to find out that Kaye lived on the second floor of a high-rise in Burlington. Hearing this, Pat slammed a fist on the table and shouted what a frigging stroke of luck that was. "Dan's girlfriend Tiffany lives in that very building!" Dan was Pat's nineteen-year-old son. They took this as a sign that their prying had the blessing of a higher power. Freed of the burden of guilt they went full steam ahead.

First they asked Kaye if she was busy the following weekend. And, if by any chance she was not, would she care to join them at Jill's for pizza and a movie? "Nothing extravagant," they said, "just us gals."

Kaye would not.

She was having yet another dinner party. Just an intimate get-together with five close friends, but it took effort even so, didn't it? She was cooking Spanish. Hal was coming to town and *paella* was his absolute favourite, bless his heart. Luckily Kaye's grandmother was Spanish and the ability to create *paella* was in her blood.

No thanks, she didn't need any bowls, but did they happen to know where she could get hold of some saffron?

They did not.

To be honest, Gertrude had some, but reading the warning signals in eight accusing eyes, she put a chokehold on her kindness.

By then they had a plan. Saturday night Tiffany was to go down and knock on Kaye's door around nine in the evening. Young and cute, wearing a T-shirt sporting a sisterly slogan, her appearance would be nonthreatening. If and when Kaye answered the door, Tiffany was to ask if she could please borrow a flashlight as she had somehow managed to blow every fuse in her apartment.

They waited at Jill's that night. The minutes, unlike the wine, barely moved. At nine forty-two Tiffany and Dan turned up to file a report:

Kaye had answered the door in her pajamas, the TV on in the background, churning out a rerun of a rerun that was predictably unfunny the first time around. She had peered out at Tiffany's harmless face through the peephole before opening the door, but left the safety chain on for the longest time, until finally disarmed by the friendly girl outside. She had acted as if she was unused to visitors.

Not only did Kaye not own a flashlight, candles or matches, she did not appear to own very much of anything. Her apartment was more or less empty.

"But she had this ugly old couch!" A frown disfigured Tiffany's pert nose. "This *puky* velveteen job in, like, shit-brown and faded orange. It was like, euhhh!"

Monday did not come soon enough.

"Sooo," cooed Jill, "how did your Spanish *paella* whatsit turn out?"

"Utterly divine," gushed Kaye and exhaled one of her sighs. The *paella* had been the genuine thing, mainly because she had invested in this enormous cast iron *paella* pan when she was back in Barcelona last year. And a friend of hers had given her a big bag of saffron.

"Really? So you had a typically Spanish dinner, eh? Dancing flamenco and fighting bulls, drinking vino and eating late?" Jill's attempt to sound light-hearted proved beyond her capabilities.

"No, not too late," said Kaye, oblivious to dark forces. "We ate around eight thirty. Hal had to get back to Toronto, he had rehearsals the next morning. He's got a major role in this new movie."

There were a lot of phone calls that night.

Tiffany was accused of having visited the wrong apartment.

Tiffany's description of Kaye proved she had not.

And so it continued until Christmas when Kaye planned to hurl herself into a vortex of parties and dinners and open houses. Christmas Eve she was scheduled to fly to Montreal where her mother resided with her new husband, a corporate lawyer of some repute. They had recently redecorated their mansion in Westmount and were preparing a huge celebration.

And what about her father?

He lived in Vancouver, was some kind of showbiz producer. On Christmas Day he would be on film business in Los Angeles.

"Merry Christmas everybody!"

"Oh, bite me," said Jill.

Early in the afternoon on Christmas Day Irene drove to pick up her ten-year-old daughter Tina from a friend's house in Burlington. Having got expensive skates for Christmas from her errant father, Tina and her friend Bethany had been out skating. As soon as she got in the car, Tina started sneezing and coughing most wretchedly. Watching green snails crawl out of her daughter's frozen nostrils, Irene decided to stop by a drugstore for a cold remedy to see Tina through the holiday. They were having Christmas dinner at Irene's parents' house and her brother Carl and his family would be there.

Ever since Kaye had entered their lives Irene had become acutely aware of the shortness of her shortcomings. Carl's kids never had green stuff oozing out their noses. They were snooty enough, but never snotty. Carl was equipped with a genuine Stepford wife. He was a bit of a Stepford wife himself. "Uptight? You should see my brother. He pulls his ass when he blinks," was how she had described him to the others.

The pressure was on.

In the drugstore Tina insisted on a grape flavoured placebo. Irene added some children's aspirin and they headed for the checkout. At the end of the aisle Irene sensed atmospheric disturbance.

A shadow fell across their path. There stood Kaye, clutching a bag of nachos and a jar of salsa with a dusty lid, the December issue of Cosmopolitan tucked under her left arm. She did not look happy to see Irene.

"Kaye!" Irene's surprise was genuine. "I thought you were going to Montreal?"

"My stepfather died on Christmas Eve." Kaye deflated in a bottomless sigh, far heavier than her usual ones. Mourning may have accounted for her pale face. It looked blotchy without make-up. Dark bags dropped under her eyes. Something ugly and crocheted clung to the top of her head. It was pink and purple and had holes where the yarn had ripped.

"I'm so sorry," Irene gushed. "Will you be going up to join your mother?"

"Yes." Kaye looked like she hadn't slept for days. "I'm leaving early in the morning. That's why I'm just having some nachos and an early night. I can't be bothered to cook. It's been terribly traumatic for everybody."

"I can imagine, especially at Christmas. How awful for you!"

Kaye looked brave.

Irene sped straight home, slid on ice through two red lights, ignoring her daughter's screams of terror. She was on the phone to Gertrude before she got her coat off. Gertrude, stuffing a turkey with her left hand while talking, reminded Irene that Kaye was supposed to have left for Montreal the same day her stepfather had allegedly united with his maker.

Gertrude was on her way to her daughter's new house where she was depositing the turkey in "a massive new oven," so she was in a bit of a rush. But she thought up an excuse to call Kaye the next afternoon when Kaye was supposedly in Montreal consoling her grieving mother.

When Kaye answered the phone on the first ring, Gertrude blithely invited her over for dinner on the 29th. Kaye said she would unfortunately be out of town, but thanks all the same. She had just got back from Montreal where she had received a call from her dad who had insisted she join him in Los Angeles. He was taking her to a big extravaganza in Beverly Hills. Kaye had always been crazy about LA.

And listen to this: George Clooney was going to be there!

Gertrude said she could certainly understand why she would want to go to LA, it being such a warm sunny place this time of year, and what with the subzero temperature we're having here, and Clooney being such a hunk and not to worry about it and Happy New Year and all that.

"Mm," said Kaye.

On New Year's Eve Margaret bribed her cousin's Mexican husband Dominic in Milwaukee to phone Kaye long distance in case Kaye had call display. Kaye answered the phone, again on the first ring, and Dominic said, *"Quiero hablar con Consuela, por favor."* Apologizing in bad English for having the wrong number, wished her a *Buen año nuevo* and hung up.

By then they could not, dared not, fathom how low they had sunk, just as they refused to acknowledge how great was Kaye's elusive power over them, how empty their own lives, for them to obsess to such a degree over Kaye's seemingly emptier one.

These thoughts had crossed their individual minds at some point over the past months, but they had hoped that as long as they said nothing out loud, they could pretend it wasn't so.

Kaye returned to work after the holidays looking elegant in a mango pashmina shawl draped over her favourite blueknit dress. The shawl was a Christmas gift from Hal. That dear man always lavished her with gifts.

"And how was LA?" inquired Gertrude. "Did you meet George Clooney?"

"And Montreal," asked Irene. "How was your stepdad's funeral?"

The questions were laden with a hefty dose of sarcasm, but it was, as ever, lost on blithe Kaye. The funeral had been beautiful. Sad, but very, very meaningful. The Prime Minister, an old friend of her stepdad's, had attended. He had given a most moving eulogy.

"And LA?"

"Oh God! How to even begin to describe it?"

"So . . . what's George Clooney like?"

"Too gorgeous for words! But he was surrounded by an army of bodyguards, so I didn't really get to talk to him or anything. He smiled at me though."

Kaye saw no reason to explain how she had managed to be in two places at once. Later that morning when they left for coffee, she stayed behind, busy on the phone bragging about her trip.

This was the day Pat took it upon herself to monitor Kaye closely. It did not take long to verify that, while Kaye was on the phone incessantly, she never actually talked to anybody. She pretended to make calls. The incoming calls were all for Dr. Billington. She simply cut them off before shrieking "Oh hi!" in a loud voice. Once you paid close attention it wasn't difficult to figure out her method. She kept one hand on the phone itself, playing with it, discreetly disconnecting the real caller while inventing a fake one. She was very good at it.

"You can tell she's had a lot of practice."

"That would explain why there are never any calls for her when she's not at her desk."

"But it doesn't explain how she's gotten away with it for so long."

After this discovery Gertrude gave up and pronounced Kaye deeply disturbed. She said there was a name for her particular condition, but that she could not remember what it was. Something long and foreign.

Gertrude also went on to pronounce the five of them, herself included, sad and pathetic.

Nobody appealed the verdict.

If it had been uncomfortable to circle Kaye's orbit before, from then on it became oppressive. Their acceptance of her lies had been disturbing enough, but living with their self-loathing for having swallowed those lies like Friday donuts now became so unbearable that over the months they started, one by one, to do the unthinkable: they applied for other positions within the hospital. At first they did not have the guts to tell each other, the way traitors keep their shameful schemes to themselves. Subsequently they suffered guilt on top of everything else.

But this they knew: life, as they had known it, would never be the same.

Four months later it was as if there had been an explosion in their midst. The blast found them scattered all over the building.

Gertrude, an office fixture for twenty odd years, shocked everybody by being the first to flee the scene, embarrassed, but too relieved to care. She had been offered a better paid job as administrative assistant down in Family Medicine.

Jill was next to go, landing a coveted spot in the Pediatric Clinic.

Margaret followed suit a month later, transferring her Personal Ads to a cubicle in the Business Office. This, she soon complained, was full of boring, sane women who talked endlessly about tidying their closets and cleaning their ovens.

Pat ended up in Audiovisual the same week Irene started a new secretarial job in Pathology.

Life had acquired a sad tint that sometimes made them avert their eyes when talking about it, a tint that had coloured them restless. They still got together for coffee and lunch, and outside work, but their gatherings were subdued, the flow of wine halted. They were bitter, quieter. They felt older, they went to bed early.

One day at lunch a pale, wild-eyed Jill steamrolled across the cafeteria towards her waiting friends, collapsed into a chair and started drumming her red nails on the table. It sounded like machine gun fire. It took a while before she was able to inform them, teeth clenched, that Kaye and Dr. Billington were getting married. Dr. B had left his wife of fifteen years.

"And get this! He and Kaye are already living together!"

No, this was not one of Kaye's fantasies. Jill had verified the facts and they checked out. It was true. According to the girls who had inherited their old desks, neither Kaye nor Dr. B had given anything away. There had been no meaningful glances, no covert touching or sly winks. Nobody had had a clue. A travelling rumour insisted that it was in fact Mrs. B. who had left Dr. B for a woman, but nobody knew for sure.

The news had a catalytic effect on Jill. First she went on a diet. She lost thirty-five pounds in less than four months, a victory she celebrated by spending a fortune on a brand new wardrobe — and nothing off any sales racks either. She could not afford such a splurge, but that was beside the point, that was why the good Lord had created credit cards. It was, she explained, a high risk investment that hopefully would result in a huge yield within a very near future.

The new svelte Jill looked in the mirror and, although thrilled with what she saw there, decided that the image was still not up to snuff. She went a step further and dyed her hair platinum blond. *That* did the trick. She was now turning heads at an alarming rate. Which she ignored because, she revealed, she had a plan.

"What do you mean you have 'a plan'?"

"Wait and see."

As the Christmas party season loomed nearer, she put her plan into action. Step One: secure an invitation to the party up in the old department.

That was easy enough.

Step Two was slightly more complicated. Its success depended on being able to lure Dr. B into the office storage room. Jill had expected this to be a challenge, what with him being in love with Kaye and all, but some men exhibit a remarkable lack of moral fortitude within sniffing distance of a svelte blonde with cleavage.

Step Three made Dr. B a happy man.

Pat was the first to find out. She found it hard to digest the news when a grimly triumphant Jill dropped by the following evening to deliver an update on the efficient execution of her plan.

"You mean you and he . . . in the storage room?"

"That's right."

"No way!"

"Trust me. This is out of the mouth that did the deed!"

"What do you mean?"

"I performed oral sex upon the good doctor."

"You gave him a blowj . . . !"

"Please! I prefer the term oral sex. It's less tacky."

"Jill! How could you?"

"Well, it did make me gag."

Dr. B — Graham in this new incarnation — spent the following Saturday night at Jill's. Eager for a repeat performance of Step Three, he arrived carrying flowers and a bottle of champagne. Once again the new improved Jill exercised her jaws.

Graham's life took on a whole new meaning.

Meghan, Jill's daughter, was at her dad's for the weekend, at a safe distance from her mother's ambitious debauchery.

Something else happened that evening. Gertrude called Kaye at the Billington residence. It was not a planned call, nothing they had decided on as a group. They no longer plotted events *en masse*. It had taken a lot of internal wrangling, a quarter of her special bottle of Scotch and six cigarettes before Gertrude was able to lift the receiver and dial the Billington number.

When she informed the others the following Monday at lunch, she did so with the haggard face of someone who has received devastating news. She had felt so terribly sorry for Kaye, she said, and had desperately wanted to do something for the poor deluded woman before it was too late, so she had called and offered her help. What else could she do? Did they see her point?

They said they did. Sort of.

It had been well intentioned, but it had failed miserably. Kaye, impatient and distracted, had informed Gertrude that she really had no time to chat, sorry, dear. She and Graham were hosting a big dinner party, catered mind you, as better parties are, but even so, there were details to see to, napkins to fold, silver to polish, fresh flowers to arrange, vintages to uncork, that sort of thing.

"There isn't a single detail to see to, except you," a frustrated Gertrude had shouted, on the verge of tears. "I know you're alone. Talk to me, Kaye, for God's sake! I'm here for you. You need help."

"Oh, Gertrude, you're so weird!" Kaye had laughed.

After Gertrude had hung up, she had cried for a long time, but that was a fact she kept to herself.

Less than a month later, Kaye and Graham split up. The evening he worked up the nerve to gently break the news about his affair with Jill to Kaye, Kaye interrupted him to ask, could she say something first, "Please Graham?" She had a confession to make, a confession so fateful it made her blush. Best get it over with. It was this: she had fallen in love with a man named Hal Watkins, a famous actor she had met at a friend's a while back. She couldn't help herself, she was in love. These things happen. They were so crazy about each other, she and Hal, they had decided to get married at once and fly off to Montego Bay for an extended honeymoon. Hal had a villa there.

There. She had said it. Could Graham ever forgive her?

A relieved Graham swallowed his own confession (far more eagerly than Jill had his semen) and assured Kaye how truly happy he was for her, and how he would have to learn to live without her.

"Mm," said Kaye.

She disappeared from their lives after that. One day she was disturbingly there, the next she had ceased to exist.

The woman who had replaced Pat later heard a rumour about Kaye and George Clooney, hastily adding, "Not that I believed a word of it."

According to another rumour Kaye had moved to Vancouver, though some claimed it was Montreal.

"Or maybe Tierra del Fuego." Margaret was still pissed off.

Graham revealed to Jill that Kaye had started to frighten him as soon as she had moved into his house. First of all, she had brought next to no belongings at all. "I swear," he said, "that woman walked through walls. And she never seemed to eat." He had suspected her of sneaking out at night to suck the neighbours' blood. They all looked a bit pale.

Was it true that his wife had left him?

He preferred not to discuss it, wounded pride, fragile male ego and all that, but yes, it was true. His wife had not left him for a woman though, unless that woman was herself. She had simply come to the realization that having a life of her own, using her considerable brain, would be far more fulfilling than being a doctor's moll. She had already been accepted at M.I.T. to do a Ph.D. in biochemistry.

As soon as the divorce went through, gorgeous platinum blonde Jill Bernice Koplek married Dr. Graham Arthur Billington. Not because she loved him, she told her friends, defensively, though she had grown rather fond of the guy, for he was not without charm and kindness. No, she had married him because she was determined to never again go unnoticed. It was her way of making a statement.

"One could do worse than marrying a doctor," she summed up, twisting the diamond ring around her finger as if it was uncomfortably tight.

They were all invited to the wedding and the reception afterwards, a fairly modest affair where they sat at a table on their own with Tina and Meghan, the bridesmaids, feeling a bit out of place. Most of the men in the crowd were doctors, all accompanied by their wives. Some of the wives were doctors too. Some were lawyers. Four of them were friends of the previous Mrs. Billington.

Only a few were molls. None were secretaries.

Jill remains part of their circle, though these days they see less of her. She is still working. In her free time she is busy redecorating the new ranch house in Ancaster. It has a beautiful view of the city below. She called Gertrude a while back to announce that she's pregnant. She sounded genuinely pleased.

Irene runs into Graham — they're on a first name basis now — at the hospital whenever he has an errand in Pathology. He looks happy, less anal, slightly smug. He has grown his hair longer. His new ties sparkle with bright colours.

Pat is dating a technician in A.V. His name is Harry. He is five years her junior. They have joined an amateur theatre group that is putting on Oscar Wilde's play *The Importance of Being Earnest*. Pat says she can't get over how much frigging fun it is. She has been selected for the role of Gwendolyn and is busy learning to speak with an upper-class British accent. Harry is playing Algernon. Everybody has been invited to the party on opening night.

Margaret has joined a yoga class and is on yet another diet. She has lost seven pounds in two weeks. The widower next door keeps asking her out, but Margaret says she's not interested. All that man ever does is watch TV and play bridge, except for once a year when he drives his pick-up truck into nature to shoot a bunch of deer for no discernible reason. "Who needs that kind of shit?" she asks. She's debating whether or not to join a theatre group as well. She used to act in high school, did they know that?

They did not know that.

Oh yes. And she can sing too.

Pat has told her they're doing a musical next and that she should audition.

Margaret says she just might.

Gertrude's daughter Evelyn is expecting her first child and Gertrude spent every evening until recently building a Victorian cradle out of expensive oak. It was coming along splendidly until about a week ago when she started complaining about the fact that she is always the one expected to perform these unnecessary duties. Last Sunday she gave the unfinished product to Mike, her son-in-law, to sand and varnish, saying it's your kid, you do it.

She is fed up with gourmet cooking as well. It's too much work, too much money and too many calories hurrying straight to her ass. She is off on a trip to Greece next month with an old friend she ran into a few months ago. She has not elaborated on the sex of the friend in question.

Irene enrolled in a pottery class a while back. Last month she made a beautiful fruit bowl in shades of swirling blues and greens mixed with the odd fleck of dark gold. Tina says she never knew her mum was such a great artist. Even her brother Carl has been over to admire her effort. He was very enthusiastic, which is not at all like him. He asked if maybe Irene would consider making one for his Stepford Wife's birthday, in shades of beige and grey to match their decor. He sounded as if Irene had finally done something worthwhile enough that it deserved a reward.

Having discovered her artistic talent, Irene has signed up for the next level pottery class, as well as an evening art appreciation class at the university. She is considering learning how to weave. She has room for a weaving loom in the basement.

Life has reshaped itself into a new pattern that is less symmetrical, but interesting in a different, less predictable, way. "Enjoyable" is a word that has cropped up lately.

And yet they are still bothered about Kaye who is long gone. It's as if they can't let go. No wonder, all the power they let her usurp without a single mewling of protest.

"What's the moral of this story?" Irene asks Gertrude at coffee one morning. They haven't had coffee together for several days. None of the others have showed up, claiming heavy workloads.

"I don't think morals enter into it."

"Every tale should have a moral."

"Why?"

"Morals are comforting."

Irene had expected Gertrude of all people to understand this simple concept, but Gertrude, who is well read, says that is certainly *not* true. Stories happen, they unfold and come to an eventual conclusion, and that's freaking well that. They are brief, or not so brief, these glimpses of life. Sometimes they are intended to mean something specific, other times not.

Irene insists. She has a stubborn need for this particular tale to have a moral attached to it. Like the list of ingredients on a can of soup.

"Morals and soup are two different things."

Irene ignores the acerbic comment and tries to explain. "Morals are for the survivors of unfairness to cling to. They're what help us survive."

"Christ, aren't we deep today." The indifference in Gertrude's voice is new. She is withholding herself as of late, and in that withholding is present a hint of more changes to come. She is drumming her nails on the table the way Jill used to. It doesn't sound like a machine gun, mind you, more like a determined march into the unknown.

Irene gets upset. "I'm perfectly serious. A moral would make it easier to cope. I crave justice. Justice makes it easier to forgive."

"Forgive who?"

"You know who."

"Say the name."

"Why?"

"Say it."

"Kaye."

"And why does Kaye need to be forgiven?"

Irene ought to have an answer to that question, considering how strongly she feels about it, but she can't for the life of her dredge up a suitable reply. She decides not to have coffee with Gertrude for a while.

UNDER THE EIFFEL TOWER

LOOK AT THAT WOMAN SLUMPED OVER THERE, the one on the third bench from the south end of the Champ de Mars. The one with the reddish blond hair, knees pressed together, feet in low-heeled walking shoes. With her shoulders slouching like that she looks like a dejected lump of dough.

Who is she? And what's with that embarrassed look on her face?

Her name is Carol Hubick. She is Canadian. From Ottawa. And she is afraid of heights, which is why she is sitting temporarily alone.

Further down the path, somewhere over her left shoulder, looms the Eiffel Tower like a giant souvenir. Carol's husband, her brother-in-law and his wife should have reached the top of that tower by now, gushing breathless over the famous view she will never get to see. Judging by the queue, the rest of the world's teeming masses are impatient to join them. Carol sighs.

Never mind.

White clouds glissade with continental elegance over the roof of École Militaire. Birds trill their *joie de vivre* — probably in French — this magnificent June day as Paris bestows its most charming smile upon the hordes of visitors. And yet Carol, more impressionable than most, is not seduced. Yesterday she would have been, but not today.

She is feeling ashamed, and that is what accounts for that contrite look of hers. The reason for her shame has nothing to do with her fear of heights, it is caused by something far more unexpected. Looking friendly enough where she sits — and she is friendly, to a fault — her docile face, apart from the unbecoming blush of embarrassment, reveals none of the clandestine thoughts whispering in her head as if afraid to get caught and reprimanded.

These thoughts of hers are best described with the two words that did not always go together but these days are attached at the hip, accusatory and shrill: Politically incorrect! Such a tricky constraint is political correctness, making deviants of ordinary folk.

Carol does not approve of negative attitudes, including her own. She considers herself a liberal person, generally kind and good and well meaning. She believes in equality. Life is so much easier when people get along. And she has not changed her mind about that, not at all, it is just that today has turned out to be different. It was not supposed to, but it has. Today she has been forced to acknowledge another side of herself. Already she is surprised at the insistent nature of it.

For the last five minutes she has been furtively eyeing a woman also sitting alone, two benches down on the opposite side of the path. This woman is the reason Carol's head is hosting a midmorning coffee klatch of thoughts that nudge and gossip, impatient to share not so much what they know as what they assume.

Well, she has no business sitting there, does she?

Of course she doesn't! She's a gypsy. These benches are for tourists who have paid a lot of hard earned cash to come here.

Exactly! I mean, look at her. She's a beggar!

No, I shouldn't think like that. It's not like I'm a bigot. I don't even know if she's a beggar.

Oh, she's a beggar all right.

Now, you don't know that.

Sure I do. The city's full of them.

The woman, whatever her profession, is undeniably a gypsy. But what does that mean? Is the pointing out of this fact equal to uttering a racial slur? She is not bothering anybody, her expression is benign, she could advise Mona Lisa on the enigma of smiles. Her eyes are focused on something far beyond the tower, secretive, hooded eyes expressing vague amusement. Her clothes — a long skirt, cardigan and scarf — are simple, a mixture of browns and blues with a splash of red in the skirt. She looks a bit disheveled, her skirt unironed, but that is not it either.

No, what Carol finds so troublesome is the forbidding otherness of the woman. She just sits there and exudes it. Unsure of how to interpret such a phenomenon, Carol takes it personally and finds offense. The word *untouchable* slips uninvited into her mental coffee klatch and joins the discussion. Allowing the term to make itself at home takes her subversive musings to a new extreme. She is shocked.

I shouldn't think like that. If she turned her head this way she'd see me blush. Maybe she'd guess why. That would be so embarrassing.

Oh, don't be stupid! She's not a mind reader, for God's sake!

Back home they might have smiled at each other, these two women of a certain age, sensing similarities, making a friendly comment about the weather.

Carol had not anticipated spending this glorious midmorning in solitary contemplation. She had every intention of tagging along with the others up to that ludicrously high point of the tower where no human was meant to set foot. Less than half an hour ago she was fully prepared to exhibit the necessary bravado, however brittle, however false, in order to honour what is a very special occasion: her and Rod's first holiday abroad. Which is not just any old holiday but a celebratory journey, for on July the fifteenth — the day after tomorrow — they will have been married for twenty years.

That, as Rod keeps pointing out, is something.

On the plane from Toronto Rod voiced a wish to celebrate at the Crazy Horse Saloon, watching dancing girls, chugging a magnum of champagne, smoking a stogie, all after a big French dinner. Carol told him what she thought of that fantasy. She had her eyes set on a restaurant she had read about called Le Grand Vélour, a very old and famous place full of distinction. Napoléon himself used to dine there.

It was an ambitious plan, but the place — apart from costing an arm and a leg and your firstborn — turned out to be in such demand that people have to reserve a table years in advance, probably at birth.

Instead they are going to celebrate in the not quite as expensive restaurant the concierge at the hotel has recommended. La Truffière it is called, on the Left Bank and *très* romantic, very suitable for an anniversary dinner, according to the concierge who kindly offered to make a reservation.

They are going to go the whole hog that night with drinks before dinner, champagne with the food, you name it. Carol plans to have a liqueur with the coffee, too, see if she doesn't.

Grand Marnier probably, she loves that stuff. Rod says he is having a three star cognac for sure. And — it goes without saying — they are having an appetizer, main course and dessert. Crème brûlée probably, which is light but delectable. Carol is already addicted to it.

Rod has brought along his good suit and the Ralph Lauren tie she bought him for Christmas. Carol plans to wear the dress she wore for their oldest son's high school graduation. For the price she paid, it will have to serve as her special dress for the rest of her life.

Maybe they can bury me in it.

They are going to bring the camera and ask the waiter to take a couple of pictures. It will be just she and Rod having an intimate anniversary dinner in the fancy restaurant, the other two will have to fend for themselves. Steve says they will feast at *le* McDonald's because they serve alcohol and he can have a couple of beers with his big Mac.

I might order seafood for the main course. Something with shrimp and garlic butter. It's so French. And I love dipping the bread in the butter. Maybe I'll tell Rod about sitting here getting all worked up about some gypsy woman I don't even know. It'll give us something to talk about.

Carol had been convinced she would conquer her fear when she finally stood before the tall metal milestone, that she would make it to the top, eyes open, world at her feet, congratulatory. God knows she had thought about little else the previous winter when the snow lay deep and the temperature hit rock bottom and still kept on plunging. In January Rod came down with pneumonia that took a turn for the worse after he was given the wrong antibiotic. He was forced to be off work for two weeks.

There had been ice on the inside of the kitchen window, a spreading white crust along the bottom pane. She had drawn little Eiffel Towers in it with a paring knife, worrying that if Rod did not get better soon, they would not have enough money to go to anywhere.

Yes, she had been as eager as the others to join the endless queue shuffling forward an inch at a time towards the coveted elevator that would transport them up into the stratosphere and spit them out where the air is thin.

When they were heading for the tower, the other three could not contain their excitement. Lynette, Carol's sister-in-law, said "Jeez Louise, it's waaay taller than I'd imagined! Though not nearly as shiny, mind you." It being so famous and all, she'd had a mental picture of men crawling all over it every morning, spraying it with a special polish through hoses attached to large canisters strapped to their backs, buffing every inch of it with enormous soft cloths until the entire thing gleamed in the sun.

Carol thought it looked a big ugly contraption built only to humiliate the likes of her.

Rod and Steve were impressed and said so. They could not wait to get up and take a gander at the view. Rod was already waving his new Camcorder in every direction. At one point he stuck it in Carol's face, pretending to be a journalist requesting a comment. Was Madame looking forward to *le* view from *le* top of *le* tower? Did she think she'd be able to see Canada from up there? How come her face was such an interesting shade of green? Was she an alien? Was this here tall doohickey her mothership?

"Leave me alone, damn it!" It was not the response she meant to give. "I'm sorry, you guys, but I can't go through with it. You'll have to go up without me. WILL YOU FOR CHRISSAKE STOP WAVING THAT THING IN MY FACE!"

At least she had the courage to admit defeat.

The other three exchanged glances. On the flight across the Atlantic they had made a bet that Carol would get cold feet when the time came. Carol, having insisted on a centre seat on the jumbo jet, had steadfastly refused to look towards any window, though she had been quick to assure them that she would be a paragon of courage when push came to shove, just wait and see. She would ascend all the 900 feet to the very top.

Then push came to shove and now she owes them thirty dollars each. Ninety dollars total, and make no mistake, they will insist on payment, she knows what they are like. She could have bought a nice bottle of perfume for that money.

Then off hurried Rod, Steve and Lynette until they disappeared in a horde of tourists all wearing identical fanny packs. Rod should talk about aliens. The entire queue looked like an army of marsupials come to rob the French capital of cheap souvenirs.

Carol is not wearing a fanny pack. She thinks it looks too touristy, a dead giveaway. It also makes her stomach look bigger than necessary. Dieting is difficult at the best of times, but in France you may as well forget it. Okay, eating chocolate almond croissants for breakfast is not strictly a must, nobody else does, but that does not stop Rod from patting his own comfortable girth, repeating the same dumb line every morning: "When in Rome, eh guys? And Paris, too."

When Carol turned her back on the others, she was not sure what to do with herself. Not wanting to look lost, she strolled down the path in the direction of Esplanade des Invalides, unaware that behind her, stepping out from the marsupial queue, Rod was filming her slumping defeat for posterity.

What she wanted to do was find a bench at a safe enough distance from the lolling sea of tourists around the Tower and the various kiosks doing a brisk trade. Her thoughts were still acceptable then, less than twenty minutes ago.

There must be millions of miniature chrome Eiffel Towers sitting on knickknack shelves all over the world from Ottawa to Oslo, Omaha to Osaka. I'm for sure not getting one. What use is a six-inch Eiffel Tower made in China?

There is a good chance she will find out. She is pretty sure Lynette will buy one each for her kids, parents, aunts and uncles, including the one who had his camera stolen on his visit to Paris two years earlier and now hates everything French. Yesterday Lynette took her sweet time selecting a tiny Notre Dame in a snowstorm, a keepsake for herself, she said. She kept shaking the plastic bauble, holding it up and declaring how adorable it looked, how real.

"How do you know?" Steve asked. "You've never seen the Notre Dame in a snowstorm."

"You have to imagine, don't you?" said Lynette, still shaking the stupid thing.

As Carol reached the end of the path, some Japanese tourists got up and vacated the third bench from the end, so she hurried over to replace them, parking herself in the middle to make it awkward for anybody else to join her.

And here she sits, hosting stubborn, forbidden thoughts about a woman she never laid eyes on until ten minutes ago, a gypsy disfiguring Carol's idea of Paris.

I wish I could shake the scenery and make it snow. Make her disappear in a cascade of flakes that look like grated coconut.

Not only does the woman lack the Parisian elegance Carol has come a long way to admire and — with a bit of luck and determination — emulate, but with her otherness she looks as threatening as the gypsies begging on the steps leading up to the Sacré-Coeur. Tucked in every corner of the steps, there they sit, like living statues.

They ought to order them to move. It's not fair that they're allowed to sit there so sneakily and pounce on people.

I shouldn't be thinking that.

But it's true! They pester people. People like us who pay our way. I was assaulted, wasn't I? Rod said it was an assault. Rod's a cop, he ought to know.

Yesterday when they made their way up the steps, walking off some French calories after a lunch of *croque monsieur* washed down with a couple of beer, one of the beggars, a scrawny young woman holding a baby, grabbed Carol by the ankle and did not let go. Just sat there, innocent as can be, presenting a pleading face to the world, though her eyes were as menacing as the claw firmly locked around Carol's ankle. Rod had to holler at her in bad French to let go, goddamn it. The gypsy ignored him.

After Carol tried to pull her foot free, she felt stupid and cheap and handed over what change she had. The young woman did not show the slightest gratitude, but did let go of Carol's ankle, shifting the baby to her right arm, acting like the people before her had become invisible.

"Your problem," Rod educated Carol for the third time that day, "is that you're way too soft. These people can tell a sucker a mile away, you gotta realize that. This is Europe."

The gypsy woman down the path is wearing a blue kerchief around her head, tied at the nape of her neck. A large canvas bag lies open in her lap. It looks like a shapeless, hungry pet, its mouth open in a rictus yawn. The woman is indifferent to her surroundings, staring with unblinking eyes beyond the imposing tower, northwest across the river towards the Bois de Boulogne. But she is not begging. Her hands are not stretched out palm up, but perfectly still, clutching one of the handles of the gaping bag. She sits immobile, bothering nobody, her vaguely amused expression never fluctuating. She could be waiting for her family to come back down from the impossible height of the tower. She, too, may suffer from acrophobia.

But she's doesn't, does she? She's a beggar. I mean, let's face it, you can tell, can't you?

I shouldn't . . .

Carol continues her internal quibbling, ashamed, knowing how bigoted it is to assume that a woman is a beggar simply because she is a gypsy. It is, she cautions herself, not very nice. Yet something in her rebels.

Tell you what, if she's not a beggar, I'll run up the outside of the Eiffel Tower like the damn Road Runner. Surprise the hell out of Rod.

She tries to concentrate on something else. Something pleasant.

Let's see . . . Well now, here I am a skip and a hop from the famous Seine, lovers strolling along its banks. Isn't that something?

The Seine is not visible from where she sits, but she knows it is cutting the city in half not very far away, and the knowledge that it is there pleases her, the fact that all she has to do is get up from the bench, take a short walk, past the gypsy woman, past the tower, and she will be standing by the river Seine, right smack in downtown Paris. She considers doing just that, going for a stroll. She has an idea of the general direction and has plenty of time before the others return to earth. They might even see her from up there — a tiny round ant in a green dress from Eaton's — crawling along the river which she imagines must look like an uneven grey pencil line from that platform in the sky where Rod will be capturing the view with the Camcorder they couldn't really afford.

Is that woman even breathing? She hasn't blinked the whole time. There's something predatory about her, she's so still. Like a snake.

Predatory.

That's another word I shouldn't be thinking.

In the end Carol does not budge. She is too afraid to get lost. Besides, Steve has the map. He is the only one who knows how to fold it properly.

Instead she lets her mind do the wandering. It is safer that way. Unguided, it meanders, not towards the Seine, but backwards into the safe distant past where it knows its way around. It continues meandering until it runs into a dark-haired little girl named Gudrun. She stands before Carol, a seven-year-old girl dressed in an ugly brown skirt and sandals two sizes too small. The encounter is not surprising, considering.

Carol's mother, Gudrun, grew up in Denmark. Over the years she has never missed an opportunity to tell her famous story about how she almost became a gypsy. It was the most exhilarating adventure of her childhood, but one that ended abruptly with the shocking revelation that you cannot *become* a gypsy. Gudrun discovered that you have to be *born* one. You *can not* make becoming one your destiny just because it appeals to you.

And why not?

Because they won't let you.

Gudrun had been devastated. Being sentenced to remain plain old Gudrun Andreasen for the rest of her life was a punishment she did not deserve. This was the point in the story where she would shake her head in profound disappointment without halting the familiar flow of words that now do a rerun in Carol's head.

I tell you, I don't think I ever got over it. Because at first it was so exciting I just about peed myself. Imagine discovering that there existed a people who lived like us kids could only dream about! And right there, on the edge of the city! I tell you, if these people wanted to sing and dance all night, they darn well did! We ordinary folks had to dress decently and behave properly, except for major holidays and birthdays. How fair was that?

But listen to this. It was an afternoon during the summer holidays. All us kids on Vedbaeckgade had nothing to do that we hadn't done a million times before. We were bored. Then one of the boys dared us to bike out to the gypsy camp. They were always doing things like that, said it had to do with inventiveness, which was a superior form of intelligence only boys were born with. Like the time we built the airplane that wouldn't fly no matter how much we flapped our arms, and Peder said it was because us girls . . .

What? Don't be so impatient! I'm getting to it! Now listen. Everybody thought it sounded like an exciting adventure, so we hopped on our bikes and got going. There must have been about eight or nine of us. We didn't bother leaving a note on the kitchen table to tell our parents that we were off to forbidden territory because we figured we'd be back before they got home from work. We wore our house keys on strings around our necks and that made us independent.

The camp was outside of town in a wooded area. These days it's all built up out there with new villas and freeways and what have you, you know, out near the airport? Remember when we went visiting a few years back? Anyway, back then we had strict orders to stay away from there. A no-go area it was, where bad dangers lurked that adults could not bring themselves to put into plain language. Nothing had ever happened in those woods, but "it paid to be careful." A dubious expression, I always thought, for no matter how careful we were, nobody ever paid us for it.

No, wait! I'm just getting to the good part!

It was very pretty there, I'll never forget it, like the woods in all the best storybooks, not a bit scary. I'd never been out that way, and was I surprised to discover paradise so close to where I lived! We walked down a path listening to the birdsong until we came to three caravans standing in a semicircle in a glen right there in the middle of the woods. Under the trees some horses were grazing. It was so tranquil and idyllic I just wanted to sit right down under a tree and fall asleep. Maybe one of those big horses would come and nuzzle my hair and I'd wake up and it would let me ride on its back through the tall grass full of wild flowers. Oh, it was lovely!

Well, we were no more than ten steps into the meadow when we heard some strange noises and before we knew it a mob of kids came careening out of nowhere, just like that, screaming at us that we were trespassing. Some dropped right out of the trees like ripe fruit. Their leader was a boy named Jesper. He was the oldest, about twelve or so. I don't know why an exotic boy like that had such a plain Danish name. It didn't seem right.

Then it turned out that the boys from our street knew Jesper. He went to the same school as Peder and Ib and was a hero because he was such a terrific football player, that is, a soccer player, and you couldn't get more heroic than that.

To us girls he was handsome in the same dashing way of pirates and cowboys in the Sunday matinee movies. Exotic. A real heartthrob. And he knew it.

Next he and the other kids began to tease us. We teased them right back, of course, and so it went on until we ran out of insults. Then we started talking normally, testing each other. And before long we were having a fine old time.

I remember we had moved to the front of the caravans and were starting some game or other, hide and seek maybe, when suddenly the door to one of the caravans flew open and a bunch of women came flapping out the door. Like giant butterflies, all dressed in scarves and skirts in blues and greens and reds. Never had I seen anything like it. And they were screeching and making a fearful racket! They must have looked out their windows and seen a bunch of brats that didn't belong there. God knows what they thought we were up to, but all hell broke loose. They tore about, shouting and waving their arms like this, gathering up their own kids like they were in grave danger or something. Us they shooed off like we were stray dogs with fleas, screaming "UD! UD!" in Danish.

But the thing is, you see, they weren't paying proper attention, because they collected me as one of their own! Well, my hair was nearly black when I was young, and I have brown eyes. And it was a long sunny summer that year, so I was very tanned. I've always tanned real easy, not like you and your father. You have his pale freckled skin that . . .

Ja, ja, I'm getting to it!

Now, after my friends ran for their lives, there I was, left behind, standing in my ugly brown skirt and blouse and last year's sandals that were two sizes too small. I swear, to this day I remember my big toes dangling over the edge of the sandals like big slugs. I felt so drab, like a housefly among those butterflies.

Funny thing though, I wasn't the slightest bit scared! Already I was planning my exciting life as a gypsy. No more living in a cramped apartment, no more sharing a room with my brother, no more being told, do your homework, sit straight at the table, hold your knife and fork properly. Chew your food with your mouth closed. My parents were such sticklers for manners. It comes from being working class and always trying to prove you're as good as those above you.

And now I was to be free from all that! Well, I figured I'd go home for Christmas and birthdays, maybe holiday weekends, but the rest of the year I would travel around in a caravan, spend my time at carnivals, eating spun sugar and riding carousels. Never use a knife and fork. Stay up late every night and dance and sing for the rest of my life. Have my ears pierced and let my hair grow long. Maybe marry the handsome Jesper when I grew up. Become a gypsy queen! Sounds good, ja?

And then that lousy Jesper betrayed me! He pointed at me and shouted, "She's not one of us! She's one of the Danish kids!" And he laughed and laughed. I could tell he'd read every silly thought in my head. He had something I wanted and he had the power to take it away. So he did, and looking mighty pleased with himself too! But I suppose there's no point in having power if you're not going to wield it, is there?

Anyway, next what happened was that the chief gypsy woman, or the loudest at any rate, I remember to this day that she was wearing a turquoise scarf around her head and long dangly earrings, she shrieked like I'd tried to trick her, and then she chased me right out of the adventure, screaming in a language I didn't understand, apart from that one Danish word, "UD!" And I fled for my life up to the street where my friends were waiting looking mighty scared. They thought the gypsies had taken me prisoner.

Nothing left to do but jump on our bikes and hurry back home. I tell you, I was so disappointed I cried. By the time I got home my mother was back from work busy getting supper ready, hakkebøf *with lots of onions, my favourite, only that evening I wasn't hungry. When I told her she snapped at me. What did I think she was, a goddamn servant, standing at the stove after a hard day's work, peeling onions that made her cry, cooking food that wasn't good enough for me? I said, "I bet gypsy kids don't have to eat* hakkebøf *if they don't feel like it," and she yelled, "What does that have to do with anything, for crying out loud! Go set the table!"*

Relax, I'm almost finished! I don't think I told you this last time, but the following month the gypsies left. Somebody said they went south to Germany and France. Others said they went across to Jutland, up to the beaches near Skagen, which didn't make sense what with the weather growing cold. The truth was, nobody really knew. It wasn't like they sent us postcards, was it? Wherever they went, we never saw them again.

And that was the end of my adventure.

Gudrun did get to travel eventually, to faraway USA as an *au pair*, then up to Canada on a summer holiday, where she met and fell in love with a man of Scottish ancestry named Gregory Marshall. Before Christmas they were married.

Carol thinks that if her mother had run away with the gypsies that long ago summer, the bench where she herself now sits would be empty. And who knows, the woman down the path might have been Carol's mother's daughter. The daughter of Gudrun Andreasen and Jesper, the soccer-playing gypsy prince.

Carol is still busy contemplating what could have been, when a boy appears out of nowhere. Standing in front of her he holds out his right hand. She stares, first at his dirty paw, then at his face, realizing it is a familiar one. And for a minute she is convinced that it is Jesper standing before her, that he has finally escaped her mother's threadbare adventure. He is the same age — more or less, hard to say with these kids — a good-looking boy at any rate, though a bit malnourished, if his bony wrists and thin face are anything to go by.

"*Franc!*" The word is a demand, not a plea. The hand ventures closer, the fingers wiggle.

No. He did not pop out of the past. She remembers where she saw him. This is the same boy who was pestering a group of Americans earlier when they were walking towards the tower, six or seven big beefy Yanks in knee-length plaid shorts, talking and laughing like they were in their own backyard. Until this boy appeared in their midst, a thin foreign reed not knowing his place, his eyes silencing their confidence with that cold, naked look.

Planted firmly before Carol he studies her with those same cunning eyes that know when and how to plead. He repeats his demand in case she is too dim to comprehend. "*Franc! Franc!*"

Having just relived her mother's famous adventure has left Carol not sentimental exactly, but softer than she might otherwise have tried not to be. She has some change in her pocket.

Well, let's face it, what's a darn franc anyway? Twenty-five cents? It's not like I can't afford it, is it? When they change to euros, these kids will demand much more.

She drops some coins into the boy's outstretched hand, three or four, she is not counting. She feels confused, she wants the damn kid to disappear, wants him to stop looking at her like that, as if she is guilty of something.

The boy's fingers close around the money. Without wasting another glance on his mark, he turns his back on her and saunters down the path. When he reaches the bench where the gypsy woman sits, he slows down and sidles up to her in an offhand manner. It is obvious that they know each other, and yet both pretend otherwise with well-practiced nonchalance. The boy's back is blocking Carol's view so she cannot see what they are up to, if anything. A few seconds later the boy swaggers off to ply his trade elsewhere. The woman continues her enigmatic gazing towards the beyond. Like a statue, she has not moved.

Marvelling at the arrogance of the boy's swagger, as unperturbed as the woman's gaze, it occurs to Carol that the two might be mother and son.

As soon as the boy has disappeared, another one pops up. Carol checks her watch and when she looks up again, there he is. His small shadow has fallen into her lap and there it lies. He is a skinnier, greedier predator, much younger than the previous one, and he repeats the same performance, only he says "*Franka, franka!*" Inside his mouth an angry pink tongue darts about. For a second it looks forked.

Carol shakes her head to make clear that enough is damn well enough, and shame on you, kid. Her halfhearted gesture is as futile as she hoped it would not be. Defeated, she does her best to ignore the little pest. She stares towards École Militaire, feigning intense interest in cloud formations.

This boy does not take kindly to being ignored. He is an expert at his job, knows how to brandish his talent without mercy, wishing as always that it were more lethal. This woman, he decides, and for arbitrary reasons alone, is *not* getting away.

It is not because he has taken a particular dislike to her. He hates all tourists.

In the end Carol capitulates and drops a couple of franc into his hand, the last of her change, acutely, defeatedly aware that she should not exhibit such weakness. His hand is so small the two coins cover his entire palm. Had Rod been there he would call her a hopeless wuss and ask what her goddamn problem is, and doesn't she ever *learn*, for chrissake?

Good thing Rod is up in the sky with his Camcorder.

I mean, it isn't easy, is it? These kids are so skinny, aren't they, the city so rich.

The persistent boy, unlike the older one, is not about to make do with two measly francs. Feeling himself to be on a roll with this gullible cow, he has no intention of walking away. His eyes — cold and calculating — are big and beautiful, his lashes long and thick. And he knows how to lower those lashes, adorable, Bambi-like, just watch him. He also knows, despite his lack of years, how to discompose his marks, how to make each one feel singled out and defenseless. It is dead easy. Most of them suffer a bad conscience at the mere sight of him. Granted, others do not, but their lack of pity pales compared to his.

His study of Carol is as intrusive as a physical touch. He knows that this woman with her unguarded eyes is easy prey. A pushover, like so many of them, you can tell by the slope of her shoulders. Has a soft spot for kids. The big ones always do, they are complacent and tend to lack confidence. That is why they squirm when scrutinized.

Stupid fucking cows. This boy despises such women even more than he despises the rich scrawny ones shopping for designer jewelry in the boutiques along rue Royale, those snooty places where they keep the doors locked. Linger by a shop window and they come and shoo you away.

Having established what kind of woman he is dealing with, his eyes fall on the small gold Saint Christopher medallion hanging on a sturdy gold chain around her neck. The way it glints in the sun pleases him. It will look even better around his neck, he does not have that mushy white fat for the chain to get buried in. It will give him status. He points to it, making sure its owner is paying attention. Utters something sharp. It may be the French equivalent of "Hey, lady!" or "Pay attention!" Carol does not speak French and has no idea what he is on about. The boy turns his hand palm up again. Impatient fingers wave, hurry up, hand it over!

He is wrong about one thing, this brazen child. Carol is not as helpless as she looks. Putting on an expression of disdain, she musters up enough courage to bark "Go away!" But again her attempt at authority fails. The words deflate on the way out, lose the power that fired them. Annoyed, she resorts to poignant gestures, turns her head away from the boy, crosses her arms like a schoolmarm displeased with his behaviour in class. In case he is unfamiliar with the English words "go away," he will not be able to misinterpret that.

Carol has had that medallion since she was nineteen. For twenty-seven years and five months it has suffered dire neglect in a chipped lacquered Japanese box where she keeps old jewelry she no longer wears. Both chain and medallion are eighteen-carat gold and look quite attractive hanging around her neck once again, but for Carol their value is entirely sentimental.

Twenty-eight years ago a young man fastened it around her neck, a dashing young man with shoulder-length golden hair and the kind of groovy moustache that was fashionable back then. His name was Stuart and he was in tears at the time.

Only a few tears — three or four — but they looked dramatic enough.

Yes, Carol too, for all her staid ways, once had an adventure, though unlike her mother, she does not go babbling about it.

Carol and Stuart met in London the summer of 1967 when they were both doing Europe. She had recently arrived from Canada with two girlfriends. He had come all the way from faraway Australia via the Far East and the Mediterranean countries. They met sitting side by side at Piccadilly Circus one evening, in a large crowd of young people in generic garb and backpacks, all waiting for something interesting to happen, under the impression that good times were delivered by some external force and required no effort on their part.

Later on, after nothing had descended to ignite the crowd, a bunch of them trudged off to a real English pub. Next thing — after several pints of Guinness — Carol and Stuart had somehow become an item. Like she asked her less lucky girlfriends who by then had decided to continue to France: how incredible is that?

She assumed that now her modest dreams would be fulfilled.

And how she cherished being an item with a good-looking guy! One who had come all the way from down under, moustache, sun-bleached hair and all! Living with him in a city that was an exotic world in itself! She was pretty and slender in those days, aspiring to be bra-less and hip, succeeding only with the former.

For a brief time, Carol and Stuart led a life of their own making. It was an existence based on nothing more than the fact that they were a long way from home and could do pretty much what they wanted. To Carol this was spectacular, unique proof of what life, with a bit of effort, could be like. She took

504 — fourteen rolls of thirty-six — pictures in case nobody back home would believe her. Not that she planned to ever go back home.

Stuart had strong opinions about being caught on camera, so she was forced to snap everybody and everything else instead, but managed in the end to sneak him into seven shots. Five of the shots were from weird angles that did not do him full justice.

When they parted three months and four days after their first meeting — involuntarily on her part — Stuart sighed. It was a tired sigh that said, let's face it, as their brief life together had never existed on a real level, why drag it out? They had to part at some point, didn't they?

Why?

Because they came from opposite sides of the planet, or had she forgotten?

Yes. Well, no. Of course not.

Their temporary nest, a draughty one-room sanctuary smelling strongly of incense and baked beans, made inhabitable with the aid of cheap Indian blankets, a tatty beaded curtain rattling by the front door, was charming enough in candle light, but it could not possibly last, could it?

Why not?

Because the time had come to return home, get a job and face the rest of their lives. She knew that, didn't she?

But why so soon?

Because, said Stuart, he was out of money.

It rained that night like it would never stop. Carol did not want it to stop, ever. If it kept raining, Stuart would not want to leave, would not want to part that beaded curtain and disappear to the other side of the world. He hated the dreariness of English rain.

Sitting cross-legged on the mattress that was their bed — the room was near Earl's Court where half of Australia had settled — he became wistful and sighed. Playing with a strand of her hair in that languid way of his, he sighed again, more pronounced this time, in case she had missed it. "Oh, Carol, baby, I wish I had something for you to remember me by."

The wish rang so false it did not manage to fool even Carol who was dying to be deluded. No, it was blatantly guilt that forced him to offer that line, so hollow it echoed, because *he* was the one who had decided it was time to return to Down Under as if *she* had meant absolutely bugger all to him. As if they had had their fun and now he wanted to go home and eat supper, loosen his belt, burp and have a nap.

Equally revealing was the fact that he did *not* ask her if *she* had anything for *him* to remember *her* by.

His rationale for wanting to return to Australia was reasonable enough. Real life unspooled elsewhere, Carol was as painfully aware of that as the next person, but that was what was so great about living the way they did, wasn't it? Didn't he understand that? It was like running away with the gypsies. Okay, so Earl's Court wasn't a meadow, their bed-sit not a caravan, and they didn't keep horses, but even so. They were free! If they wanted to sing and dance all night, they could. Sometimes they almost did, didn't they?

By then she had pierced her ears and wore long dangling earrings, ready to be as reckless and wild as required. The possibilities were endless, weren't they? They were young! What did it matter if he had no money? She'd share hers.

Don't be stupid, said Stuart.

At age nineteen Carol had never had a lasting relationship. Her friend Annie had said in grade twelve that it was because she was too clingy, too eager to please. It scared guys off. Stuart was the first guy Carol had managed to hold onto for more than a week, which seemed to indicate that he was The One. And then the bastard wanted to end it and go home. If he did, she would be so free she would not know what to do with herself.

At a loss, she decided that, oh no, he's not getting away that easily!

Guilt, although heavy, rises to the top. It is not easily masked by second-rate melodrama. Knowing this, the following day when Stuart headed for the pub to meet his Aussie mates, she snooped around. Always trust your intuition. Stuart was a tough boy from a mining town in Queensland. Not the sniveling type.

She struck the mother lode in less than five minutes, coming across a letter with a Brisbane postmark. It had been folded and stuffed deeply into a side pocket of his backpack. The tingle in her fingertips as she pulled the pink sheet of paper out of the envelope told her she was about to learn something she would rather not know.

Not that it stopped her.

The letter was from a girl named Mandy. Mandy Neill. The writing was happy, celebratory, it boogied across the page. For Mandy was writing with giddy hand to share joyous tidings: she had recently given birth to a lovely baby boy! Having got Stu's address from Gladys, Stu's mum, Mandy thought she better write to inform him that he was now a proud daddy. Oh, it was an ever so gorgeous baby! She had named him William Stuart. Wills for short. Such a sweet baby was their Wills, the spitting image of dear old dad. Old Gladys was bloody beside herself with ecstasy, having such a gem of grandson. "Well, you know Gladys, always a bit excitable, eh?

"PS. Oh Stu baby, I can't wait for you to come back and bounce your beautiful son on your lap. He's got your colour eyes! Waiting for you, your very own Mandy who still loves you madly."

Carol was nonplussed. Her adventure, so splendid with its rakish hero and exotic setting, had gone kaput, the hero revealed as a two-timing bastard. Stuart, not hers at all, but part of an already established tableau, The Blissful Quartet: excitable Gladys, delirious Mandy, gorgeous Wills and two-timing Stu. She imagined a family photo with the four of them grinning smug grins: Stuart in the centre with his arm around Mandy, his chest puffed out, all paternal and grown-up, ready to get a job and bring home the bacon. Have Mandy fetch his pipe and slippers after a hard day in the mine.

Suddenly there was a man-sized hole in Carol's happiness. Fanning her flustered face with Mandy's letter, she understood, if only briefly — as it was secondary to her own — her mother's disappointment that day in the gypsy camp.

Having read Mandy's irrepressible letter was why, in response to Stuart's badly acted wish the night before, Carol voiced a request later that night.

"I've thought about what you said, Stu baby, and I realize there *is* something you can give me, something that would mean an awful lot to me, something to fill the void now I'm going to lose you forever. Though you might not agree once you find out what it is."

"Name it and it's yours." His phony sincere look made her want to bash him in the face with a baseball bat. Good thing she didn't have one. It was the angriest she had ever been, ever would be, but she had the wherewithal to shield it with her own phony sincerity.

"Your Saint Christopher medal," she said, coolly gauging his reaction. "It's an important part of you and I need so *very* much to keep part of you with me, otherwise I don't think I'll be able to go on living."

He visibly flinched at that, just as she had hoped he would, but he did not dare protest. How could he? He had assured her that he was a man of his word, as indeed he was whenever convenient. He cried a bit as he fastened the chain around her neck, several genuine tears. They dripped down his cheeks and dampened his moustache. He was crying because he was losing Saint Christopher who had cost him a fair chunk of Aussie dollars. He had told her when they first met, that since he was robbed in Naples, this medal and his leather boots (which were far too big for her) were the only things of value he had left.

Now he told her again, sounding hopeful.

The reminder did nothing to change her mind; her own hurt was of primary importance. She was being discarded. Granted, it was an unusual situation, but when you are young and in love, hurt is of the essence. The greater the pain, the more meaningful. You nurse it and make it last, you gild it and put it in a prominent place in your heart's museum.

After Stuart had hoisted his backpack and left, London lost its allure and turned shabby and grey. Carol returned to Canada convinced that life was over, an image in her head of her disillusioned mother pedaling home from the gypsy camp, not wanting *hakkebøf* for supper. Carol, in a similar mood, never made it across the channel, never saw Paris. Not that time.

But she had lied, if unintentionally. After the first few weeks she learnt to cope without a great deal of effort. It surprised her. A few months later she took out the seven photos where she had secretly captured Stuart and sat down to reminisce.

The young man in the photos did not look much like the one who had stomped on her heart with his leather booted feet. For one thing, he looked much shorter than she remembered. And a bit squinty-eyed, now she carefully studied his face from one of the strange angles. One photo was taken from behind of him walking down the street, revealing that he was bowlegged. Carol threw out the photos and before long had forgotten all about Stuart Harrison from Queensland. Saint Christopher she threw in the Japanese box.

Well, in all honesty, she did not quite forget. Love lost, love never quite had, becomes mythical with the passage of time. It is the myth we cherish as we behold our gilded pain, no longer remembering clearly the squinty-eyed face of the person who gave rise to it in the first place.

It was not until she was packing for the trip to Paris that she recalled the medallion. Thinking, had not Saint Christopher been stripped of his sainthood? Made redundant when heaven downsized? Yes, he had. Served him right. That's what he got for hanging around the neck of a two-timing Aussie bastard.

But as she did not believe in that kind of hooey, what did it matter? She got down the chipped lacquered box from the shelf in her closet and there was the ex-saint, still clinging to his chain in a sea of outdated custom jewelry. Freeing the chain from the tangle, she held it up, swinging the medallion like a pendulum. The light from the lamp beside the TV reflected in the golden circle.

Watching it, she remembered, fleetingly. If it was the myth or the reality that resurfaced is immaterial, but when she was through, she had fastened the chain around her neck once again. For protection. For a laugh. For sentimental reasons. Maybe the old saint would be pleased to have his old job back.

"You give me!" The little pest knows enough English to conduct his business. His hand is small and grubby, his fingernails chewed, his sudden smile so wide and fake he looks deranged.

Refusing to acknowledge him, Carol turns sideways towards the Eiffel Tower as if she has only this minute noticed it looming there. The boy is not fooled, he is not the slightest bit stupid. Nor does he like to be perceived as an insect easily squashed. He repeats his command, his eyes growing cruel beyond his years.

The other boy reappears. He stops beside the younger one and embarks upon what sounds like a lecture. Carol has no idea what he is on about. It is not French. She knows gypsies speak Roma, but has no idea what it sounds like. He could be jabbering in Swahili for all she knows. Whatever it is, it *is* a lecture, for now he is wagging a finger.

The younger boy could not care less. His mind is made up. He aims to own this woman's medallion. It happens to be a very nice good-sized medallion on a sturdy chain. He is convinced that it is worth a bit of money. He turns to the older boy and hisses, turns towards Carol and cracks his fake smile, all within a split second, performing like a desperate mime artist trying to get a rise out of an indifferent audience.

Looking at the two boys, it dawns on Carol that they are brothers. They are both the gypsy woman's sons.

The two youngsters continue to argue in front of Carol, ignoring her for the time being, while the fingers of the grubby little hand keep waving their impatient message. A couple of times both boys briefly turn around in the direction of the woman. Messages go back and forth. The woman does not officially acknowledge them, but communicates something with the pinkie finger of her left hand. Confirmation flickers in the boys' eyes.

A few more minutes go by before the older boy shrugs and leaves his brother to pursue his ambition. Grubby fingers repeat their demand. The boy's eyes are fixed on the medallion. He does not budge.

Finally Carol has had enough. Ignoring the boy, she gets up and sets off briskly down the path towards the tower, past the gypsy woman, head held high. She will wait for the others over by the elevators, safe in the crowd. It is the only way that little pest will get the message. She hopes he will have enough decency to feel ashamed.

The small boy — they call him Pépé — stares at the woman's defiant back as she trots off. Her shoulders are round, her hips wide, her bum well padded. Fat rich cow, he thinks. He would love to kick that fat ass hard. He considers following her, taking on the whole herd waiting by the foot of the tower.

In the end he decides against it. He has had enough. He despises these ignorant people, always so fucking pleased with themselves, wanting humble gratitude for a lousy franc.

Dragging his feet he walks over and sits down next to the gypsy woman, halfheartedly keeping up the pretense of not knowing her. Sticks his fist in his pocket and pulls out what money he has managed to weasel out of the tourists. Clasping the coins he sneaks his hand into the open jaws of his mother's bag, making a deposit, the whole time continuing to look the other way.

The woman still does not acknowledge the boy. It is blatantly evident to any onlooker that they are mother and son, but that does not hamper their routine. They sit close together, the woman as immobile as ever, continuing to stare past the Eiffel Tower.

Pépé is pleased with himself. He has been at it all morning and now he is exhausted. He deserves a break. He is hungry too. He has had nothing to eat since yesterday afternoon. After a few minutes his body begins to relax. It is a slow, visible process. One by one the tense angles of his small frame soften and he starts to slump. It looks as if he is slowly melting. The more he slumps, the younger he looks. Then he yawns a big yawn and, unaware of the motion, leans against the woman, his mother, pressing his cheek against her left arm, getting comfortable. His thick long eyelashes flutter. He closes his eyes.

Without moving her head, without changing her facial expression, still looking vaguely, vaguely amused, the woman moves her left arm back and outward at the elbow, forming a triangle, a featherless wing. With a swift flap it hits the boy in the back, batting him forward off the bench. Like a fledgling he falls to the ground, but quickly gets up, never once looking at the woman who does not so much as glance at him.

Once again his face grows hard. Once again his skinny little body turns into a set of sharp angles. He visibly grows older as he trudges off in search of another mark.

Carol is unaware of what just happened. She is too preoccupied staring in the opposite direction, wondering if the scrawny brat has had the decency to get lost yet. She refuses to turn around and check. She has her pride.

All the excitement has made her hungry. She hopes Rod and the others will descend from heaven soon so they can argue about whether to have a light lunch or go for one of those *prix fixe* three course lunches with wine and bread included.

THE SKY ABOVE HER HEAD

SHE WATCHES THE TINY ALIENS STAGGERING AROUND like drunks outside her basement kitchen window, moon-faced and self-absorbed little freaks that howl off and on for no discernible reason, shoving each other when the spirit moves them. In between bouts of random violence they plunk down, docile in the Sunday sun, to quietly eat dirt. Sometimes, instead of eating the dirt, they shove it pensively up their noses.

Serena hates toddlers with a passion, deplores their blank intrusive eyes, their helplessness, their drooling inconsideration, their predictable tendency to explode into glass-shattering noise.

If you're helpless, show humility. If you're inconsiderate, exhibit a modicum of self-reliance. This is Serena's philosophy.

Toddlers do neither. Sometimes they gravitate towards her window as if sensing the caged carnivore pacing on the other side. They bang on the glass with sticky paws, flatten their fat faces against it, leaving marks, until the carnivore in her cage drools for blood and a cigarette.

Every weekend when it's sunny — it's the hottest, sunniest summer on record — the mothers of the aliens congregate on the strip of weedy lawn outside Serena's kitchen window. There they lie clad in bikinis small enough to fit a Barbie doll, bodies gleaming with suntan lotion, devotees of the sky above. Surrounding them are the usual stockpiles of baby bottles and boxes of crackers, fruit and pop cans, diapers and handy-wipes, squeaky toys and teddy bears, all the crap common on the Planet of Toddlers. Cozily at home, the mothers — they look barely out of diapers themselves, for chrissake — stretch out in the detritus, oblivious to their roaming barbarian offspring.

Why in goddamn hell don't they go to the pool?

Or out to the park with the waterslides?

But oh no. They're glued to the same spot during most of the week as well, these sloppy young mothers who can think of nothing more imaginative to do than breed, but at least while Serena is at work — in a sterile, air-conditioned hospital lab — she can pretend they don't exist. When she arrives home at five-thirty they and their disregard are gone.

At the beginning of summer she would return home to find fingerprints and smeared substances, mashed banana, chocolate and what looked like snot — for sure it was snot — all over her kitchen window. After a week of slimy souvenirs she put up a note in big, black letters that sarcastically snarled: "Kindly clear your children's disgusting mess *off* my window! Thank you so *very* kindly for your consideration. Your neighbour."

The mothers complied the very next day. There was never again a single smear taunting her sensibilities.

For some reason that, too, pissed her off.

Still in her bathrobe, Serena pulls the curtains on the holiday camp, pulls them so hard one curtain snags on the rod and would have ripped, had not the phone rung just then. Hers is a phone with a limited repertoire. She stops and stares at it, doesn't want to answer. She knows who's at the other end.

Hester, her older sister, calls every Sunday afternoon between five to two and five past to double check that Serena is coming for supper at Mother's. Serena has gone for supper at Mother's every single Sunday for the past sixteen years, since she moved away from home at age twenty. Still Hester calls to make sure.

She'll be calling from Mother's fading fifties kitchen where she goes straight after church to help prepare the food, giving the impression that Sunday dinner at Mother's is a once-in-a-lifetime banquet where nothing must be allowed to go wrong. The kitchen window will be open four inches, no more, just to let enough fresh air in. Hester will be wearing Mother's flowery apron on top of her church-going skirt and blouse.

If the time-space continuum went awry and sucked Hester back to those fading fifties like a slurpie, she'd fit right in. She'd simply adjust her apron and get on with it.

Not only does Serena know who's calling, she knows word for word the impending conversation. First Hester will inquire about her health, making it sound as if Serena might expire before dinnertime — Serena who has not been sick a day in her life. Relieved to hear that her younger sister is as robust as ever, Hester will request that she come over and help get supper ready. Getting the standard sullen reply, she will tut-tut Serena's unwillingness to lend a hand, no matter how superfluous that hand.

It's Hester's long-standing wish that the two of them spend more time together, especially now that Laurel, their younger sister, is not around. And what better sisterly togetherness than working side by side over Mother's avocado green stove, Hester imparting advice while the Sunday roast sizzles?

Serena would rather spend Sunday standing on her head in a bucket of shit, but what's the point telling Hester that? Hester never listens.

Serena wishes she were as brave as Laurel, the sibling untethered by family ties. She's a rebel, that one, Mother always says of Laurel, if and when people ask. Mother is still trying to figure out what went wrong with her lastborn, whether it was a malfunction *in utero* or some overlooked glitch in Laurel's upbringing.

Laurel has since the day she was born been disturbingly independent. As soon as she saw the opportunity to cut loose, she fled the confinement of her loved ones' embrace to the perilous world beyond the horizon. Last the family heard she was canoeing her way across Africa with an Argentinean medical student named Eduardo.

Serena had consulted a map. She wasn't sure how they could possibly paddle across Africa unless they planned to carry their canoe from river to river through inhospitable wilderness in politically unstable regions. According to the map, even if they made their way south — along the White Nile to the lakes edging the western border of Uganda, say — they still had to reach the Zambezi River to get to Victoria Falls, which not even Laurel would attempt to paddle down. From there they'd still have a good chunk of continent to traverse before reaching St. Francis Bay west of Port Elizabeth, where they plan to exit.

Serena often pictures Laurel and the Argentinean, canoe held over their heads, dodging bullets and machetes, running for their lives, green cobras dangling from the trees in various steaming jungles. They will survive, of course — Laurel being Laurel — to successfully slide out into St. Francis Bay as if out of a dark birth canal into the glaring light of civilization.

Hester? She has never seen the flimsy point of undue excitement. No flibbertigibbet, she's dismissive of any amusement that is not of a predictable nature. She's always the first to volunteer to set the tables for the church tea, arriving early to be on the safe side, resting assured that only *she* knows where everything is, instructing any daredevil new volunteer how to go about the task at hand. "No, not like that! *This* is how we've always done it," is her warning cry. Since the day Hester learned to talk, she has used that cry as a shield to dodge any stray bullets of change, has polished it with her special intonation to make it impenetrable.

Sometimes when Mother gazes at Hester bustling about her kitchen, she wonders if the woman wearing her pansy-patterned apron is her daughter or her mother.

Serena, the middle sister, has no knack for enjoying herself at all. Not unless she is outside, that is, feeling the distance between the top of her head and the sky above. She cherishes this particular private joy, and this is the reason she loathes the presence of the bronzed young mothers glistening like uncoiled snakes in the grass outside her window. They're hogging her bit of sky, depriving her of it.

Considering the need to feel the sky above her head, it was pretty damn moronic to rent a basement apartment, she's well aware of that. But the price and the location were too convenient to dismiss, and at the time she had to make a quick decision before her spurt of independence fizzled.

Besides, when the curtains are open, the place is bright enough. When she sits on the couch below the living room window, as she does now, phone in hand, she can — if she leans backward and cranes her neck a painful ninety degrees — glimpse a narrow strip of sky over the apartment building next door.

As usual, Serena turns a deaf ear, but is forced to pay attention when Hester suddenly raises her voice. This must be serious. Hester was born with her volume set at 'medium'. She considers a raised voice a form of violence.

"Serena! Are you even listening?"

"Sorry, Hester. I was looking at the kids outside my window. They're so darn cute. Don't you wish you had kids? Anyway, you were saying?"

"Do you want to come to St. Paul with me or don't you?"

"St. Paul?"

"Yes, St. Paul."

"St. Paul, Minnesota, USA?"

"Is there another?"

"There are seven," says Serena.

"There are?"

"Yes indeed. There's even one in Africa. Look them up on the map." Knowing Hester will do just that as soon as she hangs up, get dad's outdated world atlas from the bookshelf in the den, turn the pages, puzzled, unable to believe her sister might have tricked her.

But the question remains. "Why?"

"Why what?"

"Why go to St. Paul?"

"To research our family history. You weren't listening, were you?"

Haven't for years. "I was riveted. But why do you want to research our family history? It's bound to be boring. And why Minnesota?"

"Because," says Hester with emphasis on each word, "our great-grandparents first settled there when they emigrated from Norway, in case you didn't know."

"So?"

"And there's a Historical Society with all kinds of records available to the public. Frank found it on the Internet. His great-grandfather on his mother's side came to Canada from Germany through Minneapolis. I'm curious to find out about our past, that's all. Don't you remember when we talked about it at Mother's a couple of weeks ago?"

"No."

"Sure you do."

Hester and their Norwegian descended mother are fond of spinning tales about Norsemen ancestors crossing a stormy Atlantic in mighty longboats, singing uplifting sea shanties and never getting seasick. Altruistic Vikings who abhorred the idea of looting and burning.

It's been years since Serena last bothered to remind them that the ancestors in question arrived in the late nineteenth century by cargo ship, destitute farm folk who could have benefited from a bit of looting to see them through until they found gainful employment.

"Well? Aren't you interested? You said you were."

I lied. "I changed my mind."

"Oh, come on, Serena, you could do with a bit of a holiday. You never go anywhere."

"You'd freak out if I did. You fuss if I cross the street without consulting you first."

"Nonsense, dear. Besides, it'll be an adventure. And you needn't worry about the details, I've got it all planned. We'll drive there via Saskatchewan and visit Aunt Hilda in Regina on the way."

"Who?"

"Mother's Aunt Hilda. You know, Mother's Uncle Emmett's wife? Don't tell me you don't remember Aunt Hilda."

"I don't remember Aunt Hilda."

"Yes, you do, dear."

Serena does, but only barely. "I still don't understand. Why drive across half a continent to see some ancient aunt of Mother's? She won't even remember us."

"Sure she will. We're family."

"Oh, fu . . . forget it."

"Frank says we should make it to Regina in about four days. He drove there in three days once, but I'd prefer for us to take our time, enjoy the scenery and relax. We'll visit with Aunt Hilda in Regina, she'll like that. Then it's another two days down to St. Paul. How does that sound?"

Like fucking purgatory. "You can probably drive to St. Paul through the States in half that time."

"Could be, but that's the States, isn't it? Wouldn't you rather see a bit of our own country? I would. I've never been out of Ontario. And as we're going to Regina to see Aunt Hilda, it makes sense to drive through Canada. We can go through the States on the way back," offers Hester.

"I get carsick."

"No, you don't."

"Yes, I *do*! Why don't you go with good old Frank anyway? I bet he never gets carsick."

"Frank has to work all of August. Even Saturdays. They're short of people down at the depot."

"Go in September. It won't be as hot. Besides, I don't think I can get time off right now. The lab is really busy." Serena was recently asked to use up her holiday time or she would lose it.

"Sure you can. And I thought it might be nice for us sisters to do something together for a change. We never do. And family is so important. Aren't you interested in your family history?"

"No."

"Of course you are. Think about it. We'll talk about it again at dinner. Mother agrees with me, by the way. That we should go to St. Paul, I mean."

"If she agrees with you, it's because you told her to."

"Don't talk nonsense."

"Anyway, I can't come for dinner today. I'm busy."

"No, you're not."

No, I'm not. I'm trained never to be busy on Sunday afternoons. I don't have the guts to be busy. I lack the ability to deal with the guilt it would create to be busy. I'm that pathetic. I should just join the aliens outside and shove dirt up my nose.

The very sound of Hester's voice makes Serena pugnacious. It's like pressing a button. But as she's a coward, it remains an internal rebellion. There's no taking a stance, no verbal shoot-out, only self-inflicted indigestion and a lurch in her gut, a tensing of the muscles in her neck.

Serena's family has squeezed her so tightly to their bosom that her spirit wheezes like an asthmatic's last breath. Having found themselves unable to rein Laurel in, they are not about to let Serena slip away. They live for their sense of family, their holy institution. It's as if they only feel a sense of identity in relation to each other, like stars in an ignored constellation. They will never fathom why Laurel prefers trekking across dark continents in the company of strangers.

There is as of late a new star in the constellation: Hester's husband since a year back, the one she got secondhand: Frank of the Immaculate Garage. God knows he fits right in. Serena has already succumbed to the fact that she'll be stuck in a car for days on end, driving from southern Ontario to Saskatchewan well within the speed limit, listening to nothing but talk radio, in order to visit with the aged wife of their mother's dead uncle, to then get back into the car — Hester's freaking Honda — and drive for another two days to some Midwestern American city where they don't know a soul. All because persnickety Hester feels the need to delve into the past to find something that will shine a spotlight of importance upon the partly Norwegian stars in the constellation.

Kill me now.

Putting down the receiver, Serena fantasizes about breaking Hester in half, shoving the top half up the tight butt of the lower half. The image of Hester stuck up her own ass gives her the strength to shower and get dressed.

Outside her window comes the sudden howl of an aggravated alien.

Hester is approximately half the size of Serena, a dry little twig of a woman, but that does not mean she'd be easy to snap in two. Or even bend. Hester doesn't yield in any direction. She's modestly proud of her limitations, breathtaking in scope as they are, bound like a bride to her unwavering sense of duty.

She's by no means an unattractive twig, she has a nice trim figure, a pleasant face enviably untouched by approaching middle age, as if she has lived a life void of troubling thoughts. But it's an attractiveness that is easy to miss. Hester dresses primly to hide what others would flaunt, has never used a lipstick or a push-up bra. She doesn't see the point of vulgarity.

Hester is the backbone not only of her family, but of western civilization, born with a notion that it's up to her to set an example.

Stuck in a car with Hester for six days, how will Serena refrain from becoming stark raving homicidal? Serena examines this question with trepidation as she drives over to Mother's an hour later. Holds it up against the merciless light of her defeatism.

At the exact time Serena considers running a red light headlong into an empty Sunday bus, Hester is busy chopping the carrots, slantwise to make the slices bigger, having basted the roast, while telling Mother what a rousing sermon the minister delivered that morning, even though Mother was sitting right beside her in the usual pew listening to every word. They have the same conversation every Sunday. Hester finds all sermons rousing. They lift her spirit and propel her through another busy week with a steady smile on her face.

Mother is more than capable of cooking dinner — she would dearly relish something to do — but she has since a while back been relegated to the role of "elderly" by Hester. The elderly must rest and let the young do the work, says Hester. Having obediently settled into the role, Mother spends Sunday afternoons with a cup of tea she doesn't really want, watching her eldest daughter prepare supper. She has never been crazy about the way Hester prepares the roast; the meat comes out too dry. Father is of the same opinion, but they never say anything. It's best that way. Hester means well.

Father keeps to the den during Sunday afternoons, watching TV with his feet on the footstool Hester bought for him; now he, too, is elderly and must act the part.

Frank of the Immaculate Garage is outside, sleeves rolled up, doing something to his in-laws' car, inhaling the tempting smell of food from the kitchen window. Frank is a happy man. He loves his new wife.

The two sisters leave on their trip from the cracked driveway of their parents' pale blue bungalow early on a Tuesday morning. Mother is hysterical with worry, crying off and on. It's such a long, long way and so much can happen on the road to two defenseless women on their own. Having tossed and turned all night, Mother has come to the covert conclusion that this trip is not such a good idea after all, despite what Hester says.

Mother is looking around for a shoulder to cry on properly, but Father is hovering by the back door, saying nothing much, which is what he does best. At the moment he's wishing that Hester would allow him to smoke at least one lousy cigarette. Father is not of Norwegian descent, he's half Polish, half Ukrainian, but that doesn't mean he's not excited about his daughters' journey of discovery. When emotions get the better of him, this is what he does, he keeps very quiet and thinks of cigarettes.

In the family's eyes this is not a mere trip but an adventure of spectacular proportion, an exploratory trek by Viking descendants into the heartland of a still untamed continent.

Frank, wearing his best tie to mark the occasion, is checking the tires on Hester's Honda. He has already given her detailed advice about what to do in case of car trouble, insisting she bring the cell phone he bought for — God forbid — emergencies, and to keep the car doors locked at all times. He keeps checking the tires over and over again, putting an ear to them at one point, should they need to confide any embarrassing problems best not spoken out loud. While he does, he pulls nervously at his tie.

Only Serena is unable to grasp the importance of the occasion. Brooding like the hormone-ravaged teenager she once was, she gets bored and busies herself shoving their bags into the trunk. When she has finished, Hester appears as if on cue to rearrange them, explaining why her arrangement is preferable. Something to do with balance and easy retrieval.

Kill me now.

"I'll drive the first two hours," Hester says when they're ready, handing Serena a written schedule. It has three columns drawn with a ruler: name, date and hours. It's stapled to the three sheets of paper where she has written down Frank's instructions regarding procedure in case of trouble. "You take over at ten o'clock. Now then, I believe it's just about time to say good-bye."

The farewell ceremony takes another twenty minutes, what with Mother still fussing, insisting they take a second box of Kleenex, a box of Band-Aids, a bottle of calamine lotion for insect bites, mumbling about watching out for rattlesnakes and rapists. "It's a dangerous world out there."

"You're right," agrees Serena. "I say we need assault weapons. And a hand grenade or two."

By this time Frank's tie has sweat marks and hangs crooked. Serena leans out the car window to point this out.

Frank blushes. He's a shy man.

"Don't forget to fasten your seat belt," interrupts Hester. "And put that Kleenex box in the back, otherwise it'll slide around the dashboard. Now then, are you sure you'll be comfortable wearing those jeans?"

"I'd be more comfortable if you'd turn on the fucking air conditioning."

"Oh, watch your language, Serena. Keep your window rolled down instead. No sense wasting money when fresh air is free. But don't roll it down all the way, it'll get too windy."

It's approaching thirty degrees already. The humidity level reached a hundred and ten percent weeks ago. The air is a sodden sheet intent on embalming Serena. She would be much better off in a summer dress, she knows that, but she decided on jeans because Hester keeps pointing out that it's not proper for a woman Serena's age to wear denim. Serena is thirty-six.

Frank leans in to kiss Hester good-bye. One peck later they both blush violently.

Hester is still blushing, smiling to herself, when they pull out of the driveway and head north towards the intersection that will eventually take them out of the city towards new horizons.

It's Hester's habit to stop at green lights to be on the safe side whenever intuition tells her the orange light is coming on. She's oblivious to the honking of car horns. A great fan of talk radio, she never wants to listen to music. She finds the noise distracting. During the news she comments respectfully on events, on politicians and the wisdom of their words.

"Shut the fuck up, Hester, I'm counting trees. Four million seven hundred and ninety-four thousand three hundred and twenty nine, four million seven . . . ."

"Oh, stop it, Serena. It's not . . . "

" . . . hundred and ninety-four thousand three hundred and thirty. You almost made me lose count."

Hour after hour through never ending forest Hester never exceeds a speed of eighty-five kilometres per hour. Whenever they reach an overtaking lane, the mile long tail of cars that have accumulated behind them go flying by, drivers flipping Hester the finger. Every hour spent in the car Serena fears for her life.

In a diner in northern Ontario a great hairy hulk of a man — four times the size of Frank — strides up to their table, glares hard at Hester, points an accusing digit and growls, "You, lady, are a goddamn menace on the road."

Hester stirs her coffee meticulously, careful not to spill, smiling a smile that exhibits nothing but human compassion. "It's better to arrive safely a bit later, than not arrive at all, don't you think?"

The man's face says that were Hester not a pint-sized female, he would drag her outside by the hair and beat the crap out of her. As it is, he merely shakes his head and leaves. Serena watches him stride over to a massive eighteen-wheeler parked on the other side of the gas station. It's the same rig that strained in vain to get by them earlier, going up a steep hill before the overtaking lane petered out.

The trucker spits, climbs up into the driver's seat, lights a cigarette and drives off to get a safe headway over Hester, who is telling Serena not to order dessert as it will give her indigestion and make her sluggish.

Serena orders apple pie and ice cream, too busy being contrary to notice Hester's hand trembling as she lifts her cup.

The crust of the pie is made of cardboard, the bits of fruit in the filling held together with Elmer's glue, but Serena forces down every last crumb to prove a point. Walking behind Hester to the car, she reaches under her shirt to unbutton her jeans.

They sweat their way through interminable tunnels of dense forest and rocky outcrops of the Canadian Shield, each day more monotonous than the previous. The roof of the car is too low, Serena can't see much of the sky, can barely sense its presence. On both sides of the road, there are only trees, trees and more goddamn trees, interspersed with rock face.

Sometimes there's rock face, rock face and more goddamn rock face, interspersed with trees.

Once in a while, for a bit of relief, they're rewarded with a generous view of Lake Superior. The sight of it is what prevents Serena from bashing her head to a bloody pulp against the front windshield. Lake Superior, she reflects, is a magnificent lake as well as a lucky one. It owns a lot of sky. She imagines lying sprawled in a boat bobbing in solitude on its peaceful centre, no land in sight, looking up to where there exists nothing but clouds on a canvas of what would be blue, had the scorching sun not bleached it white. No Hester, no Honda, no talk radio, just the soft sound of water gurgling against the boat.

The thought makes her want to wail and ululate.

Hester, too, admires the panorama and says seven times what a treat it is to live in a country with a fine lake like that. But to stop more than the once to take a picture would be to waste time when they have a perfectly good view from the privacy of their car.

"If you'd step on the damn gas once in a while we wouldn't waste any time at all."

If the needle on the speedometer dares creep above eighty-five while Serena is driving, Hester breaks into a predictable lecture on road safety. Once, outside Dryden, Serena gets pissed off enough to step on the gas until the car shoots down the road at a hundred and twenty, overtaking cars, trucks and campers where there is no overtaking lane, cars coming from the opposite direction veering wildly. Hester's face goes white with terror. She screams, then starts to sob.

The rebellion — too short a thrill — ends with Serena apologizing half-heartedly, but it does add a small spark to the pointlessness of that particular afternoon.

As an added bonus, Hester is very quiet that entire evening.

When Serena has given up hope, the forest begins to shrink. The trees grow shorter, their numbers diminish. Soon they are gone altogether.

In blessed relief a great land opens up, stretching flat and golden to a very, very distant horizon. Above it the sky arches to infinity. It's a sky far more immense, far more blue, than the soiled one Serena is used to. Here she can see the edge of the world, can actually see where the sky bends down and touches the curve of the planet. It makes her heart beat so fast and hard she can hardly breathe. How she wants that sky! She wants to stand on that horizon, arms outstretched, embracing it in gratitude, begging it to rain on her, cool her off! Cleanse her and make her new, make her pure, put her ever so gently in a state of grace.

As Hester never exceeds eighty-five kilometres per hour and doesn't want to drive for too long each day, the four-day trip takes five and a half days. Six evenings of watching reruns in the roadside motels Frank has marked for them in the CAA book.

It is late afternoon when Hester's Honda Civic pulls into a driveway on Elphinstone Street in Regina and they are greeted by a small white-haired woman peering confused from the crumbling front steps of the small bungalow she had moved into thirty-one years earlier. She has no idea who the two women in the car are, does not recall that Emmett's niece's daughter ("Esther, did you say, dear?") called two weeks earlier to suggest a reunion, but she is ready to welcome them if they are family, and as they say they are, who is she to argue? The two women look respectable and decent.

Inviting them in, she offers them a glass of milk and a tuna salad sandwich, only to discover that she has no tuna. Hester offers to drive to the nearest store to buy a can of tuna and a jar of mayonnaise, after discreetly throwing out the jar in the fridge. It is two years out of date, she later confides to Serena whom she leaves behind to assist Aunt Hilda, should assistance be required. Serena helps her aged relative set the small Formica table in the kitchen with cracked plastic mugs featuring Christmas trees and dinner plates of Royal Doulton bone china with a rose patterned gilded edge.

"Whose girls are you, did you say?" Aunt Hilda keeps asking, putting a soupspoon by each plate. Under the impression that they have just arrived from Minneapolis she wants to know if it is their first visit to Canada.

Serena has to shout her answers to be heard over the noise of the TV in the living room.

They spend the night in a motel. Aunt Hilda had not understood that Hester's plans included staying a few nights in her house. As it was, the spare bedroom was full of boxes and old clothes, including an empty birdcage on a dresser beside an ancient sewing machine. There was no spare bed. Somewhere in the jumble might have been the photo albums Hester had planned to leaf through with a helpful Aunt Hilda by her side identifying different blood relations preserved in black and white.

They leave for Minneapolis the next morning, after Hester places a call to Social Services to ask that somebody look in on a Mrs. Hilda Skaerstad on Elphinstone Street. Then it is another two day prison sentence in the confinement of the four-door sauna under that all-encompassing sky Serena has fallen madly in love with and does not want to live without.

By the time they reach St. Paul two days later, Serena feels a calm so deep and still it has her worried.

"You go check in, Hester," she tells her sister in the Best Western parking lot. Her voice is angelic. "I'll get a cart and take care of the luggage."

The Laura Jane Musser Plaza at the great hulking Minnesota History Centre offers a view of an urban valley that sprawls unrestrained until halted by the big ugly Xcel Energy Centre straight ahead of where Serena is sitting. Over her left shoulder rises the downtown St. Paul skyline, looming new skyscrapers, old church towers cowering in their shadow. And in the foreground, a sinister old red brick building with the letters "Catholic Charities" painted in fading white letters on the roof.

Serena imagines Hester in a nun's habit, supervising starving, sore-infested orphans sewing their daily quota of postal sacks, telling them helpfully that their stitches are uneven.

On the other side of the valley, on its own private hill, sits the cathedral of St. Paul like a precious stone in a cheap ring. Above it shreds of clouds hurry towards downtown, grey and thinning, rapidly wearing out. There will be no rain today either.

It's the day after their arrival. Hester has long since disappeared into the hushed library section of the building, clutching two notebooks and six pens. Like her first day at school. Earlier on, passing time in the gift shop on the ground floor, Serena considered buying a bumper sticker that read *WELL-BEHAVED WOMEN NEVER MAKE HISTORY*, a quote by somebody named Laurel Thatcher Ulrich, who she probably ought to have heard of. But buying it would have been dishonest. She *is* a well-behaved woman, *that's* her problem.

She could have bought it for that other Laurel, the free one, to stick on her canoe.

Instead she bought a *Cabin-Cooking Cookbook*. She has no use for it, but it seemed the kind of item one ought to buy in a gift shop in the Midwest, land of pioneers. It might come in handy should she ever feel like marinating a moose or stuffing a beaver.

Also, she felt it a duty to purchase at least one souvenir in the gift shop. If nobody buys these gifts, she reasoned — and nice gifts they are, all attractively displayed — such shops will be forced to close down, and then where would one ease one's holiday boredom? At least a cookbook is useful. She could have chosen an eight-inch birch bark canoe.

Leaving the gift shop she walked across the central circle to the cafeteria. The stone floor was so smooth and shiny she could see her reflection in it. She felt a strong urge to kick her shoes off and slide around on it, skate with her arms stretched out, shriek like the moon-faced aliens outside her kitchen window back home.

She refrained and headed for the cafeteria in an adult manner. Got a coffee and — because she's on holiday and she can if she wants to — two giant muffins, an apple-cinnamon and a chocolate-walnut, still warm from the oven. With her loot on a tray, she walked upstairs to the outside plaza. There was a free table at the very end beside two women eating fruit salad out of plastic containers.

This is where she now sits, eating her apple-cinnamon muffin. It's a terrific muffin, moist and warm, full of apple chunks. From her table she has a clear view of the face of the older of the two women at the next table. It blocks most of the view of the ugly Catholic Charity building where Hester was a nun in a previous life.

The woman has a round face that has long since settled into a harmonious expression. The bouquets of laugh lines around her eyes are nothing but attractive. Her hair is short and grey, thick and springy. She seems entirely at home in the rotundity of her body. This is what impresses Serena about her, this at-homeness in herself. The woman's sleeveless sundress exposes her generous upper arms. The flesh on her right arm wobbles slightly when she lifts her glass of water. She looks like a woman unburdened by regrets.

The woman's younger companion looks equally relaxed — at least from behind. There's no tension in her slim tanned shoulders. Serena guesses they are mother and daughter of the get-along variety. They sit without talking for long periods. Their silence is undemanding.

At the table behind them, a young man is studying, a pile of books before him, sunshine on his face. He's drinking mineral water and eating a baguette with ham and cheese. Once in a while he looks up and gives the woman with the laugh lines a quick glance before returning to his reading, as though he draws reassurance from the solidity of her presence.

Breaking the silence, the woman's younger companion, reining in some interesting reflection, leans forward and begins to talk in a low voice. Whatever she is sharing makes her older companion laugh. The younger woman joins in the laughter.

"It reminds me of when we drove through Montenegro once," the older woman says when they're done laughing. She doesn't bother keeping her voice down, she has nothing to hide. "This was way back when it was still called Yugoslavia.

Ages ago, the kids were still small. We were on our way down to Greece from Paris, to visit Jim's aunt Esther who was married to a Greek businessman, they're both dead now, and we'd spent the last few days driving down the Dalmatian coast. It was absolutely beautiful, by the way, but people drove like freaking maniacs, speeding up to overtake in the wrong lane on hairpin curves, coming right at you. I was scared witless.

"Then, just after Dubrovnik, we turned left and drove up this steep mountainside full of more hairpin curves, and I mean hairpin, up and up until we arrived in a different landscape. It was like we'd travelled back in time several centuries.

"Later that day, somewhere in Montenegro, we stopped for a break in this weird and wild uninhabited place. It was a kind of disturbing little happening."

"How so?" asks her companion, leaning back, tilting her head, settling in for the story.

The shadow of a small cloud passes over the terrace. Serena, pretending to be deep in her new cookbook, has been caught up in the story from the word go. She, too, settles in. She's no longer hungry, but curbs her impatience by starting in on her second muffin.

"Well, we stopped beside the road near a very deep canyon, or crack in the earth, I'm not sure what the proper term would be, I never saw anything like it. We didn't even know it was there until we strolled off the road and damn near fell into it. There wasn't any fence or sign or anything, and the sides were as steep as walls. And then, down at the very bottom, and it looked a mile deep, we see this lake completely covered with water lilies, it was just so amazing, hidden right there in a crack in the earth. I tell you, it was such an incredible sight it damn near made me weep. White flowers infused with pink and purple. Absolutely effing gorgeous. You know, the photo of me and the kids on the wall in my den? That's where Jim took it. Unfortunately you can't see the bottom of the canyon."

So they are not mother and daughter.

"I know the one."

"Are you sure I never told you this?"

"Trust me, Liz, I would have remembered."

"Well, anyway, it was the usual roadside break. Lily went to pee behind a bush. Alex wanted me to peel him an orange, then ate half of it and threw the rest down to the water lilies. It was so far down you couldn't hear it splash.

"Anyway, while we were there a large van drove up and parked a bit further down from us. An old-fashioned sort of van with English licence plates, a bit rusty. A large family. Mom, Dad, grandparents, several kids, that kind of thing, came spilling out, obviously stopping for a break, but we didn't pay much attention to them.

"Then as we were walking along the rim of the canyon admiring its water lilies, we heard the mom of the English crew shout that it was time to get going, so they all piled into the van and continued south. And that was that, or so we thought.

"A while later we got into our car to drive off in the same direction, which was southeast to the capital of Montenegro. Titograd it was called back then. But just as we were pulling out, who do we see but the grandpa of the group come tottering up the slope from the canyon. First a black peaked cap appeared, followed by his head, then his upper body dressed in a knitted cardigan, next his legs dressed in black pants and last his feet. He was wearing green rubber boots. That's how I'll always remember him, appearing bit by bit, hat, cardigan, pants, green rubber boots, looking happy, then perplexed, finding his family and the van gone, standing forlorn looking about."

"Did you stop?"

"No, because by the time it occurred to me that we ought to, Jim had stepped on it, wanting to get to Greece as soon as possible. 'The old guy's not our business,' he said. He was sure they'd come back for him. 'What if they don't?' I said. 'I can't see them not coming back,' was his response. 'People don't go depositing aged relatives by the side of the road in foreign countries, do they?' He was right, I suppose."

"Did they?"

"Did they what? Come back, you mean? I've no idea. We didn't pass their van at any point. Odd, don't you think?"

"I'd say. So you never found out what happened?"

"No. He might still be tottering about somewhere. Though he'd be well past a hundred by now. I've always wondered what happened to the poor old coot."

"You're sure he wasn't a local?"

"I wondered about that too. But he looked so English, what with his cardigan and all. And I'm pretty sure I saw him walking and talking with two of the children earlier on."

"What a curious tale."

"It is, isn't it? I almost wish you hadn't reminded me of it."

What it was that had reminded the woman of an old man forsaken on the brim of a canyon filled with water lilies, Serena will never know. But as she looks up from her book at the white shimmering sky, she wants to embrace the woman named Liz, pat that springy hair and say, "Thank you, my good, sweet angel, my patron saint. Thank you for letting me listen in on your story."

Smiling at nobody in particular, Serena turns a page in her cookbook, looking to the world like a woman planning a dinner party.

Later that afternoon she feels an overwhelming need to distance herself from Hester who is meticulously printing the same paragraph beginning with "Serena and I" on postcard after postcard, cheeks flushed with the pleasure of her work. Topping the growing stack is one still to be addressed. It's for Laurel who, as far as they know, is still paddling a canoe somewhere in darkest Africa.

"Where're you going to address it to? The Okavango Swamp?"

"To her apartment in Vancouver, of course. I'm doing the addresses last. Besides, she might be back by now. And she'll want to know about our adventure."

"Yeah, she'll be green with envy."

Serena walks out the door without saying good-bye, leaves the hotel to trek into downtown St. Paul, crossing the bridge over the highway, passing the colossus that is the Historical Society before turning left. The afternoon heat sears her skin.

The city centre is a cluster of tall buildings with corporate names like The Pioneer Building, The Empire Building, The Agro-Bank Building. Confident names. There seems to be no street life to speak of. Serena goes inside one of the buildings and ambles through the connecting walkways. They're refreshingly cool, but gloomy and deserted.

Too spooked to linger she hurries back outside onto the melting sidewalk, makes her way down Kellogg to the river, happy to find it. She continues along it as far as Robert where she flops onto a bench in the shade under a tree. Sits and watches the Mississippi flow by under a bridge that looks brand new. It's the colour of golden desert sand. She imagines an Egyptian bridge might look like this.

The new bridge spans the river importantly, crowding out the rusted old railroad bridge next to it. Serena sympathizes with the rusty bridge, quiet and forgotten, minding its own business, having done its job without reward.

And then she thinks of Hester — God knows why. If Hester were the rusty old bridge, she would immediately put the new bridge in its place by showing it how to properly span an abyss: "You have to remain inflexible and rigid, never buckle. It's how we've always done it."

Or she would tell the new bridge that its kind is not needed. It's what she once told Brian O'Shaughnessy, the boy Serena fell mindlessly in love with in grade twelve. Hester, seven years older, took the hapless boy aside in the street one day and explained — her voice as kind as ever — why it was in everybody's best interest that he stay away from Serena. One: he was a *Catholic*. (Feeble excuse Serena now thinks: Frank of the Immaculate Garage is a freaking Catholic.) Two: he was *not* what the family had in mind. Hester did not elaborate what the family *did* have in mind for seventeen-year-old Serena, but it's a well-known fact that Hester does not trust good looks in a man, however young. Manly good looks are a sign of moral decrepitude.

It took moonstruck Serena three weeks before she found out why Brian was avoiding her after those first promising dates of teeth-colliding kisses and padded bra-squeezing. It took far longer to get over him, far longer to let go of her sugarcoated dreams of marriage and children, two girls and two boys, all with same intense blue eyes and dark curly hair as their father.

Serena O'Shaughnessy. Mrs. O'Shaughnessy. She'd had the signature down pat.

Brian eventually married a girl named Catherine, also Catholic and Irish. They have four children, two girls and two boys. All but one are dark and handsome like their father.

Serena ran into him a couple of years after he got married, a moon-faced alien drooling on his arm.

The last wedding party Serena was obliged to attend was Hester's. Hester surprised the hell out of everybody by getting married at age forty-two to Frank Dubrowski, a man unburdened by good looks, but famous for keeping the most spotless garage for miles. A forty-eight-year-old widower who since his first wife's death ten years earlier had lived alone in the modest split level with the famous garage that holds his pickup truck and a lawnmower the size of his front lawn. These days it holds Hester's Honda Civic as well, when Hester isn't busy trekking Viking-like across the continent in it.

Frank sometimes leaves the garage door up — by mistake, he claims — to flaunt his organizational skills. Inside this sanctum clean tools hang in alphabetized rows according to size, including three garden hoses, two of them unused but of superior quality.

"You could eat off the floor in there," Hester complimented Frank at the church Christmas party the year before their nuptials. Every person in the room could tell by the look on Frank's face that he'd suddenly realized that before him stood the insightful woman with whom it might be worthwhile to continue a spic-and-span existence.

They're truly happy, Hester and Frank.

In bored, petty moments Serena pictures them at their kitchen table, sipping tidy cups of coffee, a coaster under each cup to protect the table, smiling smug smiles as they relish the supreme order of their universe. It's a picture that forces her, wherever she is, to flee outside to drown herself in fresh air, gulping it, looking towards heaven for reassurance, lest she falls off the precarious tightrope that is her life. She has a poor sense of balance.

The same furtive way she fled Hester's and Frank's wedding feast, escaping at the moment she always escapes such gatherings: when the dancing starts and half-pissed relatives begin to flaunt their staggering lack of rhythm. As always, the very sight of them plunged her into dark despair. Emotions that strong must lead their own dance, so she followed them — as always — out of the room, which at a wedding was the dreary banquet room of some local hotel — always, always — down the stairs, out the back — always, always — to the parking lot. Uninteresting territories, these behind-the-hotel parking lots — always, always — oil-stained, bleak and without hope.

But above the pitiless concrete, stars blinked in the night sky — always, always — as though it was tradition when mortals celebrated their paltry achievements, blinked and winked in her understanding piece of heaven — always, always — letting her know they were there. And she wished upon those distant stars — always, always — for what she was never sure, some calming influence, the strength to break free, to rid herself of the confining identity imposed upon her. And it helped. The deep heavy sighs that lodged like stones in her chest became weightless and floated out of her, rose into the universe like bubbles.

Serena knew the family assumed that she had run away because she was jealous of Hester tying the knot with a fine fellow like Frank Dubrowski, remembering how she had fled Cousin Joanne's wedding in the same manner. Just as she had fled Cousin Torben's wedding before that, when he married that tall girl from Vancouver, whose dad had been to prison for some white-collar crime.

Just as she knew that that was why they had made a point of consoling her at supper the Sunday following Hester's wedding, their limited minds figuring she was bothered that not only Hester, but girls whose parents had a criminal past, ended up happily married. They employed their usual version of subtlety during the consolation process ("You'll find a man too!") until Serena got up and stormed outside, over to the back fence where she stood, arms crossed, staring hard into the sky as if waiting for an incoming mothership to beam her up. Stood there knowing full well that in the house they would stay at the table, Mother saying, "Eat while the food is hot!" They would be eating and craning their necks to stare discreetly out the window to see what she was up to.

Just as she knew that Hester would be the first to put down her knife and fork and say, "I'll go and talk to her. I know how to handle her."

Just as she knew that Father would mumble, "Oh, leave her alone," and that as ever nobody would pay him any attention.

Just as she knew that Mother would reply, "You do that," and then do something like hand Frank the mashed potatoes and say something typical like, "Home grown russet, Frank. From out back. Have some more." As if her eldest daughter's second-hand husband might fade into thin air if she did not keep feeding him.

And sure enough, there came Hester looking purposeful. Serena watched her approach, then fled to the driveway, hopped in her car and tore out of there. Hester was still wearing Mother's flowery apron. It flapped around her hips as she ran to the sidewalk to peer after Serena's fast disappearing car. She stood there for a while, nonplussed, fingering the top button of her blouse.

Serena always keeps a pack of cigarettes and a ten-dollar bill in the glove compartment; they tend to come in handy. She also leaves the key in the ignition. That Sunday, it was close to midnight before she returned to Mother's to retrieve her coat and handbag. Hester and Frank were long gone. Mother and Father were asleep (or pretending to be), when Serena slipped quietly into the house, reeking of cigarettes, coffee and the cloying fat of deep-fried donuts.

They stay in St. Paul for another two days. Serena tries hard to be obliging, even when Hester insists they eat the nondescript food in the generic hotel dining room rather than go out to a restaurant where the food might to be worth chewing.

After a mainly silent dinner Hester wants to hurry back upstairs to work on her notes. Most of the copious information she has gathered has nothing to do with their ancestry, but unrelated subjects she finds fascinating and wants to tell Frank about.

"Why would Frank give a shit about what quilting patterns were popular with early Scandinavian settlers?"

"Frank is interested in everything I tell him. He has a very open mind."

"Frank . . . " *doesn't have a mind. He's exchanged it for a garage.*

"What dear?"

"Nothing."

Serena breaks loose each night, desperate to get outside, running down the stairs if the elevators are heading upwards. She does this even though there's nowhere suitable to walk in the vicinity. She has to. She craves the sky, longs to feel the cooling night wind in her face. She needs to look up and see those reassuring stars, that comforting moon, those unencumbered clouds on their way to distant horizons. She would circle the large deserted parking lot between the hotel and the Sears Bargain Centre, pace it like a caged animal, wear a groove in the asphalt if she had to.

She crosses the street instead, stops on the bridge over the highway and watches the lights of the night traffic below, two uninterrupted red lines streaming one way and two yellow ones hurrying in the opposite direction. Wonders where they are all in such a rush to get to this time of night. Imagines candlelit, garlic based dinners, glasses of wine, people to talk to. Lives well lived.

Up by the cathedral she turns left and heads towards downtown St. Paul, trying to look like she has a destination, that she's at home here, that she's afraid of no one. She ends up going farther than intended, inhaling the fresh air after another long hot day. No gun-toting criminals lurk in the shadows. There's nobody out at all and it's a bit eerie.

Soon it becomes too eerie. A few blocks past the Xcel Energy Centre, afraid of getting lost in streets that look different at night, she turns to go back to the hotel, walking faster now, chased by her own footsteps. By the time she gets to the bridge, she's running, out of breath.

Hester is still sitting at the round table by the window, haloed by the glow of the lamp above her head, busy categorizing and transferring the notes about their ancestors from Norway. There are few notes to categorize, so she prints each word with care, giving it its own symmetrical importance, determined to imbue their slender family tree with weight and substance.

Relief floods her face when she sees Serena, out of breath and sweaty, walk through the door.

Serena greets her with a comment. "Still at it?"

"Oh, I've been busy." Hester gives Serena the rundown on the family.

Originally from Haugesund on the west coast of Norway, Great-grandpa Johann and his brother, Mother's Uncle Emmett's father, Niels, arrived by boat in New York from Bergen in 1892, together with their parents and younger sister, Ulrike. From New York they took the train to Minneapolis, where Johann eventually got a job as a private chauffeur. His only son, Hans, moved to Toronto after he married a Canadian girl. After months of doing odd jobs Niels continued up to Saskatchewan, where a few years later he bought a homestead by the Frenchman River near the Alberta border. Ulrike's branch was stunted; she never married. Uncle Emmett, an only child, married Hilda, and they had one son, Carl, who was killed in the war, pruning that branch before its time.

"So we no longer have any relatives to speak of?"

"Not on Mother's side, no. At least not here. But I'm sure we have lots of distant ones in Norway, in this Hoggisand place."

"Hardly worth the trip, was it?"

"You haven't enjoyed yourself?"

"I've been thrilled to bits, Hester. But now, if you'll excuse me, I must have a shower."

"Don't forget to hang up the towels. That's what the sign says. Hang them up to indicate that you will use them again to save energy. I think it's the least we can do to help out."

"Absolutely," says Serena. She's been nice all day and now it's late and she's beat. She stands in the shower until the water runs cold, then dries herself and throws the towels on the wet floor. The dry ones too.

Fifteen minutes later, after a cold shower, Hester shakes the towels out and hangs them up. Using a length of toilet paper she cleans the counter top until it's nice and dry, wiping up the gobs of toothpaste Serena left in the sink.

When Hester is in her flannel nightgown and has hung up their clothes, smoothing them with the flat of her hand, she folds her bedspread and slips between the sheets. She requests Serena turn off the TV.

"You can watch TV at home," she says. "It's a rerun anyway. That guy hasn't been on the show for ages. They killed him off, remember?"

"I like him."

"No, you don't. Turn it off."

"Why?"

"Well . . . so we can talk. We're on holiday."

"Fine." Serena turns off the TV and throws the remote on the floor. "What do you want to talk about?"

"Anything, dear." Hester's fount of goodnaturedness is not about to run dry. "Why do you always go walking late in the evening? You do the same at home. I've never understood it. It's always worried Mother, if you must know. It's not safe, not these days. Especially not here where everybody carries a gun."

Serena's too tired to lie. "I need to see the sky."

"The sky? What on earth for?" Hester's tone reveals that now she has learned the nature of her sister's ailment, she'll do her best to cure it.

"Turn out the light," says Serena before Hester has time to open her mouth again. "I'm going to sleep."

When Serena was little she assumed that if you owned a piece of land you also owned the matching piece of sky above it. If you didn't own any land you were the proprietor of only the area of sky directly above your head.

Uncle Emmett had inherited a lot of land in southern Saskatchewan from his father Niels. After he married Hilda, he sold it and they moved east to Ontario where the winters were less harsh and the soil more fertile. He bought a farm near Orangeville.

When you stood at the end of the long driveway leading up to the farm, all the land rolling to the horizon was all his, every bit of it, consequently Serena assumed that he also owned the considerable chunk of sky directly above it, perhaps farming its stars.

At Uncle Emmett's funeral she overheard two of the neighbours, Mr. Harding and Mr. Leskinen, discuss the land. Apparently there was too much of it for Hilda to handle alone, so she had decided to move back out west to a place called Regina, where her only sister lived. Somebody named Gruber had bought the farm. It was no longer in the family.

It was, they agreed, too bad.

Serena was five at the time. "Did the man buy the sky above it too?" she inquired, thinking he must have. Or could heaven be sold as a separate parcel of land?

The two neighbours — they'd had their fair share of funeral whisky in Mr. Leskinen's pickup truck — looked down at the little girl in her Sunday best. "Did you say something?"

"The sky above this land. Did the man buy that too, or is it still Uncle Emmett's now that he is up in heaven?"

They snorted and chuckled and shook their heads.

This was a matter of importance and she needed clarification, so she pressed on. "Well? Is it?"

"Sure, kid. Emmett's right up there behind that cloud."

"That big cloud over the trees?"

"That's the one."

"So you can keep your bit of the sky when you die?"

"You bet, toots. It's all yours."

She was relieved to learn this, though it raised another question. "Then what bit of sky do the people get who are taking over Uncle Emmett's land?"

"That's up to God to know and us to find out. And seeing as we're not dead yet, we'll have to wait and see. That's how it works."

"I see." At the time she thought she did.

After the funeral, Mother's Aunt Hilda moved to Regina to be close to her sister. Regina was way, way out west they said, in the province called Saskatchewan. It was all prairie out there. They pronounced the word "prairie" as if it was something substandard or contagious.

Did they have the same sky on the prairie? Her mother said they did, but that it was way, way bigger on account of the flatness of the land.

A day and a half later they're back in Canada, back on the prairie where the sky is as omnipotent as ever. In Regina they stay at the West Harvest Inn, not bothering to bewilder Aunt Hilda with another visit. Hester is unable to check with Social Services about her because it's Saturday. She says she'll call them on Monday.

The following day as they set out, Serena suggests they wait until she has to go to the bathroom before they stop to get gas. "It'll save us a bit of time."

The timesaving aspect wins Hester over.

They are just east of Indian Head when Serena confides that her bladder is about burst and that they better stop at that gas station over there. Hester fills up the car while Serena runs to the bathroom.

"That was quick," says Hester approvingly when Serena returns.

"I pee like a pro. Did you pay for the gas?"

"I'll go do that now."

"Hey, want to get me a bottle of diet pop while you're there? I'm dying of thirst."

Hester says she'll be happy to.

When Hester reaches the door to the gas station store, Serena slips out of the passenger seat and hurries to the back of the car, opens the trunk and lifts out Hester's strategically placed bags, puts them neatly side by side on the tarmac before nipping around to the driver's side. She slides in, buckles up and turns the key in the ignition.

Hester must have heard the car start, watched it roll forward, not comprehending, for there she comes, careening out of the store. Serena hears her scream, "What are you doing?" as the car hits the highway and shoots off in the direction they just came from, sees her wave her arms at the runaway vehicle, screaming louder and louder. In her pale face, incomprehension is growing in tandem with her fear.

Ignoring her sister — though far from oblivious to her — Serena switches the radio to a music station serving golden oldies. Mungo Jerry! She cranks up the volume. *In the summertime when the weather is high, you can stretch right up and touch the sky.* Snorting with laughter, she steps on the gas until she far exceeds the speed limit. There's not a lot of traffic on the prairie. She drives faster still, switching on the air conditioning to High. Cold air blasts into the hot car. She can feel the sweat on her forehead dry.

Hester's runaway Honda shoots west while in its back mirror Hester herself grows smaller and smaller until all that's left of her is a thin exclamation mark on a receding horizon.

Ahead the road stretches and stretches far into the distant future, ruler straight beneath a sky so infinite Serena is convinced she can accelerate right into it if she tries hard enough. She presses the gas pedal all the way to the floor.

The Rebel Doll

JOAN IS TIRED AND CRANKY. It's been a long and tedious journey. Her clothes smell of jet fuel. Now she worries that her sister has forgotten that this is the day she arrives from Canada for an overdue visit. Everybody in the immediate family has travelled to England to visit Abigail but Joan. Then again, Joan is busier than any of them.

Now here she sits. The bench is hard, its wood worn and slippery, not compatible with her bony butt. She keeps shifting her legs, scissoring her right over her left, left over right, conscious of the fact that crossing one's legs is disastrous not only for the body's natural alignment, but leads to varicose veins and blood clots and God knows what. No doubt it's disastrous for spiritual enlightenment as well.

Abigail was supposed to be waiting when the 2.19 train pulled in (at 2.36), arms flung open in welcoming embrace, but she wasn't there. There wasn't a soul on the narrow stretch of platform that makes up the quaint end of the line of this small branch railway. Joan, having had the foresight to get some English change, headed straight for the waiting room to find a public phone. There was no phone. She strode up to the old man behind the ticket counter to ask why.

"There's a call box across the street, dear." The man pointed across the street to a red phone booth.

There's an old-fashioned black phone sitting by his right elbow. Joan points to it. "Do you mind if I use it?"

"Sorry, madam, no customers allowed inside this area."

"Listen, I'm a crown attorney in . . . "

"Be that as it may, dear." The old man stirs a spoonful of sugar into his mug of tea.

Stunned by the man's indifference, Joan, at a loss, concedes defeat. "Can I at least leave my suitcase here while I go to call?"

"By all means," says the man, stirring his tea as if it was a pleasure to do so.

There is no answer at Abigail's house. Hopefully this means she is on her way. If not, Joan will be royally pissed off.

There is, of course, another scenario: something has happened. Abigail being Abigail, it is entirely possible.

Joan returns to the train station. The old man ignores her.

It's a muggy July afternoon. The waiting room is dead quiet. Apart from Joan there is only the old man half dozing behind the safety glass of his ticket office, his mug apparently empty already. Joan wouldn't mind a cup of tea. Or coffee. Something to wake her up.

She is about to slide into jet-lagged slumber, when the door to the platform flings open. A man strides in. He does so as if entering a stage, a not very good actor, too self-conscious and stiff, but eager to perform, craving the spotlight. Though he does not utter a word, there is something decidedly noisy and invasive about his sudden presence.

Joan straightens up at the sight of him. Maybe Abigail sent him to fetch her.

A second look tells her this is not the case.

The man's acute self-awareness renders his movements graceless. His white holiday hat, meant to be dashing, perches at an odd angle. It looks as if it resents being stuck on this particular head and is determined not to cooperate.

If hats could make wishes, reflects Joan, this one would wish it was angled on a more compatible noggin. The hat looks so new she is surprised not to see a price tag dangling from its brim. The man's jeans and white sneakers are also brand new. So is his shirt. She can tell by the sharp creases that it was until very recently folded into a neat rectangle.

This stranger with his slightly bulging blue eyes, moist fattish lips and pompous expression, is no friend of Abigail's.

Joan takes a fervent dislike to the man. It's not the first time she suffers an irrational reaction to a complete stranger.

(Her husband finds her behaviour disturbing. Abnormal. "Joan has issues and, trust me, *that* is putting it mildly," he has revealed to his colleague, Fiona, to whom he has grown very close over the past two years.)

Joan interprets her own behaviour as insightful and intuitive. Looking at the man before her, she deems it fair to conclude that the person he now assumes himself to be did not exist when he bounced out of bed this morning. Only when he stepped into these brand new togs did his new self — his holiday self — emerge, looking pleased, the hat a bit iffy, but everything in its proper place.

Now here he is. "Pompous Twit on Holiday" is the title she arrives at. It's this insight of hers that inspires the creation of amusing titles, that and her keen ability to analyze people and situations. Her title for this man, while not hugely original, is thoroughly fitting.

Did the man request that his wife, assuming he has one (and something tells Joan that he does), purchase these holiday garments for him? Did he hand her an itemized list of his precise requirements? Saying, "And please note, dear, that the shirt must have very, very thin stripes, preferably a discreet blue, and be of the finest quality cotton."

Or did he undertake the task himself, trusting only his own immaculate taste?

Yes. A second glance tells Joan that he did just that. He was off to the shops, as they say over here, probably after work one evening, having consulted a Men's Fashion magazine, a Sunday paper colour supplement catering to the upwardly striving. Afterwards he took a later train from the city, carrying his bags in a manner that prominently displayed the names of the upmarket shops where he had purchased his clothes as though shopping in these places had long been his habit.

How can Joan, newly arrived in the country, presume to know all this?

Because it's obvious. Her first impressions are seldom wrong. It's a talent she takes pride in. She is well known in legal circles in Canada, the fearsome Joan Deacon, crown attorney, she of the tailored two-piece suits and cold silver jewelry. Deciphering people is her business and, by God, she's good at it.

As she points out to friends and colleagues when the subject comes up, deciphering people is not half as complicated as it sounds. It does not require great insight into the complexities of the human psyche. Most people are easier to read than a mass-produced paperback with a pre-fab plot. People may be devious, but ninety-nine percent of the time they are devious in the same predictable manner.

Thus a quick read of the new arrival informs her that here is a pompous fool as supported by the evidence in a standard dictionary: Pompous: *pretentious, as in speech or manner;*

self-important. Fool: *a person with little or no judgment, common sense, insight etc.* That's easy enough. *Why* he has decided to reinvent himself at this point in time, unless it is a regular quirk of his, she can only speculate on, and so she does, for no other reason that it amuses her, and because she has time to kill. It stops her from having to worry about Abigail.

The waiting room in the small railway station somewhere in the northwest of England is an insignificant relation of the vast crowded cavern of London's Euston station where Joan caught the train to Manchester earlier that morning, having arrived from Gatwick on a train crowded with overseas travellers with bad transatlantic breath.

She arrived at her final destination on the nearly empty two-carriage toy train that trundles up a modest branch line from Manchester twice a day. Where, expecting to find her sister, she found nobody at all.

The small town of Bendlesfield is the end of the line. The train could not make it any farther should it want to make a run for it. Twenty feet from the station the rails ends at a brick wall that once was the opening of a tunnel. Trailing down the brick wall are green rivulets of ivy and climbing up from between the rails to meet them, a tangle of wild roses. Beyond the ex-tunnel, green hills billow in the summer haze.

Five years ago, Joan's sister Abigail, unexpectedly widowed at a young age, surprised everybody by getting married again. Her new husband was an Englishman named Ian Burke, a cheerful, burly man born and bred in these faraway parts. They met when Abigail was on a week's holiday in London. The enforced trip was a birthday present from her parents, two brothers and sister. They hoped a change of scenery would help her forget the recent tragedy.

It was her first holiday since Wallace, her husband, died in a car crash on a wintry Calgary thoroughfare. He had been driving home drunk from an office Christmas party — straight into a sixteen-wheeler coming from the opposite direction — after having promised Abigail that morning, cross his heart and hope to die, that this time he would for sure stay sober, and what's the matter, Abby, you don't believe me?

Less than a year after they first met, Abigail and Ian settled staidly, contentedly, on the farm half a mile north of Bendlesfield. Ian had recently inherited the falling down barn, the two-storey limestone house, and a suitable number of acres from his grandfather. They grow their own vegetables, but do not actually farm. Ian is the co-owner of The Toad and Jockstrap, a pub on the outskirts of town — village really, together with his grown-up son Ned from a previous marriage. The pub keeps him busy, especially in the summer when thirsty hikers crisscross the countryside on the network of public footpaths. He works full time, pouring lager and ale and serving ploughman's lunches and steak and kidney pies (made by Abigail) to save money on staff.

And — he has sworn to Abigail — he always walks back home along the winding country lane if he has had a pint or two.

Abigail has found a worthwhile brand of felicity in this most unexpected of places. She has recently had modest success as a writer of cookbooks: the *Abby's Country Kitchen* series. A new one is due out in the fall.

Joan has not seen her sister for more than three years and is impatient for her to show up and reveal if, and how, life in the

English boondocks has changed her. She worries that Abigail might have acquired odd habits, common in these parts. Forgetting how to tell time or something. Joan, a big-city woman, finds rural areas picturesque enough for short visits, but would not actually want to waste her life in one.

She checks her watch. Abigail's lack of punctuality has not changed.

A minute after the man has entered the waiting room, the door to the platform opens again — unobtrusively this time — and a woman and three young girls timidly file in. The man does not hurry over to hold open the door for them, though it's clear that they are his wife and daughters.

Joan's first impression is: what a long-suffering quartet! It's the rigidity of their upper lips that give them away. That and their uniform posture: shoulders hunched in a desire not to be noticed. The look in their eyes is evasive as if to prevent the world from detecting any subversive thoughts that well-brought-up people are loath to acknowledge ownership of, but that sometimes, if you're not careful, shine through.

The quartet reveals no visible trace of excitement over the start of their holiday.

It's Joan's opinion that the English middle class has a greater flair for polite long-suffering than anybody else on the planet. Either it's in their blood, a mutant gene expressing itself in that Mustn't-Make-a-Fuss attitude they're so damn proud of, or they enroll in obligatory government sponsored classes to perfect it, perhaps some kind of middle class finishing school. Abigail, given to loud and immediate complaining when displeased, has written lengthy e-mails to Joan about the unreasonableness of this odd phenomenon, confessing that she will never comprehend, nor does she wish to, the reasons for such self-inflicted limitations.

It's with great interest that Joan observes the phenomenon in these specimens in their natural habitat.

The wife and three daughters are nicely dressed, but their clothes are not new. Their plain cotton dresses are freshly laundered and ironed (a good mother sees to that), but they are far from the latest fashion. People sporting brand new clothes tend to walk in a manner self-conscious and expectant, tense from a secret wish to be complimented, especially if the clothes are more expensive than they can normally afford.

The female members of this family are entirely without expectations.

If they were on the same train as Joan they must have sat in the other carriage. If not, where did they pop up from? There has been no other train. Have they been standing out on the platform until now? And if so, why?

The wife is toting a bulging straw bag. The eldest girl, not more than ten years old, carries a tennis racket in each hand, awkwardly as if unsure what such implements are for. The middle one, a few years younger, drags a skipping rope like a leash with the dog missing. The youngest is clutching a smugly grinning doll that breaks drastically with family tradition by flaunting the gaudiest get-up imaginable. The cheap synthetic material — the shiny kind that never wrinkles — is bright orange splashed with purple and green polka dots. The sleeves are wide with purple flounces. Pink and green beads rattle and clang around the doll's neck. The grinning lips are a violent red. It's a naughty grin. The doll resembles a small vampire recently arrived from New Orleans, having celebrated Mardi Gras by feasting on fresh blood. From the hem of the dress dangle two thin legs ending in a pair of oversized blue shoes.

When the door has closed behind the quartet, the man issues a command, a sudden nasal honk. Their attention to it is automatic. Without a word they march over to the long bench facing the street and sit down, one after the other in a choppy wave.

The bench is at right angles to the one where Joan is sitting. The twit parks himself closest to her. The youngest child sits at the far end. From the doll comes a clatter of beads that sounds like an unrepressed giggle. When it stops, the room once again succumbs to silence.

There they sit, saying nothing, doing nothing. Perhaps this is how they spend their holidays, sitting in waiting rooms at train stations raising questions in the heads of strangers, staring out windows, down at smooth stone floors, up at ceilings, never uttering a word.

It rained earlier in the day and the room is damp, exuding a stuffy smell of mould. A determined fly buzzes frenziedly in one of the two windows, demonstrating how one ought to frolic now the sun is shining. After a while the buzz inspires the eldest girl to start fiddling with her tennis rackets, thudding them rhythmically against her feet.

Unexpectedly the fool springs to life. "I'd better call the office," he declares to the room at large.

Nobody responds to the announcement. Joan is the only one to show an interest as he hauls out a mobile phone and proceeds to dial.

The fool — like most of the world's mobile babblers — has nothing of interest to impart but is driven by the need to communicate all the same, louder than necessary, if only to confirm his existence.

"Vanessa? Derek here. How are things at the office? Oh, good. Listen, I thought I better leave you my holiday number.

Our cottage has a phone, you see. So . . . I thought . . . you know, just in case . . . Have you got a pen?"

It's a bad habit of Joan Deacon's, this fixation on complete strangers. In her defense, it has always been a harmless compulsion.

The objects of her present fixation take no notice of her. There is no reason why they should. She is a middle-aged woman sitting alone in the waiting room of an insignificant railway station in the middle of nowhere, a suitcase at her feet, a deceivingly plain purse on the bench beside her. She is comfortably, but not elegantly dressed, looking somewhat disheveled — the result of having spent the night on a transatlantic flight. She has stowed her impressive assortment of rings, including her wedding band, in her purse. Her fingers tend to swell up when she travels by air.

Somehow she has already sensed that in the eyes of this awkward tribe she is, as they would put it, not their sort.

"All right then? You'll know where to get in touch. What? Oh, I don't know, we're not there yet. We'll be picked up any moment now, I should think. I've hired a car from a local firm. I've been out and about looking for the man bringing it and . . . I just thought that as we were waiting . . . you know . . . I might as well . . . what? Oh, sorry. Well, mustn't keep you then. Bye now." Tucking away the phone, he turns to his wife, "Well, that's that taken care of."

His wife offers no audible response. She does not inquire — as would Joan — why the office needs the phone number to the cottage when they no doubt have the number of his cell phone, should they feel the urge to hear his supercilious drone.

A good, pliable woman, reflects Joan, does not indulge in sarcasm.

The enthusiastic fly buzzes for dear life. There is no other sound. Joan half expects the fool to commence lecturing his flock about something or other. The buzzing of flies, the architecture of small railway stations, the flora and fauna of Northern England. The perfect angle of a gentleman's hat. He strikes her as the kind of father who whips out flash cards in front of defenseless offspring, demanding they live up to his expectations by showing instant proof of prodigiousness.

Joan relishes her sarcasm.

No lecture is forthcoming. The man does not open his mouth. Sitting straight and tense he contains only pent-up energy waiting to be put to use.

The eldest girl stops fiddling with the tennis rackets. The middle girl slumps and wiggles her left foot in a half-hearted manner. The youngest kicks her legs in the air for a bit. Once or twice she holds the doll's face up to her ear, concentrating hard on what the doll has to say. She nods attentively at the confidence imparted before lowering the doll back onto her lap with a raucous clatter of beads. There it lies sprawled, a gaudy, grinning twenty-inch rebel.

The wife sits so still she might have moved on to a happier place.

Eventually the fly starts banging itself against the window. The atmosphere feels increasingly heavy, the room about to sink deep into a hundred-year sleep. The sun disappears behind a cloud, the day grows darker. Soon this forgotten little building will disappear under a tangle of ivy and roses and . . .

"I wonder if I ought to give Martin a call?" The fool's thinking out loud breaks the spell. The old man twitches awake behind his counter. A pen drops to the floor. The fly falls down dead. The sun reappears. Roses and ivy halt their advance.

"Can't it wait?" It's the wife. She is still alive. Hers is a soft voice, not expecting to be heard.

"Better call now." Once again he dials, but this time there is no reply. Reluctantly he slides the gadget back into his pocket.

A minute later he consults his watch, restless, cranes his neck for a while and then lets out another honk. "Well, what do you know, the bloody driver has finally seen fit to show up with the rental car. Ought to have a word about his tardiness."

"Please, Derek, don't make a fuss," mumbles the wife. "We're on holiday."

He does not reply as they rise in another choppy wave and head for the door like a row of wind-up toys. The wife follows a few steps behind her husband with her tail of small girls.

As the wife passes by her, Joan looks up, offering a glance of solidarity, the strength of the sisterhood. Feeling sympathy — having nothing better to do — she decides to bestow support and understanding. The poor woman looks like she could use a boost.

It's a keen look, and the woman turns her head as though Joan has called out her name. She throws Joan a glance that, while vaguely alarmed, lets it be known that she has no use for whatever Joan has to offer, she can manage, thank you very much.

Out she marches, head held high, upper lip in a state of rigor mortis. The eldest child follows close behind, tennis rackets drooping. In her footsteps trudges the middle daughter dragging her skipping rope. With their pale freckled skin and dark blond curls they both resemble their mother. Neither gives Joan a glance.

Trailing them by several feet is the youngest girl with her doll. She is in no hurry. As she passes Joan she stops and stares with unabashed curiosity, head cocked like an alert bird, one mahogany pigtail falling over her shoulder, the other resting against her neck. She does not look a day over five and bears no resemblance to either of her parents. Her lips are soft, trembling slightly, as if a secret is trying to break free from between them. Her large green eyes give the impression of wanting to take the strange woman into her confidence.

"Have a nice holiday." Joan feels she ought to say something. Her voice has the false cheer grown-ups resort to when addressing small children, assuming that lacking in years and stature they are far too dim to perceive blatant insincerity.

The girl gazes at Joan for several seconds, earnestly, solemnly, never blinking, before asking, "How do you know we're on our holiday?"

"I could tell by your daddy's hat."

Briefly it looks as if the child might crack a smile, but in the end she does not. Perhaps she does not know how.

At that moment a piercing voice drills through the door. "Hermioneee! Don't dawdle!"

The girl sighs. "Lizzie doesn't like holidays," she whispers. She has a slight lisp.

"Who's Lizzie?"

"Lizzie's my doll." She holds it up for a quick introduction. Before Joan gets a chance to inquire about Lizzie's anti-vacation stance, the little girl has scuttled out, clasping the doll in a tight grip, preventing any sudden escape.

The door slams shut. Outside Hermione's father is having a word with a short skinny man leaning bored against the open door of a red Ford Escort. After a while the skinny man shakes his head with scorn and the twit disappears around the station building. He returns dragging two large suitcases. The skinny man opens the trunk of the car and points. Looks amused as the know-it-all, red-faced, heaves the cases in one by one.

When skinny has slammed the trunk shut, he hands over the car keys and saunters off, leaving the fuming customer to order his brood into the car.

Two minutes later Abigail storms into the waiting room in her usual whirlwind fashion, hair uncombed, a thorough lack of stiffness in her upper lip.

"Shit, Joan, I'm so sorry! It's that goddamn piece of crap of a jeep!" she hollers, sounding the same as ever. "God, I've been dying to see you!" Five years on British soil has not robbed Abigail of her tendency to speak in sentences followed by at least one exclamation mark. "Forgive me!" She throws her arms around Joan and waltzes her around the waiting room, shouting "Hello Sidney!" to the delighted looking man behind the counter.

And Joan hugs Abigail and all her careless faults, stumbling and stepping on her toes as she follows her sister's twirling. Crown attorney Deacon was never much of a dancer.

The Burkes country home is exactly as Abigail has described it: a perennial mess scattered over threadbare oriental rugs. The floor slants in different directions. Exposed oak beams draw lines in the low ceiling in the living room. In this house, with its thick stone walls, every room remains cool throughout the summer.

The upstairs guestroom window faces the side of the house where the kitchen garden has exploded into profusion. Tomatoes hang heavy on the vines, monster zucchinis nestle like large green billy clubs on their hills. Lettuces, spinach, carrots, radishes, beets, green beans, yellow beans, cucumbers, broccoli, cauliflower, peppers, you name it, everything is swelling with obscene fecundity. At one far end rows of cabbages sit like fat gluttons too lazy to battle the horde of raspberry bushes about to usurp their turf. Lining the other end a united force of hollyhocks, like those of T.S. Eliot's, are aiming too high. And in between and all around, in random splatters of red, yellow, blue and white, wildflowers flourish uninvited. Birds sing in harmony in the willows on the other side of the wall. Two rabbits hop about in the field beyond.

It's all a bit much.

In the days to come Joan will look out this window onto this dewy dream and know why her sister sings in the morning as she toasts her uneven slices of homemade bread. Yet wondering how the hell Abigail can stand it.

Two days later Joan is strolling along the town's meandering high street, when around a bend who should coming marching towards her but the fool and his troop. The man has switched to the role of pukka sahib, suitably kitted out in knee-length khakis, crisp and new. The walking stick in his right hand is tapping time on the sidewalk at a steady clip. They are approaching in their usual formation, anti-holiday Lizzie reluctantly bringing up the rear with Hermione.

The first four pay Joan no mind. Perhaps they fail to connect the woman from the train station with the stylish lady dressed in a Calvin Klein beige linen dress and Italian sling-backs, sporting two diamond rings of an in-your-face size. The fool is staring straight ahead as if hypnotized by some vision up the street. His wife and two older daughters are still wearing plain cotton dresses, though different from the ones they were wearing when Joan saw them last. All three have discovered things of intense interest on the pavement by their feet. Hermione is the only one aware of the world around her. She immediately recognizes Joan and slows down. Lizzie, gaudy in full synthetic vulgarity, hangs limp in her arms.

Joan stops. "Hello there, Hermione."

"How do you know my name?" Like she did at the train station, the girl cocks her head, birdlike, peering up at the tall woman. A ponytail has replaced her pigtails. Unlike her sisters, she is dressed in denim overalls.

"I heard the tw . . . your father call you at the station the other day, remember?"

"Did you?"

"I did."

"Oh yes. I think I remember that."

"Are you having a nice holiday?"

The girl offers no reply, but her deep sigh is answer enough. After a moment, having pondered whether to bring up the sensitive subject, Hermione lisps, "Are you really a silly old spinster?"

Joan, taken aback, could tell the child that silliness is not the characteristic she is known for. Also, she is not that old, thank you very much, and she is certainly not a spinster. She is married and has three grown sons and two grandchildren. She could also educate this outspoken child on the subject of language, inform her that the word "spinster" is, in this day and age, an obsolete term that holds meaning only in prissy Jane Austen novels. But why confuse the poor thing?

"Why, yes," she replies. "How on earth did you know?"

"Daddy told me."

"He did, did he?"

"Yes. He says all spinsters are silly. That's why nobody wants to marry them. And that's why they have to travel places all by themselves, you see. He says if I don't behave, I'll grow up and be a spinster too."

"Why that's . . . "

"Hermioneee! Don't dawdle!" The fool has turned around and is waving his walking stick. He might be waving it in a hurry up sort of gesture, or he might be brandishing it at Joan. Both he and his wife are throwing her fearful glances, as if spinsters are not only silly, but armed and dangerous.

"Good-bye, silly old spinster."

"Good-bye, Hermione. Good-bye, Lizzie."

Hermione puts the doll's face up to her ear and listens with a surprised look on her face. "Do you know what? Lizzie doesn't think you're silly." She discloses the news while lowering the doll with the usual rattling of beads. "She thinks your dress is too posh for a silly person."

"That's very observant of her."

"Hermioneeee!"

The girl sighs and trudges off. Over her shoulder, Lizzie grins with wicked red, red lips at Joan.

Before Joan enters the cheese shop to get "a nice piece of Stilton and a chunk of red Leicester," as per Abigail's orders, she gazes down the street after Hermione. The girl has stopped and turned around. She is holding up Lizzie's right arm, helping the doll wave to the posh lady by the cheese shop.

Behind her, her father is shaking his stick like a mad peasant keeping the devil at bay.

Joan waves back, regally, to both of them, sunlight reflecting in her diamonds.

It's two days later when she again spots the troop marching steadfastly down the opposite sidewalk licking ice cream cones in unison. All except Hermione.

She is lagging behind, preoccupied, trying to feed Lizzie her ice cream. Lizzie with her usual contrariness is averting her head. With Hermione's help the doll lifts an arm and points first to the ice cream, then to Hermione, indicating that *she* should eat it all. Necklaces dangle around the doll's limp body, carmine lips smile at the folly of mankind.

If it's observing Hermione offering her doll ice cream that triggers it, or if there is another cause, from that day on Joan takes to roaming the village and surrounding countryside in search of the fool and his flock. She is aware that it's a meaningless, dimwitted pursuit, and a bit perverse, yet she is helpless against the urge. It's not very often she becomes obsessive to such a degree, but when she does she finds it imperative to follow through her investigation. It turns into a case, and a case is always a challenge. Every stone must be turned in search of evidence.

("There goes Joan playing detective again," her husband would have sighed, had he seen her. He would not have been amused. He would have rolled his eyes, thinking of divorce, not for the first time.)

"I'm going for a walk," she repeats to Abigail and Ian every day after lunch. "I need to be alone to think for a bit. There's this case that's bothering me. Hope you don't mind."

Before she takes off, she turns into a silly old spinster. To look the part, she has begun to dress in as dowdy a manner as she can. If Abigail wonders about her sister's transformation, she never comments, never shakes her head, never grimaces, though she has an expressive way of performing all three. Nor does she remind Joan that she has come to Bendlesfield to spend time with *her*. She never reveals the slightest annoyance when Joan heads for the kitchen entrance to put on the muddy wellies Ian wears when working in the garden. The rubber boots are the perfect accessory to the old cardigan with the baggy pockets she discovered on a hook in the closet of the guestroom. (It once belonged to Ian's grandmother and has several suitable runs in it.) For full effect Joan ties an old paisley scarf of Abigail's around her head, hiding her pricey haircut. She's thrilled with her disguise.

"I can't believe the way she's dressing all of a sudden," says Abigail to Ian one day as they watch Joan shuffle down the road in the green rubber boots. "She's always been such a snob. Even as a kid she was picky. Everything had to be a perfect match. Fussy, fussy, fussy, that is Joanie. Seeing her like this is so refreshing, I don't dare say boo."

"I could have used my wellies today, mind you. Planned to do a bit of gardening," Ian grumbles, but doesn't take his complaint any further. Nor does he says anything about how his poor gran would have turned over in her grave had she known that her old cardie was being paraded up and down the village high street.

Joan relishes the invisibility her new role brings with it; it gives her a feeling of freedom. As a badly dressed spinster she has nothing to live up to, nobody to outperform. There is nothing she has to get done before the day is out, no meetings, no decisions to make.

Other dowdy people bestow friendly nods upon her as they pass in the lanes and public footpaths. "Lovely day," they chirp, their faces wholesome and ruddy. "Simply lovely," twitters Joan in her best English accent.

Twice she observes the fool's column at a distance. The first time they have just turned onto the footpath down by the river. It's a narrow path, walled in on both sides by an impenetrable jungle of blackberry bushes and muddier than usual after an early morning downpour. The column marches ever forward through the muck, shunning the ripe bounty lining the path. Only Hermione stops to sample the berries, encouraged by the observant Lizzie who points suggestively, first to the berries, juicy and plump, then to Hermione, tired and thirsty.

During the second sighting, the wife and the girls are taking turns climbing a stile leading into yet another field full of yet more grazing sheep. Pukka sahib is standing on the other side holding out a helping hand, administering advice. "No, not like that, dear, you put the *entire* foot down, heel and all. Better balance that way. Come on, Blanche, your turn. Don't dawdle. That's the ticket! Okay, Beatrice, you're next. Up you go, there's a good girl. Hermioneee! Wake up!"

Hermione clambers up the stile only to linger on the top step, turning left and right to admire the scenery. Approving of what she sees, she lifts up Lizzie so she, too, can enjoy the pastoral idyll. Lizzie takes her time gazing about with round eyes. Feels a sudden need to impart another reflection into Hermione's ear. Listening and nodding, Hermione refuses her father's impatient hand.

"Lizzie and I can do it ourselves!" Slow and stubborn, she climbs knock-kneed down the stile, her doll in a tight grip. By the time she is safely on the other side, her father has already charged halfway across the field, scattering sheep in his wake. Watching his back and the obedient tail that is the rest of her family, Hermione sits down on a stone, chin in hand, Lizzie gossiping in her ear.

Something about the scene bothers Joan, but she can't for the life of her figure out what it is. Shrugging off a sense of unease, she continues in the opposite direction, not wanting to be seen.

After that episode the troop eludes her for several days. Joan wonders if they have left. It's late on a Wednesday morning when she unexpectedly stands face to face with Hermione again. The encounter takes place at the end of the short lane leading to the high street from the car park. A horde of little old ladies have poured out of a large tour bus and are tottering frenziedly towards the single public toilet at the entrance.

Hermione's family has escaped the stampeding biddies and is turning the corner up ahead. Hermione, heading for the same corner, stops when she spots Joan and at once demands to know why she is wearing wellies when it's not raining? When it's not even going to rain? This she knows, because there's not a cloud in the sky, is there?

"It is," she informs Joan, "ever so silly."

"But I *am* silly, remember?" says Joan, slightly peeved.

Never in a hurry, the girl ponders the statement. "No, I don't think so," comes the verdict. "I think maybe Daddy was wrong. Sometimes he is, you know."

"You don't say?"

"No, I don't. Lizzie does."

Best change the subject. "And how is Lizzie?"

"She's ever so tired of going for vigourating walks. It makes her feet hurt awfully."

"Well, she has rather small feet, doesn't she?"

"Yes. And Daddy walks very fast, you see, cause it's good for the cari . . . cari . . . car-*dee*-vaksular system."

"I see."

At that moment, Hermione's mother pops her head around the corner looking for her youngest. Seeing Hermione talk to that strange woman again, she hurries forward and, grabbing her daughter hard by the arm, shoots Joan a look that spills dread and disgust. Joan feels amused pity as she watches the woman drag her stoical child to safety.

It's the last time she sees them. Afterwards she deems it best to cool her compulsion lest she gets arrested for stalking small children. It would not look good on the record of a well-respected Canadian crown attorney.

The following Saturday morning Abigail drives in to Bendlesfield train station to pick up the new laser printer she has ordered. It arrived by the two-carriage toy train on the Friday afternoon. She struggles through the door an hour later with a cumbersome box which Joan helps her lift onto the desk in her study.

"I saw the funniest thing at the station," says Abigail. "Not ha-ha funny, just funny odd. A bit sad too." Her voice is matter-of-fact, her eyes wistful. She glances sideways at her sister.

"Well," says Joan, "I'm all ears."

"Okay. Well, there was this couple waiting for the train, you know, stiff, silent, awkward people, repressed middle class on the lower side of the scale, that sort of type. This place is full of them during holiday time. Private people that keep to themselves. They rent cottages all around the countryside. Trek along the footpaths for a week or two. The wife was of the patient yes-dear variety, the husband this supreme fool decked out like he was going on a damn African safari."

"Interesting. Go on."

"Well, they had three little girls, but it was the youngest that caught my attention. She stood by herself by one of the waiting room windows clutching the gaudiest doll you ever saw. Once or twice she held it up to her ear pretending it was whispering to her. Then she widened her eyes and shook her head in amazement. It looked so cute. When the dad ordered them out onto the platform, she kept standing there with her back to him as if she hadn't heard him."

"She just stood there?"

"Yes, she stood by the window looking at two little girls on the opposite pavement. They were dancing along, those two, hand in hand, twirling and skipping, merry as can be. She seemed fascinated by them. When her dad shouted at her not to dawdle or they'd leave without her, she turned around and tried to imitate the girls on the sidewalk. You know, trying to do a similar dance with her doll. Only the poor thing couldn't pull it off. Her little legs were too stiff. It made her stumble and drop her doll. In the end she gave up and trudged after the rest of her family. Trying hard not to cry."

"The poor thing!"

"Yes, that's what I thought." Abigail falls silent for a moment, throwing Joan a quick glance before saying, "You know, and you'll have to forgive me for saying so, but she reminded me of Kevin."

Kevin is Joan's youngest son. He recently turned twenty-four. A young man of defiant spirit.

"How on earth can a little English girl remind you of six-foot-two Canadian Kevin?"

"I'm not talking physical resemblance, Joanie. But remember when he was little? Always lagging behind? You always shouting, 'Keviiin! Wake up already!' Remember?"

"I most certainly do not." It's true, she does not. She has no recollection of anything of the sort, but Abigail's talk of Kevin upsets her all the same. It's not what she came to England for, being compared to some pompous pukka-sahib.

"Oh, come on, Joanie! You can't possibly have forgotten?"

"And Kevin never had a doll."

"I know Kevin never had a doll, for chrissake! But he had that ugly black and white bear with the pink baby socks, didn't he? And that polka dot bow tie his brothers put on it as a joke, only Kevin decided the bear liked it just fine. Surely you haven't forgotten *that*?"

"What bear?"

"You know the one I mean! He never went anywhere without it, for God's sake, Joanie! What was its name? Tilley? No, wait . . . Talley . . . no . . . Tooley! Yes, that's it, Tooley the Bear!"

"I don't recall any bear." Joan does not remember. Nor does she not remember. "How can you compare a boy to a girl? And how dare you compare me to some pompous twit of an Englishman?"

"A child's a child. An overbearing parent is an overbearing parent."

Joan explodes. "I BEG YOUR PARDON?"

Abigail does not bat an eyelid. "Oh, don't look like that, for crying out loud! You know what I mean! It's not like you were a bad parent, Joanie. You just had firm opinions."

"I see no comparison at all." Joan feels her face heat up. It's a blush of intense fury.

Abigail forgets to bite her tongue. "How can you *not* see the comparison? Are you selectively blind?"

Joan sputters. "Because there *is* no comparison!"

"You just won't let yourself remember, will you? You're so damn stubborn!"

"Remember *what*, for heaven's sake?"

"Kevin pretending to be deaf. Walking off to talk to strangers. Whispering to that raggedy bear. Daydreaming. Rebelling. Then blaming it on the bear, saying 'Tooley told me to'. And you going, 'Keviiin!' And you're telling me you don't recall any of that?"

"That's right. I don't." Each reply shorter, more clipped.

"Amazing! Could be early Alzheimer's, I suppose. Maybe you should have a brain scan when you get home."

Abigail can tell by Joan's stare that she has donned her well-worn suit of armour. It's what she always does in the face of criticism. Abigail decides to cut it short without giving in. "Oh, don't be so damn huffy! You're a grown woman! And a grandmother. Kevin's a grown man. Anyway, you'd have liked the little girl at the station. She was the sweetest little thing, her ponytail bobbing up and down when she tried to dance. I felt rather bad for her."

"She'll be all right, I'm sure. You always exaggerate." Thinking, repeatedly, I'm *not* like that.

"I do *not*! Besides, Kevin turned out all right. So he didn't go into law, big deal. He's doing just fine, isn't he? Didn't he get a scholarship to do his doctorate in archeology?"

"He did. Top of his year. He's . . . Was I really that judgmental?" Joan asks the question in order for Abigail to gush her protestations, to say of course not, darling sister, you were a role model for us all.

"You certainly were," says Abigail. "Now then, do you know how to hook up this frigging printer?"

"Of course I do." Resentment coats Joan's face like an early frost. She can't stop thinking of Hermione's little legs being unfamiliar with the simple rhythm of joy. Kevin was never like that. "Kevin was a good dancer," she blurts out, aware of the supreme idiocy of the statement.

"He was okay. But only because you made him go to dance school even though he hated it."

"I sent him because he was good at it. He had talent."

"Think again."

"What do you mean?"

"Well, he didn't exactly skip and twirl with natural grace, did he?"

"Of course he did!"

Abigail sighs and slides a hand over the new printer as if trying to calm it, and looks at her sister, wondering why pompous people have such a raw talent for self-delusion. Maybe you can't have one without the other. She shakes her head and bursts out laughing. No point arguing with a brick wall. "I'll leave you to it," she says and disappears.

Standing alone by the laser printer, the warmth of the afternoon sun trying hard to melt her frosted features, Joan, against her will, looks back. Then farther back. Squints. Looks farther still. It takes courage to do so. Her hands are trembling, but she does not give up.

And sure enough, when she goes back far enough, she sees it, the memory waving back at her, shouting, How the hell are you, Mrs. D! Bet you didn't expect to see me here today?

No, says Mrs. D. I did not.

Tough luck, says the memory and slaps her in the face.

They had been on holiday in Cornwall. It was their first trip to England, their first holiday abroad since Kevin was born. He had just turned five. They were hiking on the moors of the Land's End peninsula. Up in the empty landscape where the wind wailed like a live thing, sentineled by two tall megaliths, stood the donut-shaped stone known as Men-an-Tol.

According to legend the mysterious stones had once been part of a larger stone circle thought to be an ancient burial ground. They were supposed to have stood there for thousands of years. Men-an-Tol was believed to have curative powers, and people had for centuries brought their children there to pass them naked through the hole in the stone three times in the hope of curing rickets, scrofula and other diseases common as dirt at the time. The procedure worked best if performed at dawn against the sun.

Adults, harder to cure, had to crawl through nine times.

One by one, the Deacon family crawled through the hole. They did so for fun and only once, not suffering from rickets. Nor were they naked. They did not do so at dawn, or against the sun. There was no sun.

The mist began to roll in unexpectedly when they arrived at the stones. In no time at all the fog had grown so thick it obscured the horizon. By the time they had made it through the stone — all except for Kevin — it had eclipsed everything else as well.

They pretended that if they crawled through the stone to the other side, they would end up in a different world, a place of sunshine and blue summer sky. Joan, taking the lead, was the first through. Kevin was last because he flatly refused.

Or, rather, Tooley did.

Kevin stood pigeon-toed, red baseball cap back to front, mist twirling around him, about to embrace him and carry him away. He clutched the black and white bear wearing pink baby socks and a red and white polka dot bow tie, while all around the mist rolled, roiled, got thicker by the minute, more sinister.

She felt the cold fear of losing him.

"Keviiin! Come on! Or you'll be left behind in that foggy old world all by yourself!"

Was that her voice? *That* shrill?

"I don't care." Kevin stood firm, peering angrily at her through the hole in the stone. "Why do I have to be in *your* world? Tooley doesn't like it there. He says you hate him."

"Don't be silly! You can crawl through the stone and still be in your own world." Thinking, screw that fucking bear. I'm going to throw the damn thing out when Kevin's asleep. The night before we leave England. Pretend Tooley ran away to join the circus.

Kevin repeats his question. "Why do I have to live in your stupid world?"

"Sweetie, there's only one world. This is just a game."

"That's not true!"

The idea had been for them to have a family adventure, to wiggle snail-like through the stone, taking pictures for posterity. It's what you do when you're on holiday.

When Kevin still refused to move, Joan reached through the hole, grabbed him by his bony little shoulders and dragged him through the stone in one swift motion. He screamed in rage at this violent rebirth, being forced against his will to pass through another small opening into a world where voices screamed at him out of the fog.

"Tooley and I don't want to be in your world!"

She ignored his childish tantrum.

Craig did not take any pictures of Kevin being dragged through the stone, arms protectively around his bear.

She did not mean to be bossy, and it certainly was not her intention to upset her youngest son. Only by then the fog had made the empty moor invisible. She was afraid they would get lost, afraid Kevin would be left behind, afraid they would never find him again. She did not want to lose him, because she loved him too much.

She had assumed he understood that.

Kevin had always lagged behind.

Kevin and Tooley.

That day, having dragged her protesting five-year-old and his bear through the magic stone into the other world that was not supposed to be foggy, they got lost. It was like being surrounded by a grey concrete wall.

"Is this fog real?" asked Jeff, their oldest.

"Of course it is."

"It's creepy."

They were forced to stop, fearful to take another step, when through the fog there appeared a tall dark shape followed by a small squat one. They were almost face to face before the tall shape turned into a woman. The small shape at her feet was a black terrier. An ordinary woman, as far as they could make out. They could not see her clearly, but there seemed to be nothing remarkable about her appearance. She was dressed in a cardigan and rubber boots, a scarf tied around her head, looking like she knew her way about.

Relieved to see her outline, they asked for directions.

"Straight down this path," she told them, pointing in the direction she had come from, "then turn left when you come to a gate." They thanked her and began walking in the direction indicated, step by careful step. The woman and her dog had already disappeared in the fog.

At the outline of the gate were they were supposed to turn left, Kevin erupted in another furious protest. "No! She's wrong! We should be going that way, over *there*! There's a tower over there. *That's* where we should be going." He pointed in the opposite direction.

"No, Kevin, the woman said . . . "

"I don't care! It's the wrong way! She was lying!" He shouted the accusation.

"Honey, that woman lives around here. Don't you think she knows her way about?"

"She's lying! That path goes away from the sea! I know it!"

By then something in his face had caught his father's attention. "How do you know, Kev?"

"Because Tooley can hear the ocean breathing way over there." He pointed again. "I can hear it too."

Nobody else could hear a damn thing. As Joan told Kevin, the ocean was too far away, and besides water doesn't breathe, so stop your nonsense.

Before they had time to react, Kevin had marched off into the dense fog. They had no choice but to run after the stubborn child before they lost him, all of them shouting "Kevin, wait up!" By then Joan was cold with terror. Craig looked like he might burst into tears.

Hurrying blindly after Kevin they arrived at a tall brick structure that looked like a tower. Just then the fog began to lift. As swiftly as it had descended it was gone. It was with immeasurable relief they were able to discern first Kevin, then the path leading down to the road, and, as they walked towards the path, the sea and the faraway horizon. The tower turned out to be the remnant of a building at an old mine site.

"How did you know there was a tower, Kev?"

The sun appeared, the sky turned blue, the world was a safe place.

"I saw the top of it from far away before it got foggy. In the old world. You know, when you carried me on your shoulders, Dad. Remember?"

"Good for you, Kev." Craig clamped a hand on his youngest son's shoulder and did not let go of him until they reached their rental car.

In the car they debated whether the woman had lied or if they had misunderstood. Craig's opinion was that she had mistaken them for Americans and, being anti-American, had sent them in the opposite direction.

Jeff and Russell, the two older boys, were convinced she was a ghost. "And the dog too."

"Ghosts don't wear rubber boots," Joan informed them.

"How do you know? Have you ever seen a ghost?"

"There are no ghosts."

According to Kevin, Tooley knew exactly why the woman had lied, but that Tooley would never tell because they'd never believe him anyway.

A comment Joan dismissed with "Oh, Kevin."

She had not thrown the old bear away, that much she remembers.

What happened to it?

Does he still have it?

Kevin never knew how to dance. He was not a graceful child. He was tuned to a different wavelength, which, while providing no sense of rhythm, gave him an unwavering sense of direction.

When he moved away from home at age eighteen, Joan assumed that it was his inner voice guiding him, the voice of Tooley, and that he knew where he was going, and why. And he did know, by the looks of it. He is doing splendidly in his own world and has no intention of ever crawling through a magic circle back into the confinement of his mother's well regulated one.

Because there is, Kevin discovered early in life, more than one world.

It's not until now, standing by the window in Abigail's study with its low ceiling and slanting floor, arms crossed, shoulders tensed, that Joan wonders for the first time whether

Kevin prefers to pay an inflated rent for a small one-bedroom apartment in faraway Vancouver in order to escape his mother rather than live at home for free. If it's his way of impressing upon her that her world is not for him.

He doesn't call very often. She calls him at least once a week to ask why she hasn't heard from him, trying not to sound like a nag. "I just got back from a dig in Iran," he will say, or some equally solid defense. Excavating in Brittany. Digging holes in Uzbekistan. Looking for Neolithic treasures beyond the reach of her judgment.

Jeff and Russell are both lawyers, still living in Calgary, their hometown. Not because they are particularly obedient; they take after their mother.

Next time she calls Kevin, she will ask if he still has that bear of his. Tooley. Ask him if he remembers where it came from. (Did they buy it for him? She can't recall.)

Craig will know, but Craig is in Canada. Craig talks to Kevin all the time. He calls him from work. They talk regularly, and they e-mail back and forth on a daily basis. Only if Joan asks, does her husband tell her what Kevin is up too. If she reminds him that Kevin is her son too, he just looks at her with his own brand of hostile amusement.

Joan and Craig do not eat supper together very often anymore. They blame it on their hectic schedules, things getting in the way, meetings and such. But once in a blue moon they dutifully sit down for a meal, giving it a chance, trying their best to make amicable conversation with the aid of a good bottle of wine.

"Kevin should be back in Canada soon, shouldn't he?" she asked the last time they had supper one on one. It was in a Thai restaurant; she so seldom has time to cook.

"Oh, he's been back for a couple of weeks," replied Craig, twirling his pad Thai noodles.

"He has? How is he?"

"He's just fine."

"What's he up to?"

"Right now he's at home working on his thesis, but he's going back to Uzbekistan in the fall for another stint."

"Oh. For how long?"

"I'm not sure. For the winter, I think."

"I see."

Joan looks out the window onto the old meadow. At first it's just a blur. She blinks. Blinks some more. As it slowly comes into focus, she sees how drenched in flowers it is, wildflowers blue and white, red and yellow. It was yesterday too, but today the flowers appear more abundant, more vivid. Mossy boulders lie like sleeping trolls among the flowers. A rabbit sits on one of them, its nose twitching.

The meadow slopes down to a row of crooked pear trees growing along the crumbling stone wall to the east. Their branches droop with the burden of excess fruit. It's been a benign season. Behind the wall — it's as mossy as the boulders — over to the right, there is a secret clearing where, according to Abigail, a golden carpet of primroses grows thick in the spring.

Joan has no idea what a primrose looks like.

Beyond the clearing a heedless little river dances and skips, ever sure of itself, gaining momentum on its journey to the open sea.

CHARMED

EMMA WAS YOUNG WHEN THEY FIRST MET, but not as young as Pierre. Pierre was so painfully conscious of his lack of years, the fact that he was legally a child still, that he was forced to lie. When Emma said she had recently turned nineteen, Pierre, not batting an eyelid, claimed that, well, what do you know, so had he.

The truth was he had turned seventeen less than a week earlier, an accomplishment so unimpressive he had not dared reveal it for fear of being shunned. A cowardly attitude for a social rebel and freethinker, and don't think he wasn't aware of the irony.

But he was right. She *would* have shunned him. Called him a presumptuous beanpole of a brat.

When Pierre revealed the truth three years later (he was basically honest, only in no hurry about it), Emma had the grace to receive the revelation as an endearing offering rather than a desperate lie begging for retroactive forgiveness.

These days she thinks: Oh, that nonconformist, avant-garde Pierre! That one-of-a-kind Pierre! He would have been so easy to forgive no matter how grisly his crime.

Not that Pierre would ever commit a grisly crime.

He came sauntering into the second-rate art school one night, straight out of a dimension Emma had until then been ignorant of. Half an hour late for class, and unperturbed by the tardiness, he suddenly stood among them, dressed in purple velvet pants that looked like they had been painted onto his long skinny legs. So relaxed he appeared slightly somnambulant, he politely announced to the room at large that his name was Pierre, that he was a new student, and say, where is the teacher? Is it too late to register?

It was hard to tell if his calm was due to confidence or indifference.

"Can I help you?" Gunnar had come scooting from his office. Gunnar was the art teacher. His voice sounded threatening. When he disapproved of something, two sharp creases appeared between his black bushy eyebrows, making him look demonic. That evening the creases grew deep as soon as he laid eyes on purple-legged Pierre standing with arms crossed in the middle of the room, gazing about like a potential buyer of the property, large sleepy eyes sliding over the sixteen students busy at their easels, each one more preoccupied with trying to look artistic than with actually producing anything with artistic merit.

Suddenly the newcomer stopped looking sleepy and became too distracted to pay attention to what Gunnar was saying. The reason for the distraction was Emma, or, as she had her back to him, Emma's long black hair. It began pulling at Pierre's eyeballs in a peculiar manner, and then — once her appearance got proper hold of his attention — hypnotized him.

"EXCUSE ME!" roared Gunnar. The creases between his eyebrows deepened as he reached up and tapped Pierre on shoulder.

"Huh?" Genuinely surprised, Pierre peered down to discover a pissed-off demon fuming at him. "I'd like to enroll," he informed it.

"Then come with me to the office," ordered Gunnar, frown intact.

Pierre would later confess to Emma's friend Helen — who would never tell Emma — that he fell in love with Emma even before he saw her face. There was something about the way her hair hung halfway down her back, so heavy and thick — and later, when he took a few more steps into the room and saw her face in profile, the way her bangs flopped into her eyes.

It had reminded him of a wild, ungroomed pony, he said.

Helen hated ponies after that.

Pierre was too absorbed beholding Emma's hair that night to notice her staggering lack of talent. The nude on her canvas had swelled towards the edges like dough spreading unrestrained due to an excess of yeast. The peculiar dimensions looked nothing like the bored naked woman perched on a barstool on the podium waiting for the next cigarette break.

When Pierre eventually did acknowledge the boundless distance between Emma and artistic genius, he merely concluded that this irrelevant detail had nothing to do with Emma's special essence. The way he saw it, there were too many artistic geniuses milling about the world as it was, but only one Emma.

Emma had always considered herself the artistic type and did not see why she should let a lack of talent stand between herself and artistic expression, for if she did, how would she ever develop any latent gift?

Pierre, not shy by nature, became so preoccupied simply watching her during those first few classes that it tied his tongue in a knot. He could not think of anything interesting to say. A truly extreme situation.

It took two weeks before he worked up the nerve to start a conversation with the wild-haired pony who by then was busy adding various shades of purple to her nude. The purples gave the swelling curves on her canvas the appearance of a rotting carcass. Strong emotions crashed inside Pierre like a stormy sea. It was tricky, for while these emotions made him feel giddily alive, his internal tidal waves had to remain nonchalantly hidden. Starting a conversation that exhibited obvious indifference required concentration. He had to make it clear to her that her response — or lack thereof, heaven forbid — did not matter to his emotional well-being.

Emma, knowing nothing of Pierre's inner hurricanes, and suffering no unforeseen weather patterns herself, explained to him on the Thursday evening when he took the first step and admired her hair out loud, that she was part gypsy, which was why her hair was so black.

It was a story she was fond of telling. Sometimes she claimed to be the adopted offspring of Spanish aristocrats killed in a car accident when holidaying in Scandinavia. The version depended entirely on her mood and the gullibility of the listener.

She was neither part gypsy nor an orphaned Spanish aristocrat, but the lies were romantic, and romantic allure is not to be sneezed at. Adhering to the unyielding fact that she was just another kid on the block was simply tedious. Certain truths are irrelevant. Emma merely refurbishing her ancestry for the benefit of mankind. The world was too full of ordinary people as it was.

With Pierre she used the gypsy variant, sensing it would have been his preferred choice had he been able to choose.

If Pierre believed her — he said he did — it was because he felt like it.

Her natural hair colour was a common working-class brown. It would, she was convinced, not have held Pierre's attention. (It is true. It would not.) As it lacked poetry, she never revealed this fact, not even retroactively, not wanting to mar his illusions. For make no mistake, Pierre was a master illusionist. That was his charm. He created illusions with acute attention to detail, the overall effect being that there was much more to Pierre than first met the eye.

Ordinary people and tedious facts held no place in Pierre's dimension either. It was a place deliciously free from restraint, but full of possibilities, an Aladdin's lamp that he invited very few people to rub against.

The first time he spoke to Emma, he dragged his right hand through his dark shoulder-length hair and she noticed the ring on his finger. In its solid silver custody sat imbedded a sizeable chunk of green amber full of shadows and secrets and something that looked like a prehistoric species of ant. Emma grabbed his hand and asked where he got that amazing ring. Leaving his hand in hers, he wanted to stroke her wrist with his thumb. It would have been so easy to give in.

But Pierre did not give in. He might have been young, but he was no weakling. He pulled himself together and told her about a silversmith he knew. Down by the coast, he said, halfway between Ystad and Simrishamn, thereabouts, down by the Baltic Sea where the winds are salty, there's an old man in an ancient limestone cottage who makes jewelry. He works alone in his studio, close to shore, the waves of a restless sea crashing almost onto his front step. Obliging, Pierre let her lift up his hand, turning the ring to the light so she could get a closer look. The amber had dark secret areas and a bright patch like a tiny meadow filled with sunshine.

"Is that an ant?"

"Yes," confirmed Pierre, "that is an ant. A peculiar kind of ant, for sure. At least part of one."

Emma studied the large stone for a long time that evening, imagining the sea tossing and turning, the wind howling, the old man working alone in his cottage by flickering candlelight when the storm killed the electricity. And she thought, as she watched the light play with the stone's secret, that there must be times when the sea is calm and the man leaves his work bench and goes for walks on the beach. Looking for gifts of amber that the Baltic Sea has washed onto shore for him to find.

If creating special effects came naturally to Pierre or if he at worked at it, Emma did not bother to determine, for what did it matter? It was such effortless magic, why pick at it?

Pierre's family, unlike most of the people Emma knew, was not working class. They lived in an old apartment in an area of the city that had once again become fashionable. It was many-roomed and had high ceilings, but was more or less unadorned and purposely so, full of echoing empty spaces and modern pieces of furniture with sharp angles. The two oversized paintings in the living room were ultramodern, showing little, offering nothing to an eye hungry for meaning. That's because they were status symbols, Pierre explained during Emma's first visit. He was delighted that she viewed them with contempt.

"My mother loves status symbols," he said. "She thinks they define her."

"And do they?"

"Unfortunately."

In the kitchen where Pierre got them a bottle of orange juice there were two refrigerators side by side, one for fancier food and one for ordinary everyday food. There was not a great deal of food in the one assigned to common comestibles. The other one was padlocked.

Emma's family lived in a much smaller, two-bedroom apartment where china figurines decorated the linen cupboard and sports magazines and women's weeklies lay scattered on the coffee table beside the ashtray that held her father's pipe. Her mother's knitting nested in one of the chairs. Emma had to share a bedroom with her brother and his smelly soccer shirts.

They only had one refrigerator, not nearly as big as the ones in Peter's kitchen, but it was full of food.

She did not tell Pierre this.

On the door to Pierre's room hung an old-fashioned sign that read: *Café Unwirklich*. Café Unreal. It was shaped like a cloud, smoky and shapeless. Pierre admitted to having stolen it in Munich the previous summer.

How?

By standing on a friend's shoulder, detaching it with a screwdriver.

Where did he get the screwdriver?

He had stolen it in a department store earlier that day, with that very purpose in mind.

And nobody tried to stop him stealing the sign in the middle of a public place?

Well, it was late at night, there weren't many people about, just two drunks who kept cheering him on. Also, it wasn't a very nice place, the unreal café, full of loud, pretentious people, too disappointingly real. But he had taken a liking to the sign. Had decided he deserved it more than they did.

He kept to himself the fact that he had been barely sixteen at the time, on a school trip.

Emma had to agree that the sign was totally suitable, for stepping into Pierre's room from the stark trendiness of the rest of the apartment was like leaving cold reality behind. Even though the room was not very large, the dimension that was Pierre's appeared limitless.

The most capacious piece of furniture was an old-fashioned dresser, bowlegged and imposing, covered in twirling patterns of purple, red, orange, green and some colours that Emma was sure did not exist outside Pierre's room. He had painted it himself, he confessed, paying respectful attention to detail, having sensed at a young age that beautiful objects would be important to him, a buffer between him and the mundane.

"These purple bits," he pointed out, "are all different body shapes. And see this orange pattern? All animal shapes. Notice how beautifully they fit together with all the stars and moons and clouds in between?"

"It must have taken you forever." Emma's shining eyes pleased him no end.

"It seemed like it. I stayed up late every night until it was done. Twenty-two nights. But it was worth it, don't you think?"

"Oh, I do," she sighed. "I do."

That Pierre! Such a fantasist!

The top of the dresser was crammed with what Pierre referred to as *objets d'enchantement*. Who else but Pierre would keep a glass slipper on the dresser, claiming it belonged to Cinderella? A fragile piece of footwear three inches long?

"Did she really have such small feet?"

"Yes," said Pierre, "Cinderella had very small feet. Like you, Emma-gemma."

"I'm a size 38," said Emma.

"To me your feet look very small," said Pierre.

Beside the slipper sat a wooden box. It was painted in the same uninhibited colours and patterns as the dresser and looked like a rectangular outgrowth of it. The box contained his Viking jewelry. Rare and precious-looking replicas of original, excavated pieces.

Where had he found them?

Here and there.

There was a Byzantine coin made into a pendant for a necklace, though it lacked a chain, a bracelet braided with thick strands of silver, a small animal shaped with silver wire "unearthed just outside the village where my grandmother was born." Pierre was unsure if it was a deer, but agreed that it looked like one despite the strange horns.

The fourth piece was a clasp, presumably meant for a shawl or a belt, a twisted slim golden band, heart-shaped with a curl at the tip. He held it up to Emma who was wearing a red and yellow scarf. "Do you want to try it on?"

"Can I?"

"Of course you can."

What she wanted to ask was, "Can I keep it, can I, can I? Can I be special too? Please?"

What he wanted to say was, "You can keep it if you stay with me forever."

She handed it back to him and he returned it to the box and slowly closed the lid.

There were several other containers, all made of wood, each one painted in colours that would make a rainbow blanch with envy. Some were shaped like sea chests, others like caskets and snuffboxes of various sizes. On the floor, near the door, a large clay amphora sat lodged in an umbrella stand. It contained all the marbles Pierre had won as a child. He had been the unchallenged champion of his neighbourhood. On her first visit he invited Emma to try and lift it. It did not budge. He gave her a marble instead, one of the biggest ones, a smooth globe full of purple and yellow swirls. It rolled around in the palm of her hand, cold at first, then warming up as if it had decided it liked her.

The walls in his world were painted green — like a forest in spring, said Pierre, full of the lightness of hope — and hung with paintings that resembled some kind of psychedelic folk art. Each painting was signed by Pierre, the earliest one dating back six years. In their midst hung an MFF soccer shirt, its back to the room, displaying the number nine.

In the window between two yellow begonias stood a vase of flowers surrounded by statuettes of stocky peasants dancing. The bouquet on that first visit consisted of a thick dark gold circle of marigolds surrounded by pale blue forget-me-nots. A red rose had been placed in the centre of the arrangement, making the bouquet look like a single flower, the forget-me-nots providing a becoming lace edge.

Emma had never met anybody her age, male or female, who kept fresh flowers in their room. "You really do live in unreality, don't you?" she asked, her eyes wide, not disappointing him.

"Of course I do," he confirmed. "And you can live in it too. It's not that difficult." He crossed his arms, standing before her like a proud master builder.

She felt barren in the face of his splendour, having nothing to offer in return for having been allowed into the tantalizing bit of universe he had conjured up, with its apt sign on the door: *Café Unwirklich*.

Yet the moment demanded reciprocation. She concentrated so hard her brain hurt. Luckily one single distant memory heeded her desperate call. She had not thought about it for years, but discovered during a run-through in her head that all the important details remained more or less intact. Just as well, it was the only *unwirklich* incident she had ever experienced. She decided to share it, blushing at first, thinking it was probably not enough, not very interesting, stupid even. He might laugh. For sure Pierre would laugh his head off.

Or not. It *had* been a special moment in her life, so she gave it a try. "Your room makes me think the world is not at all what it seems."

"The world is *not* what it seems, Emma-gemma, don't you know that?" And then, as if he knew she had something to share: "Please go on. What were you going to tell me?"

This boy! So wise beyond his years! He would never laugh at her.

Realizing that she was safe from ridicule gave her the courage to continue. "It reminds me of this one time when I was very little, one morning when my mother was taking me to my grandma's on her way to work, the way she always did. I was sitting in the child seat behind her on her bicycle, so I must have been about three or so, I guess. Maybe younger. It was very early in the morning and summer, you know, just another day. We were going the usual route when all of a sudden the street disappeared. I swear, that is what truly happened. The street was there one second and gone the next, and instead there is my mom pedaling her old bike through an absolutely unearthly garden. Or forest, I'm not sure how to describe it, it was so green and dense, almost like a jungle, but there were flowers everywhere, covering the ground and the bushes. I could reach out and touch them, feel the dew drops on the petals, smell their fragrance. Leaves from branches overhead slid across my face. Their touch felt so nice and cool. They, too, were moist with dew.

"But did my mother stop? Oh no! She was always in a hurry, having to get to work on time, so she just kept on pedaling. But I needed to know where we were and what was going on, so I leaned forward and asked her, 'Mommy, what *is* this place?' And she replied, 'What do you mean? It's the street behind the school, what's the matter with you?' 'No,' I said, thinking how strange that she wasn't speechless with awe, 'not the stupid old street. The garden!' 'Oh, stop talking nonsense,' she said, not even slowing down to look around. Then I realized that she couldn't see what I was seeing. I didn't understand how that could be, so I never said another word about it. Until now, that is.

"We never biked through that forest-garden-whatever-it-was again. It took only minutes, maybe less, and it was gone like a bubble had burst. It was a one-time event.

"But wasn't that weird? What do you think happened? My face and my fingers were still wet from the dew of the flowers after we returned to the everyday world."

Pierre was thrilled to learn about her experience, envious and impressed. But he could not explain what had happened to Emma that day, for which he was glad, he said, because he would not want to sully it with something as crass as speculation. A memory like that ought not to be tampered with.

He did offer, "What I do know is that the brief visit to that place was a gift given to you because you're special. And *that* you must never question."

Emma was delighted. She had proved herself to be in his league.

The bond between Pierre and Emma remained firm over the next five years. During the last two of those years — years both short and long — they did not meet very often, but that was inconsequential. Their bond was elastic; it held. The relationship defied classification. It was not a boyfriend-girlfriend tie, nor was it a platonic friendship. Nor could it be pinpointed on any convenient scale in between. Like Emma's ride through the dewy garden that was not there, it was not subject to speculation.

Three years after Pierre started evening classes at the art school, he was awarded a scholarship and went off to a prestigious art institute in Paris to learn to do clever things with metals. Pierre, unlike the ragtag wannabe artists at Gunnar's school, was blessed with unique talent, a gift he remained remarkably modest about, but which explained the ease with which he created illusions.

Everybody agreed that one day that freaky boy would make a name for himself. Most said it without envy.

In no time at all another two years had gone by. Then one evening Pierre called Emma. He had returned from France earlier in the day and was eager to hear her voice. It was a month or so after Emma herself had arrived back from Italy where she had worked in a bar earning money that she subsequently spent in other bars. In this manner she had been helping prop up the Italian economy for nearly four months.

Pierre said he wanted to see her. Those were his words, straight to the point, wasting no time on chitchat: "Emma-gemma, I want to see you."

It was December already. They had not met since June. It had been a wet fall in Paris, Pierre complained. Grey and dismal, sidewalks full of umbrellas. Streets clogged with traffic, horns honking. He now needed the warmth and colour of her presence.

Could they meet soon? Later that evening?

Emma had never told him that if the colours of her presence shone brightly around him it was only because he inspired her to light up. The reason she never had said those words, and certainly did not utter them that day, was because he might take them the wrong way.

There was something else she also did not tell him. Something important. She knew she would have to spill the beans before the conversation was over, it was only fair — if fair was the right word. But it would be difficult. How to explain that since they last met, life had rearranged itself in a pattern so extraordinary it would sever their special bond? For, sadly, this much she was aware of. Why it had to be so she did not know.

Pierre did not raise his voice, but his unhesitating want pushed through the receiver like a moist breeze in her ear. It was not at all unpleasant, this want of Pierre's. "What are you doing in the near future?" he asked. It sounded as if he had some suggestions, should she lack ideas.

Oh shit, she thought. I have to tell him. Get it over with. I have to. Somehow. She felt awkward, like she had done something highly inappropriate. Committed a morally offensive crime. But why would it matter? They were just good friends, it was no big deal. He might be happy for her.

"I'm moving to Canada." She felt like a supreme twit hearing herself utter those words because, although true, they sounded ridiculous. It was not the kind of statement people went around making in those days.

She could tell by unflappable Pierre's dead silence that the sentence had thrown him.

After he pulled himself together, he wished to know *why* she was moving to such a pointless place. He was the first to recognize that it was in vogue to travel to all kinds of far off countries, exotic, dangerous destinations cheap to survive in. Hot, poor, dirty countries riddled with incurable diseases.

Nobody ever went to Canada. Canada was not exotic. It was just a wasteland on the map. Didn't she know that?

She said she did know that.

It just so happened that Canada's lack of danger and dengue fever was immaterial. Because it was not so much the *where* as the *why*. At first she did not dare tell him *why* she was moving to such an absurd place so unexpectedly, only she could not bear lying to him. He was her special friend.

To be honest, he was more than a friend.

Wasn't he?

Yes, she thought, somehow he was.

Then it wasn't as if he meant nothing to her, was it?

No. But he was *not* her boyfriend, was he?

Well, no.

So tell him then, for God's sake! Don't be so stupid.

The truth — shameful all of a sudden — was that she was getting married. She was tying a respectable, legal knot with a Canadian graduate student she had met in a bar in Rome one weekend. But how to tell Pierre that she had fallen in love with a Canadian? Pierre had probably never met a Canadian. Emma had only met one and now she was marrying him — as if he was a rare specimen she must preserve like an insect in amber.

How to tell Pierre that the object of her affection was good-looking and blue-eyed, and so normal and so conventional, so free of modern angst, so unconcerned about the meaning of life, that it made him utterly exceptional?

How on earth to reveal that to Pierre?

And then expect him to convey his heartfelt congratulations? For the thing was, she wanted his blessing. Needed it.

She was at a loss as to how to go about telling him. In the end, what came out was, "Well, you see . . . uh . . . I'm kind of . . . you know . . . like . . . uh . . . getting married . . . He's Canadian." Uttered in the same manner you might when confessing to having contracted venereal disease.

The description of her immediate future sounded bland when toned down to a vapidly stuttered utterance. At once she regretted her honesty. It was as uncalled for as confessing to dyeing one's hair. Pierre was still very young. Well, he was not a child anymore, he had turned twenty-two. Legally that made him an adult, but "adult" is a loose definition at the best of times.

Emma resented his weak spot for her. That too, was uncalled for.

She should have told him that she was going to Canada to do anthropological fieldwork, or some such appropriate lie. Analyze the mating call of the prairie farmer. (She had scraped together a degree in anthropology along the way. It had proved a good background for hanging out in Italian bars.)

The man she was going to marry came from a town in an area of western Canada called Alberta. It sounded effeminate, though her blue-eyed beloved had been quick to demand — with unexpected force — that she get one thing straight: Alberta was *not* effeminate, and she better believe it. Men are men in Alberta, make no mistake, my Swedish rose.

She did not pass on these tidbits to Pierre for fear he might laugh. Never tell the whole truth unless your life depends on it.

"Have a charmed life," said Pierre, emphasizing the word *charmed*. His voice was so low she could hardly make out what he said, apart from that one word, *charmed,* which raised itself from the whisper with bitter resonance. Then he hung up. He did not slam the receiver, Pierre would never do that, he replaced it very gently, as if he had all of a sudden grown fatigued.

Emma imagined his silver ring glinting on his hand, the secret in the green amber growing dark and melancholy. Waves crashing against a shore where an old man still sat alone in his cottage perfecting the shape of a silver ring, lodging in it a chunk of amber the sea had bestowed upon him. She thought of Pierre's hands, how they were always so warm and inviting. She thought of how she had never seen him without that ring.

And she thought how something important had just ended, quietly and without fanfare. Something she would have to do without for the rest of her life. Acknowledging the loss was a task she would have to work on.

It was the last time Pierre called her. She did not call him, nor did she question why she sometimes stood and looked at the phone with palpable reproach.

That aside, she was sufficiently in love with the conventional Canadian from the place with the feminine name that she sometimes managed to forget about her conversation with Pierre.

No, to be honest, she did not forget, she never would. But she tried to rearrange the past to fit the future, making it easier for herself, for she had always wanted to be in love in the bourgeois manner that the general population approves of. She was under the assumption that conformist love lasts longer, buoyed by that very approval.

But she *was* aware, despite all the conventional pre-approved love, that life would never be the same. It might be a happy life stretching ahead, decades of placid contentment filled with the pitter-patter of little Canadian feet, Alberta drenched in sunshine or snow or whatever the hell such a place is drenched in, but it would not be *charmed*. This was the word that sat lodged in her heart, impairing its beat ever so slightly. That quality, *charmed*, required a talent neither she nor her normal, pleasant Canadian beloved were equipped with.

Through the years she often wished that Pierre had not left her under the curse of an impossible word.

Emma does love him though, now, years later. Pierre, that is. Somehow. Still. Retroactively, if that's possible. Years later, thousands of miles away, Emma sits thinking of Pierre, thoughts tinged with a contained, persistent nostalgia. It's sometimes very faint, sometimes nearly nonexistent, but it's always present.

She polishes the memory like she would some old trinket discovered to be a valuable object worth a small fortune. Like the green amber in Pierre's ring and what it held, the prehistoric ant of sorts, a secret, and the little point of light that resembled a sunny meadow in some distant dimension. Like one of the *objets d'enchantement* he used to keep, the boxes carved and painted, his paintings, statues, flowers and marbles swirling with colours. Something to take to *The Antiques Roadshow* for admiring comments and the pleasant surprise of a generous appraisal.

Had she stayed in her hometown, and had she gone to see Pierre that day of his last call, there is no telling where she would be now, but strangely, inexplicably, it would not be with Pierre. That was not meant to be. She never loved him like that. There had been times when she wanted to, but you can't force love. Nor can you mould it into a specific shape to reflect your own needs or somebody else's.

Fate had saved Pierre for something more lasting.

That was always her explanation and it will have to suffice.

So she polishes her trinket. Polishes and polishes. It sparkles and shines, and still she keeps polishing as if trying to penetrate the shine to reach another layer, to discover what is hidden underneath. She thinks of all the objects with which Pierre created the illusion of magic in the drabness of everyday existence.

At the art school Emma had assumed herself to be in love. Not with Pierre, that was something different, her relationship with Pierre had its own unique importance. No, the object of her assumption was a young man named Leo. It was Pierre of all people who brought him to the school, Pierre who introduced her to him.

Yet Leo is absent from Emma's bouts of nostalgia, which is strange, considering that he was the one strumming the strings of her heart until she was convinced she heard a melody. So it goes. When the sand of time runs through the hourglass, some people are left untouched, others are buried. Some people matter, others do not. Leo was irrelevant despite his kinky auburn hair and funny green eyes.

Or were they brown? Grey?

It doesn't matter. He is buried in the sands of time. Should Emma try, she would be unable to see as much as an outline of his face in those endless dunes. Where he could have been, might have been, the winds of eternity have whistled by, hardly stirring the surface.

The man from Alberta, Darryl, mattered for a long time, might have mattered still had he not been more concerned with football than with marriage. Not the kind of football Emma was used to, which was called soccer in this new country. Darryl's obsession was with the North American variety where padded men lined up facing each other, only to hurl themselves into large heaps of arms, legs, and helmets. When she pointed out the homoerotic aspect of this game, Darryl was horrified, insulted, outraged. It was tantamount to being called a fag, he informed her coldly. He refused to speak to her for a week after that. Emma realized that being called a fag was something he abhorred. Perhaps when coming from a place with a feminine name, men had to try harder.

Emma remained married to Darryl for ten years. After a decade, to continue the relationship would have been meaningless. Having been more or less accused of being a fag, he never looked at her the same way again. Eventually he turned to women with bigger hair and larger breasts. In their arms he found the respect a man deserves.

After the divorce other men were invited to visit Emma's life periodically. First there was Jerry what's-his-name, the camping fanatic. That was when Emma learned that she did not like to sleep in the close vicinity of large bears and small insects. Jerry was followed by Colin the chemist, who was humourless, but a gourmet cook. Then there was Marshall the poet who was sensitive, not only needier than a newborn but proud of it. After Marshall came Neil the lawyer. She stayed with him for four years before breaking it off. Years of unsuitable men. None of them mattered in the end.

The main problem was this: their lives were not *charmed*.

Emma has not had a man in her life for quite a while now. She likes it that way.

Pierre, ageless wherever he is, still matters. Unlike the others, the shifting sands of time are powerless to contain him.

So how can Emma not love him — for lack of a better word — as the sun sets on another Alberta day? She needs something to shine a meaningful light on her life. It cheers her up. And what could be more meaningful than a person in whose heart she will remain eternally young and beautiful?

If and when he ever thinks of her, that is.

But he does.

She knows he does.

Not every day, that would be disturbing, but at special times. For example: when he buys a cardboard Easter egg for his children. Or grandchildren.

Yes, that is for sure when Pierre will think of Emma-gemma.

There had been no outrageous people in Emma's hometown back then. "Outrageous" as in exotic, avant-garde, fuck-the-status-quo. It was a respectable place, her hometown. Staid. A place where you could only be different if you were different in the same predictable manner as everybody else.

Some people nibbled at the edge of daring only to spit out the pieces, finding it did not agree with them. Most did not bother.

Then there was Pierre. Pierre took large bites, assuming the whole dangerous cake was his to sprinkle with sugar and devour. He gobbled each bite whole and burped contentedly, then asked for more.

When Pierre entered the art studio that Thursday night, Gunnar had not only frowned, he had turned pale. Had not known what to do, which was idiotic. Gunnar should have known better, he was an art teacher who claimed to have studied in Paris and Berlin, for heaven's sake. Surely he ought to be used to the true artistic type. This was what the students had whispered to each other when Gunnar ushered Pierre into the office to have him fill out the appropriate forms, unsure if Pierre's kind bothered with forms.

Ought Gunnar not to have relished the outrageous, the new? Why had squat pear-shaped Gunnar felt so threatened? Was it because romance in Gunnar's paint-splattered life was of the borrowed kind? Screwing the nude model on the couch in his office after class? As if nobody knew? He a married man and all?

Pierre was tall and slender. His high-heeled leather boots added another inch and a half to his six-foot-plus frame. His dark hair flowed thick and straight onto his shoulders. You could see every muscle in his spidery legs in their painted on velvet pants. The pants were nicely topped off with a turtleneck and a hand-embroidered vest. In the vest's embroidery, if you paid close attention, there were pictures. Pierre called it The Illustrated Vest. His grandmother had embroidered it. The pictures were from the fairy tales she had read to him when he was little. Pierre himself was a prince out of one of those stories. Moving with regal ease, ethereal but solid, prepared to live happily ever after.

And on his left hand, that solid silver ring with its large green chunk of polished amber. When Emma looked at it up close to discover more of its secrets, she had asked him if the darkness and light were caused by irregularities in the stone or something more forbidding, something secret.

"Well, if we knew that," Pierre had reflected, "it wouldn't be a secret, would it? What do you want, Emma-gemma, the unknown or certainty? There's not such thing as certainty, don't you know that?"

His eyes had been calm and superior as though they, like the amber, held some hidden knowledge Pierre thought it immodest to flaunt. It had been a while since he had bothered to notice the commotion his appearance caused. Aware that he was avant-garde, he knew this brought with it certain responsibilities.

He started at the art school that Thursday night and commenced not so much to stare at Emma as rest his eyes upon her. This continued through the entire three-hour lesson that first night, as well as Monday and Thursday the following week. He never said a word. To his chagrin she never paid any attention to him. So he thought.

After three lessons he could no longer resist. Be that girl standoffish or not, he was determined to talk to her. He struck up conversation, only to find that she wasn't standoffish at all. He could not believe his luck. What he really wanted to do was to kiss her right there and then and for the rest of the evening.

They began having conversations that grew longer and longer until they became long ribbons tying them together.

Pierre took to complementing her on the painting she had recently started, having given up on the nude. The new painting was a still life featuring an empty wine bottle (cheap Spanish), a bust of Beethoven, a rubber duck, and an economy-size pack of condoms (lent to her by a fellow student). It's possible that Pierre meant what he said, blinded by love or some other crippling condition. He took to sneaking up behind her when she was attacking her canvas with a dripping brush, putting his hands on her shoulders, leaning his cheek against her hair in a gesture that would have been forward had it not been Pierre. Doing so, he would watch her work for a while. "That's good, Emma-gemma," he would say. "I like the way you're contrasting that. That's an unusual shade of blue, how did you mix that? You have a great eye for colour."

Soon it was as if they had been close since long before they met.

Almost as close as Emma and her friend Helen had been for the last six years. Until Pierre showed up.

Helen was Emma's best friend. Her soap opera partner, as she now thinks of her. And what a soap opera it was. Up until Pierre's entry into their lives, only the tawdry, like Gunnar's affair with Hedvig, their middle-aged nude model, had added piquancy to their pseudo-artsy lives.

When Pierre had been a student at the school for half a term, he brought an acquaintance of his to the studio. Leo attended briefly, though why he bothered was anybody's guess. He had even less talent than Emma.

Emma took one look at him and it was hatred at first sight. He was an inch shorter than she was, and she could not stand the sight of the little weasel. That is, until the day when she without warning fell madly in love with him. It did not make any sense at all, least of all to her. True, she had wanted to be madly in love for as long as she could remember, but it was not supposed to be with anybody vaguely resembling Leo. Loving Leo was unambitious, defeatist, pointless. It was truly baffling.

Pierre noticed the change in her behaviour immediately. He grew pale, he mumbled when spoken to, refused to come to the coffeehouse after class. Instead he left early, making vague comments about being late for a date.

Around the same time Helen carelessly threw caution to the wind and confessed to Emma that she had been in love with Pierre for some time. Somehow Pierre found out and at once — for some reason — pretended to be in love with Helen, which wasn't very nice, but Leo and Emma were spending all their time together, putting their easels side by side, whispering exclusive confidences that were a thick wall shutting him out.

The night when a laughing Leo smeared a dab of chromium yellow on Emma's nose, Pierre packed up his stuff and left, claiming flu symptoms, coughing and hacking, looking suitably pale. He stayed away for two weeks.

When he returned, he and Helen arrived at the art studio holding hands. They continued to do so. One evening they sauntered in wearing identical scarves that Helen said she had bought on sale, though they looked uneven and homemade. Their cheeks were flushed from what Emma assumed was love (and how it bothered her that it bothered her), but was in fact only the cold winter wind slapping them in the face on the way from the bus stop.

It was a short-lived romance for all parties. A month later Leo disappeared and Emma found out that he was a drug addict. She also realized that she didn't know his last name. Overnight Pierre lost interest in Helen. Then Helen got upset because Pierre was still in love with Emma, and Emma got upset because Helen got upset because she couldn't stand the idea of hurting Helen who'd had a traumatic childhood that had left emotional scars. It did not take long for Pierre to get upset because Emma was avoiding him in order to make Helen happy, which did not work either, because Helen got even more upset because Pierre was upset. She told Emma that it was all her fault for being thoughtless and never thinking of anybody but herself. Emma apologized. Helen ordered Emma to be nice to Pierre. Emma in turn got upset that Helen got upset because she, Emma, had upset Pierre, when she had only upset him in order not to upset Helen.

How they cared in those days! How exhausting it was! The simplest act was weighed down by an excess of emotion, broken hearts and shattered egos.

Last Easter, as Emma, her daughter Frida and Frida's best friend Jane, lay tanning in an early heat wave in the backyard, Jane asked Emma how they celebrated Easter in the country where she grew up.

"Celebrate, not celebrated. They still do, you know."

"Whatever."

Emma, always eager for a chance to talk about the past, told Jane about Easter witches riding their brooms through the night sky with their kettles and black cats every Thursday before Good Friday.

"Where are they going on their brooms? An annual witches' convention? Joy-riding?"

"Sort of. Every year at Easter all the witches congregate at a place called Blåkulla. It means 'Blue hills.' Apparently witches in olden days claimed to have actually flown. Some experts today say that the so-called witches were strung out on Belladonna, which they either ate or rubbed on their brooms, or some such thing, so they were probably under the impression that they really were flying, cats, kettles and all. But I don't really know."

"Stoned out of their skulls, eh?

"Probably."

"Talk about pagan traditions," sneered Jane, who is Roman Catholic. Jane likes hanging out at her friend's house. Frida's mom has made it such an interesting place. She's a very artistic person, Frida's mom. Very charming. She always keeps bouquets of fresh flowers even though it's nobody's birthday. And stuff. Lots of stuff. She has this little glass shoe, for example, a man's shoe, which sits in one of the living room windows beside the fireplace. She once told Jane it was one of the glass shoes that had once been worn by the prince who found Cinderella's glass slipper and won her heart.

"That's right," Frida's mom said, "the prince wore glass shoes as well. I bet you didn't know that."

Freaky, but kinda cool.

There is a marble in the glass shoe, barely fitting into the opening. A large marble with purple and yellow swirls. Jane wanted to know, had the marble belonged to the prince as well?

Frida's mom said, yes, as a matter of fact it had.

She has a crazy imagination, Frida's mom.

That afternoon in the hot sun, Emma continued to tell them bits of myth and fact, not going into detail, lest she offend Jane's Catholic sensibilities. "Little girls dress up like witches and tour the neighbourhood, borrowing their mothers' brooms to ride on. And if you're lucky," she said, "you get a cardboard Easter egg, beautifully decorated, full of candy and other gifts. Frida used to get them every Easter when she was little. My mother used to send them. But it never meant as much to Frida. She threw the egg out when she'd finished the candy."

"Well, who needs all that candy anyway?" The girls are teenagers, full of modern anxieties about dieting and other measures necessary to attain physical perfection.

It was the talk of Easter eggs that reminded Emma of the last Easter she spent with Pierre. Pierre, home for the holidays, had been given a cardboard Easter egg large enough to hide a small child in. The outside of the egg was beautifully decorated, the inside stuffed with every kind of sweet, chocolate, and licorice ever produced, and not the average street kiosk offering either. Pierre's mother — she was half French, as one might have guessed, him having a name like that — had a friend who owned a confectionery called Lulu's Sweet Dreams. It was located in a fancy area of the city and sold only expensive chocolates and an impressive assortment of imported candy, including twelve kinds of Dutch licorice. The kind of shop where snooty old ladies in fur coats shopped, tying their equally snooty lapdogs outside while they went in to select their next batch of sinful treats.

Strange that his mum would give him so much dressed-up sugar, Emma thought at the time. By then he was twenty-one years old. Hardly a child. And as Pierre had never been a mama's boy to start with, it didn't make sense, though he did like chocolate an awful lot.

Like Emma said to herself at the time, who doesn't?

She had not seen him for a few months before that Easter, but had heard that he was home on leave from the art school in Paris. More important at the time, she had caught a recent rumour that Leo was in the hospital dying of some terrible disease he had contracted in the Far East. The rumour said he might not have long to live. Hoping Pierre would know the truth of this tragedy, she decided to give him a call. She was not in the habit of calling Pierre, she always waited for him to call her. It made her feel wanted.

Pierre was so ecstatic to hear from her that he nearly raised his voice. He asked would she please come over at once and share his Easter egg?

"You got an Easter egg already?"

"A big one, Emma-gemma. Wait till you see it. Are you on your way?"

She was. She caught the next bus, not even checking her makeup and hair, and in no time at all they were cozy on his bed, attacking the giant egg. She gazed fondly at all his objects, feeling at home. As usual a vase full of flowers sat on the windowsill. That day it was white narcissus and daffodils, it being almost Easter. On each side of the bouquet, among the dancing peasants, sat a pot with a single purple hyacinth. Outside a curtain of spring rain shuttered *Café Unwirklich* from reality.

Pierre had hidden some joints at the bottom of the Easter egg. They lit one and got stoned before digging into the several pounds of candy. After a while they smoked another joint, ate some more candy, smoked another one, munched some more sweet treats, until Emma heard music that was not playing. She closed her eyes and became equally convinced that she heard the glass slipper dance on top of the dresser, a rhythmic one-legged tap dance.

It was in the middle of the music that was not playing that Pierre metamorphosed. Before Emma could grasp what was happening, her eyes conveniently closed, Pierre went from a big kid eating expensive candy to a young man with more advanced interests.

(It's entirely possible that she pressed up too close to him, knowing he was far from immune to her presence. Could be that she leaned her head against his shoulder while pretending not to, the better to hear the nonexistent music. It's also possible that she felt a sudden need for physical closeness, a need to respond to a need, though she never was sure. She also liked the way he smelled.)

Then he kissed her. It had taken him years to get around to it, though he had badly wanted to since day one.

Which, to be honest, she had sensed all along.

To make up for lost time he continued to kiss her ravenously for more than an hour, by which time they were both exhausted and had to rest. Luckily he was extremely good at kissing. The discovery came as a delicious surprise. He buried his hands in her hair and went at it as if Emma were Easter egg candy, licking, tasting, savouring, devouring, while she wondered fleetingly where he had acquired this experience. He was far tastier than the imported chocolates, and God knows the chocolates were exquisite. Emma went limp and surrendered, savouring him right back, hoping poor Leo would not die for another day.

Pierre kissed her with persistent passion, and with gentle gratitude for the fact that here she was, Emma-gemma of the dyed gypsy hair, yielding in his arms, her face in the cup of his hands. Every so often those hands broke the cup in half to find their way into her hair once again, holding on to it.

"Pierre," she gasped the first time she surfaced for air, "I like the way you kiss."

He smiled but did not reply, simply went on kissing, outdoing himself. That was all he did, he never went on to grope or try to undress her, he simply kissed her as though it was an act of reverence. And Emma loved it despite the imposition of the reverence, which she preferred to close her eyes to. As far as kissing went they were hugely compatible.

It was a marvelous afternoon.

Before she left, she lingered in the doorway, her normally straight mane a tangled bouffant, her face blotchy from a million kisses. She had arrived with a question, and now she remembered to ask it, off hand, pretending it had just occurred to her, which in fact it had, as for the past few hours it had completely slipped her mind, dancing like a solitary glass slipper straight out of her head.

"Pierre?"

"What, Emma-gemma?"

"Do you by any chance know if it's true that what's-his-name, you know . . . that friend of yours . . . Leo? . . . is in the hospital? I have . . . some books of his I want to return."

"No," said Pierre. She could tell by the way his eyes clouded over that he was lying. But so was she. She had nothing that belonged to Leo. It was a safe bet that Leo was not a reader.

"Do you at least know his last name, so maybe I can mail the books to him?"

That much he offered, but with a startling lack of grace, before closing the door in a manner that made her feel locked out. Dismissed.

She worried all the way home. What if he refused to ever kiss her again?

With the help of a last name she was able to confirm Leo's whereabouts when she called the hospital. He had been admitted a week earlier. Sweet Leo with his curly auburn hair, she thought. Or what was left of him. It had been three years of non-Leohood since she last saw him, though God knows she had coped remarkably well without him. Now here he was, within reach, somewhere in one of the buildings in the hospital compound.

Emma was so nervous she felt faint late Sunday morning when she pushed open the door to a hospital room, knowing that on the other side would be long lost Leo, a languishing stick figure beneath a white sheet, unable to speak as she bravely held his skeletal little paw in hers.

"Hey!" he hollered as the door opened, before he could even see who it was.

Emma was so frightened she shrank in the doorway. She wanted badly to turn around and run, only by then it was too late.

"Hey!" she replied and entered the room.

There was Leo sitting up in bed, smaller than she remembered him. Unless it was the big hospital bed than made him look so puny. He looked uglier too, somehow. "Oh," he said when he saw her. He looked surprised, puzzled, trying to place her. "Oh, right. It's . . . you!"

"Yes, it's me. Emma"

"Right! Nice to see you!" His smile was so insincere she felt a strong urge to slap him in the face.

He was not alone. He was sharing a semi-private room with his girlfriend who sat, knees drawn up in an equally large bed. She said nothing, but Leo introduced her as Cara. It sounded invented. (It was. Her real name was Klara.)

Leo and Cara had been shipped home from Turkey, riddled with cheap drugs, hepatitis, jaundice and whatever else that part of the world bestows upon careless travellers. They were, however, in no danger of dying, though they were fond of claiming it had been touch and go, each disease an adventurer's badge of honour.

It was horrible, but Emma forced herself to stay for nearly half an hour — it felt like a year — and looking relaxed, said she had been to visit her grandmother and had heard he was here, so she thought she'd drop in, kind of thing, you know? "And Pierre says to say hi." She sat on the edge of the huge hospital bed that contained the Leo-person, whoever he was, conversing strenuously with him and his girlfriend.

Cara was a scrawny thing with long brown hair, limp and greasy, freckled arms and strangely pale eyelashes. She studied Emma with unblinking childlike indifference, so unabashed it could only be genuine.

Emma and Leo had not a thing to say to one another.

Had they ever?

No, they had not. They had seen each other at the art school twice a week for less than two months, had giggled and dabbed each other's noses with paint, gestures she had imbued with profound meaning. They had lived the last three years in different places with different people, thinking vastly different thoughts. The Leo in the hospital bed had no place in Emma's life, as she had none, wanted none, in whatever mess was his.

It was an inopportune time to find this out. She was glad she had not brought flowers and chocolate. Or an Easter egg. Thoughts of Pierre and his Easter egg cheered her, gave her strength.

To have something to do until they could politely get rid of their guest, Leo opened the drawer in the bedside table and retrieved a pipe and a chunk of hashish. It was a noteworthy lump, as big as an average fist.

"You keep that stuff right here in the hospital?"

"Hey, we know how to live!"

They quickly smoked what he stuffed into the pipe and the tension eased. The pipe continued its rounds. Cara kept busy in between turns spraying the room with air freshener, confiding that "The nurses don't trust us freaks. They think we smoke dope and fuck in here! Can you believe it?"

"Really?" said Emma, wishing she had that kind of outgoing confidence.

Handing her the pipe, Leo exhaled a cloud and informed Emma with pride that Cara sometimes didn't eat for days, because she just didn't see the point. He continued to hint about the greatness of Cara. Cara read incomprehensible Third World poets. Cara knew the meaning of life and didn't bother with a coat in winter. Cara talked about her orgasms with complete strangers.

How could Emma compete with that? She'd never even had one.

She could not wait to get out of that unadorned room and Cara's fulsome air freshener.

Her heart was not sure quite what rhythm to beat, which was a pity because her emotions were light on their feet, ready to twirl their toes in glass-slippered dance. She had got rid of the self-imposed heartache she had been prepared to carry forever, bravely, like a war widow. It was the bittersweet heroism of her situation that had infatuated her. Nothing to do with that wispy little twit sitting in the hospital bed with a stupid grin on his face. She stared at the unbecoming yellow of his teeth.

"See you around," smiled Cara when Emma got up to leave. Cara, who kept spraying the room with her lethal aerosol weapon, was a kinder person than Leo, who by then was too stoned to notice that the chick from the art school was leaving.

Cara's nightgown was see-through. Emma could see her mosquito bite breasts, the right one raised higher than the left one, following her bony right arm into the air.

The smell of lilies of the valley was nauseating.

She called Pierre later that afternoon and asked if he wanted to go to a movie.

Pierre, a forgiving soul, said, "I surely do, Emma-gemma."

The last time Emma spent time with Pierre was later that year, on a hot summer day aboard a fishing boat bobbing on the sun-dappled surface of a docile sea. Hans and Camilla, two students from the art school, had recklessly pooled their savings and bought an old fishing cutter that — for an exorbitant fee — they docked in the fishermen's harbour out near the museum. It was a quaint little harbour lined with fishermen's huts, smelling of fish and salt. Hans and Camilla had invited Emma, Pierre, and their friends Johan and Laila to go for a picnic out on the water, eager to show off what accomplished seafarers they had become, having owned a cutter for two weeks.

They gathered at nine in the morning down on the tiny dock, toting bags full of wine bottles, fruit, bread and cheese, and boarded the swaying old vessel.

"Does it leak?" Emma looked around. Maybe a stupid question. It was still floating.

"We'll find out," said Hans, lighting a seafaring pipe.

"Does it have a toilet?" asked Laila.

"Gentlemen piss over the edge. The ladies may feel free to use a bucket."

Pierre didn't say much that day.

It was peaceful out on the water. Far away rose the silhouette of the city. A foreign ship had docked in the harbour the day before and downtown was swarming with sailors in dark blue suits. Emma had been propositioned by two sailors waving a wad of money in her face as she walked from the bus stop to meet her friends.

A seagull sat shrieking atop the mast. On the sunny deck below, the human passengers drank wine while they fished, or pretended to, catching nothing, as nobody had remembered to bring bait. The fish did not go for small chunks of cheese. The sun kept shining. At one point, as they were lying around dozing, not talking, listening to the creaking of the hull and the slopping, slurping sound of the sea, Emma opened her eyes and looked right into Pierre's, catching him unaware.

That was when she knew that he loved her. While it made her heart stop, as if out of respect, she was equally convinced that she did not love him back, not the way he deserved to be loved. It made her unbearably sad not to be able to reciprocate such generosity of feeling. Because that was the kind of love his was. Generous.

Her own heart was not as big.

To deflect him from reading her thoughts, she smiled at him and took his hand. And he squeezed that undeserving hand, then kissed it, neither of them realizing that it was a farewell kiss.

How could she be so sure she did not love him? Was it because loving him would have transformed their relationship into something less manageable?

A moment later Johan, half asleep, rolled over and into the sea and they had to spring to the rescue and drag him out. Easier said than done, as nobody was sober and Johan — he couldn't swim — had grown very heavy, what with his soaked clothes and boots and all. For a moment it looked as if they might have to let him sink into a wet grave.

The seagull on the mast fled the human tragedy.

When they finally managed to heave him back on board they found a little fish squirming in his shirt pocket. Hans was overjoyed with the find. "Let's hurl him in again and see if he catches another one."

Apart from Johan's near demise, it was a perfect day, a summer moment that Emma will always cherish.

It was the last time she saw Pierre. Three days later she took the train to Italy. The following week Pierre returned to France to finish doing whatever he was doing with various metals.

The following December came the brief phone call when she shamefacedly had to confess to him that she was moving to Canada. To marry to a man from a province with a woman's name. What kind of person does that?

But that was it. No more Pierre.

Never ever

Emma stubbornly moved to Canada. Seven years went by, then one day Emma learned that Pierre had got married. The news came in a well-informed letter tucked into a Christmas card from Helen. Pierre's wife (Helen did not reveal her name) had recently given birth to a baby boy. Yes indeed, Pierre was a very happy man, wrote Helen, her handwriting gloating.

Very, *very* happy. She had repeated it twice, adding emphasis to make sure it sank in. For she had been to see them, had Helen, she was always welcome at their place, didn't have to call ahead, not her, felt free to drop in whenever she felt like it. Pierre and his wife were living in a beautiful apartment near their old school, in that Jugend building with the turrets, remember? The city had renovated the entire area around there and the apartments were very expensive, almost impossible to come by. Not that Pierre had to worry about things like that, he was doing quite well for himself these days. He'd just had another exhibition.

They had four bedrooms. Huge bedrooms. High ceilings. Big tall windows.

Well, Helen would write that, wouldn't she, if only to upset Emma. And at the time Emma had got very upset.

Even though she never loved him.

If Pierre ever asked about Emma, Helen never said.

Well, she wouldn't, would she?

Did he still have that dresser?

The glass slipper?

When Frida, Emma's seventeen-year-old daughter, one day asks, "How do you know what love is?" Emma has no idea what to answer. She could make an aging fool of herself and reply, "Well, it's sort of like an Easter egg, wonderful to look at and full of sinful sweets."

She knows better than to say that, but allows herself to think it, smiling at the thought.

What she offers from the bottom of her never-stilled human heart, is: "I haven't the faintest idea. Go ask an expert."

"Who?" Her daughter makes a snarky sound. "Dad? His dimwit wife?"

Meanwhile Emma remembers Pierre's reverence that Easter when they first kissed. The tastiness, chocolate and licorice mingling with the flavours of raspberry and violet. Pierre turning into a man before her closed eyes. And Emma, convinced she did not reciprocate, feeling guilty about it, greedily accepting those candy kisses she can still taste.

Blushing, she says to her daughter, "I don't know who to ask. Why don't you just wait and see? You're still a child."

Pretty Frida who is the age Pierre was when they first met.

Emma sometimes dreams that one day her daughter will come home with distorted lips and messy hair (not too distorted, not too messy) to announce that she has met a man from Emma's country, and that the man will turn out to be Pierre's son. They will get married, their two respective children, and a year or two later Emma and Pierre will cradle the same grandchild, scanning its little face for likeness.

At the wedding Emma will meet Pierre again. She'll be wearing one of those ridiculous hats mothers always wear at weddings.

What if he doesn't remember her?

Oh, he'll remember.

"Pierre," she'll say. And she'll look into his eyes.

"Emma," he'll reply, thinking how beautiful she looks despite that silly hat. How well she has aged.

He will no longer wear purple velvet pants. His hair, if he still has hair, may or may not be grey, but it will be shorter. He may have grown a beard, but she hopes not, there is something self-indulgent and vain about men with beards, especially those big bushy evangelical ones. It would not go with the person her Pierre always was.

Her Pierre?

Who is *she* to make such claims?

Well, he's *her* Pierre in *her* memories, isn't he?

Somewhere in the background will be his nameless wife. She is bound to be a nice woman if she is married to Pierre. Good-looking too. Tall and slender and confident, graceful in high-heeled shoes, is how Emma imagines her, feeling no ill will.

Not much anyway.

He may be divorced. There's always that possibility.

Or a recent widower.

She tries to imagine Pierre middle-aged, but it's impossible. Unless she does meet him again one day, he will remain the prince from her favourite fairytale, a charmed prince in purple pants and an embroidered vest. Forever young, holding out from the past a hand adorned with a ring where sits enthroned a stone containing a secret no one was meant to decipher.

His hands were always warm.

At the wedding reception, when the band starts to play, he'll walk towards her.

No, he'll do nothing so simple; he'll *materialize* by her side, is what he'll do, without a sound. Then he'll ask her to dance. "Emma-gemma," he'll say, holding out the hand still wearing the green amber ring. "Do you want to dance?"

"Yes, Pierre," she'll respond, "I surely do."

And Emma and Pierre will dance an old-fashioned waltz, these two people of the rock-and-roll generation. They will not be clad in glass footwear. Their eyes, no longer new, no longer expecting or wanting surprises, will reveal hints of a love that never quite was but could have been.

Or that clamoured for attention but went ignored.

Or that, despite everything, simply was.

Should they drink too much wine they might become convinced that it's still not too late and do something foolish. Start kissing with lips less plump. Hoping the clock will never strike midnight.

That must never happen.

"Whatever love is," says Emma to her unimpressed daughter, "don't let me drink too much wine at your wedding." She ignores the look in Frida's eyes, pretends not to see that bottomless embarrassment teenagers drown in when their parents say something stupid.

Parents, for some reason, always say something stupid.

The truth is, Emma does not want to meet Pierre again. Not in the here and now. Why would she? It would ruin everything. *Her* Pierre is forever young. So is *his* Emma.

It is a memory that must remain the treasure that it is, a *souvenir d'enchantement*. It must never be tampered with. Should she run into Pierre, her treasure would lose its sparkle, for this is not really about love lost. Nor is it about what could have been.

It might not even be about Pierre, though he is certainly the embodiment of it.

So what is this *it* then?

It's the sweetness of the chocolates in the Easter egg, the swirling yellow and purple in the marble, Cinderella's fragile glass slipper, the secret in the amber, a nonexistent garden, this *it* that does not, must not, need not, have a name.

BRITT HOLMSTRÖM was born in Malmö, Sweden, and came to Canada in 1970. She has published three critically acclaimed novels: *The Man Next Door* (1998) won a Saskatchewan Book Award, and *The Wrong Madonna* (2002) and *Claudia* (2008) were both shortlisted. Holmström lives in Regina, Saskatchewan.